## "YOU'RE BEAU

Nick placed his fir
and tipped her hea
eyes.

The words went to Eden's head like strong drink.
She'd never even considered herself pretty. While she
knew she was passably attractive, she'd always
thought she was the "plain" Calloway sister when
compared to Jo and Tess and Mariah.... But Nick
made her feel beautiful, feminine—every inch a
woman. And Eden wanted to experience the ultimate
expression of her femininity, finally, with him.

"Make love to me."

"I'm a drifter," Nick said, as if those three words
explained everything.

A woman less wise might have taken the statement as
a warning, or perhaps even a rejection.

But the light of the moon revealed the inner struggle
in his eyes, and she knew he felt the same longing,
the same hunger.

"Make love to me," Eden repeated softly.

## ABOUT THE AUTHOR

Penny Richards's hometown of Haughton,
Louisiana, served as a model for the fictional
Calloway Corners. She lives happily in Haughton
with her husband, their three children and several
Thoroughbred horses. The multitalented Penny
paints, collects folk art and cooks when she isn't
writing. A self-confessed "incurable romantic,"
Penny is as warm, loving and wise as any of the
heroines she creates.

## Books by Penny Richards

HARLEQUIN SUPERROMANCE
323—UNFORGETTABLE

**Penny Richards**

# EDEN

## *Harlequin Books*

TORONTO • NEW YORK • LONDON
AMSTERDAM • PARIS • SYDNEY • HAMBURG
STOCKHOLM • ATHENS • TOKYO • MILAN

FORTY YEARS OF
Romance

Published April 1989

First printing February 1989

ISBN 0-373-70350-3

Printed in U.S.A.

For Sandra, Terri and Kathey—
friends, sisters, partners.
And for Nancy, who helped
make the dream come true.

# CHAPTER ONE

HOW TIME FLEW! Eden Calloway regarded the serene face of the sleeping child cradled against her breasts and marveled at how quickly the two years since Molly's birth had passed. It seemed like only yesterday that the plump toddler with the blond flyaway bangs and the dimpled smile had been a squirming infant. She'd been left in Eden's care three days a week since then while her mother worked at her part-time secretarial job. Now Molly chattered like a magpie.

For that matter, it didn't seem all that long ago that school had let out for the summer, yet the new school year was halfway through the first six weeks, and Labor Day was only a memory of charcoal-grilled hamburgers and happy laughter. No doubt about it. Time really did go faster the older you got.

Molly shifted in her arms and Eden's bare foot set the rocking chair—the same rocking chair her mother, Grace Calloway, had rocked her babies in—back in motion. The rhythmic *squeak, squeak* of the chair, which sat on the front porch of the huge white, green-shuttered house Eden had called home all of her thirty-three years, quickly lured the child back to dreamland. Eden knew she should put Molly down, but lately she'd felt the need for more human contact. More touching. More love. And love and kisses were two things Molly had in abundance.

It was that very need that had prompted Eden to sit down in the rocker with Molly shortly after her mother had dropped her and Jamie, Molly's five-year-old sister, off

thirty minutes before. As usual, Jamie had headed straight
to the living room to watch cartoons, while Eden and Molly
rocked and talked, and Eden drew comfort from the small
body resting so trustingly in her arms.

She sighed. Her jade-green gaze shifted from the sleeping child, restlessly roaming the arid, cattle-dotted pasture
stretching out beyond the picket fence and the circle drive,
all the way to the distant railroad tracks running parallel to
the highway. Haughton, Bossier City and Shreveport lay to
the west. Calloway Corners—nothing but a crossroads with
the Calloway home, a small grocery store by the same name
and a lumber mill that sat well off the road—was situated
almost halfway between the outskirts of Haughton and the
small town of Doyline to the east.

Eden closed her eyes and let her head rest against the
rocker's high ladder back, picturing the gray ribbon of interstate highway a few miles to the north and wishing she
had the courage to see where it led. But the truth was, she
didn't have such courage or any of the other qualities she'd
need to go out to look for the excitement missing in her life.

In a moment of honesty, she'd admitted that the new
restlessness growing inside her, the feeling that she needed
to do *something* with her life besides raise a garden and
baby-sit, the new realization that life and love were passing
her by, all had a lot to do with the fact that all three of her
younger sisters had married within the past few months.

Mariah, the youngest, the wildest, the will-o'-the-wisp
who had seldom stayed in one place more than two weeks
since she'd graduated from high school, had miraculously
fallen in love and married Ford Dunning, a local counselor
who had taken over preaching in a small local church. She
was now several months pregnant, and the brightness of her
smile put the shine of the hot September sun to shame.

Pregnant. Eden's heart contracted and she glanced down
at the child resting peacefully in her arms. How would it feel

to have a new life growing inside you? What would it be like to care for a baby who was truly yours and not just on loan for a few hours a week? How would it feel to have a child call you "mother" instead of "Auntie Eden"? The hot prickling of tears stung beneath her eyelids. Like so many other things, motherhood was something she'd longed for and never had a chance to experience.

Until last night.

Dan Morgan had proposed last night, offering her the chance to have what she envied her sisters for. Marriage. A home. And besides two well-behaved girls of ten and thirteen, she would have the opportunity to know firsthand the joys and trials of pregnancy and motherhood and to experience the sweet invasion of her body by a man who loved her.

*So why are you hesitating, Eden?* she asked herself as another long sigh soughed from her lips—lips unadorned by so much as a whisper of gloss. *Why didn't you say yes before he left? Why wait? Time's apassing, as Daddy used to say, and you certainly aren't getting any younger.*

Unable to face the taunting questions tumbling around in her mind, Eden stood with her slight burden and crossed to the screened door. Shifting Molly higher on her shoulder, she used her free hand to open the screen. She let the door slam against her hip to keep from waking Molly and carried the child through the living room to the master bedroom.

Gently, she eased her precious bundle down onto the center of the peach, cream and pale blue quilt that covered the four-poster bed. She brushed aside a lock of hair from Molly's damp cheek and turned on the oscillating fan sitting atop the matching dresser. Then Eden pushed a wisp of stylishly frizzed strawberry-blond hair away from her own perspiring face and padded silently across the hardwood floors.

She wished it would cool off. Even though she liked the house open so that she could hear what was going on outside and smell the scents of the changing seasons, Eden supposed she should turn on the air-conditioning, especially since her father had paid a small fortune to have the central air-conditioning system installed in the old house several years ago.

As usual, thoughts of her father brought a resurgence of grief and loneliness. Ben Calloway had died the previous December, and Eden secretly felt that his death had brought him the first real peace he'd known since her mother had died giving birth to Mariah twenty-six years before.

Eden still missed him. She'd been closer to him than any of his other daughters. Not because there was any less love involved, but because Tess, Jo and Mariah had scattered to the four winds, while she had elected to stay home and take care of him. She'd stayed, not out of any noble feelings or a martyr complex, but because she'd been taught that when you start something, you follow it through to the end.

The end had come at early morning, peacefully. He had called for Grace with his last breath, which hadn't surprised Eden at all. As the oldest, she'd known—perhaps not understood, but known—how much he missed Grace, how deeply he mourned her loss, even after twenty-six years. Eden prayed that her sisters had found a love as strong as that their parents had shared.

A sudden thought momentarily halted her progress to the kitchen. Was that why she'd put off answering Dan's proposal? Because she wasn't certain she loved him that much? Or whether she loved him at all?

The muted sounds of a Daffy Duck cartoon followed her as she crossed the kitchen, which was decorated with spring-green gingham, antiques and copper kettles. She was reaching for a small cast-iron skillet when the phone rang.

She grabbed the receiver so that the ringing of the bedside extension wouldn't wake Molly.

"Good morning," she said, forcing cheerfulness into her voice and putting to use that disgustingly optimistic platitude Mariah was always spouting since she married Ford: act yourself into a state of being. Ergo, Eden surmised, if she acted cheerful, she would somehow miraculously become cheerful.

"Eden?" came the cautious query from the other end of the line.

Eden recognized the voice of her next-to-the-youngest sister, Jo. A wide smile curved her lips, and the note of joy in her voice was genuine as she cried, "Jo! Hi! Why on earth are you calling so early?" She glanced at the clock. "It's only—"

"A little after six California time. I know. E.Z. woke me up when he left."

Jo and her new husband, E. Z. Ellis—affectionately called Easy by his bride—were in California, where the handsome rock star was working on several deals, among them the founding of his own record label and a benefit concert for the homeless. They hadn't decided on a permanent home yet, even though E.Z. was leaning toward Louisiana and the Lake Bistineau area since he'd gone into semiretirement.

"He woke you up, huh?" Eden said suggestively.

Jo laughed at the unspoken innuendo, but refused to rise to the bait. "Yeah. I was feeling a little homesick, so I thought I'd give you a call. How's life treating you?"

Eden leaned back against the cabinets, unable to help the wry twist of her lips. "Ignoring me as usual."

A slight hint of the despair she was feeling must have been obvious. There was concern in Jo's voice as she said, "Sometimes you've got to thumb your nose at the world to make it stand up and take notice, sis."

"Maybe," Eden agreed. "But the problem is that only two of the Calloway girls were born with enough guts to do it."

"I don't know. Tess might not have been born with any, but she certainly gained some along the way somewhere," Jo, the brash, take-on-the-world-and-all-its-problems Calloway sister reminded her thoughtfully.

Eden knew Jo was referring to Tess's recent marriage to the small community's reformed bad boy, Seth Taylor, a marriage that still had the townsfolk talking.

"How are the newlyweds anyway?" Jo asked, almost managing to mask the worry in her voice.

"As right as rain," Eden told her. Unlike Mariah and Jo, Eden had had no qualms about Tess marrying Seth. Despite his reputation, she and Seth had been friends for a long time, and she'd watched as he fought to overcome the stigma of being the son of the town drunk and his common-law wife. It had been a long battle, but now Seth's reputation was one of an excellent housing contractor.

"You really think he's going to be good for her?" Jo asked.

"As sure as I am that E.Z. is good for you," Eden said.

"How's the situation with Jason?"

Jason, Seth's thirteen-year-old son, hadn't been thrilled about his father's marriage at first. It was a problem that had worried Eden and Mariah as well as Jo.

Eden sighed. "Tess says things are much better. Jason is still communicating with her." Determined to change the subject, she asked, "How's the adoption coming?"

"Good." There was unmistakable excitement in Jo's voice. Jo and E.Z. were in the process of trying to adopt a homeless, two-year-old child who had stolen Jo's heart during her brief, stormy courtship with E.Z. She had laughingly told everyone that she and E.Z. "had to" get married. They both wanted Carmen.

"We saw Judge Thibideaux when we were in New Orleans last week. We're supposed to sign the papers any time now."

"That's great, Jo," Eden said, trying to ignore that tiny bit of envy that sparked again.

"Yes, it is, isn't it?" Jo said with a laugh. "And speaking of kids, how's Mariah?"

"She's fine. With Ford's help, she's finally overcome the worst of her fears and seems really happy about the baby."

"I'm so glad," Jo said. "Just because Mama died in childbirth certainly doesn't mean that history will repeat itself."

"I know. I'm glad she's worked through it."

"Did I tell you that I'm having lunch with the producer of E.Z.'s latest video?"

"No," Eden said. "My, my, I'm impressed. To whom do you owe this honor?"

"E.Z.," Jo said succinctly. "He's determined that I'm going to be in the video. You remember 'Take It E.Z. On Me, Girl,' the song he wrote for me in his *E.Z. To Be Hard* album?"

"'You're satin sheets and fire; you're the heart of my desire,'" Eden quoted softly, her heart filled with a sudden emptiness. "How can I forget?" She drew in a deep, fortifying breath and tried to sound enthusiastic. "So you're going to make your television debut?"

"It's beginning to look that way," Jo said with a laugh.

*And I'll be the one home watching you.*

"You'll be great, Jo. Oh, darn!" Eden exclaimed, forcing the proper amount of remorse into her voice and fighting the tears gathering beneath her eyelids. "I've gotta go. Jamie wants her breakfast. I'll talk to you later—okay?"

"Sure. Give the girls a kiss for me."

"I will. G'bye."

"Bye," Jo said. Then, before Eden could hang up, she called, "Eden!"

Eden brought the phone back to her ear. "Yes?"

"Are you sure you're all right? You sound sort of... I don't know... down or something."

Eden faked a laugh. "I'm fine. Nothing but a bad case of PMS."

"That'll do it every time," Jo said with a smile in her voice. "We'll see you Thanksgiving if not before."

"Wonderful!" *Please, Jo, let me get off the phone!*

"And Eden?"

"What?" Eden said with a hint of exasperation.

"I love you."

The simple, unexpected words from her no-nonsense sister unraveled the tattered remains of Eden's composure. She swallowed the obstruction clogging her throat and wished she could call back all the uncharitable thoughts and petty jealousies she'd felt.

"I love you, too, Jo," she choked out. Then, before Jo could say anything else and before Eden broke down completely, she uttered a soft goodbye and pressed the button on the receiver to break the connection.

Then, because she was lonely, because there was nothing in her future except the same boring things of yesterday and because she was feeling more than a little sorry for herself, Eden Calloway sat down at the long, rectangular walnut table and cried.

NICK LOGAN DREW his mirrorlike sunglasses down the bridge of his nose, shifting his weight to one leg as he scanned the room's occupants. There she was, sitting alone in a booth situated near the back of the café. His well-shaped lips twisted into a wry smile. In a white linen suit, she looked as out of place in the homey eating establishment as he would have if he'd walked through the doors of a ball-room in his faded jeans.

Raking a hand through his windblown hair and tucking the sunglasses into the pocket of the black T-shirt he was wearing, Nick wove his way through the tables to where she sat, desultorily stirring a cup of coffee.

When he'd pulled his Harley Davidson into the Little Rock motel the night before, the first thing he did was call her apartment. As usual, she had demanded that they meet, and he named the spot, a small, unpretentious café with good down-home food.

She must have sensed his approach, because she looked up as he neared the table, her incredibly large, ebony eyes lighting with pleasure as she recognized him. He didn't speak; neither did she. Drawing her to her feet and pulling her against him, he touched his lips to the powdered smoothness of her cheek. The sultry, sexy scent of an ex-pensive perfume enveloped him briefly before he drew back and rubbed her straight, patrician nose with his in a gesture of affection as old as they were.

Their faces a scant inch apart, they smiled into each oth-er's eyes. Nick gave her a final squeeze. "Hello, sis."

Her mouth curved into a happy smile. "Hi."

Nick released her and sat down on the opposite side of the booth, looking her over with brotherly concern and plea-sure. Nicole was his twin, and as he looked at her perpetu-ally tanned complexion—a compliment of some recessive Italian gene from their mother's side of the family—her dark-brown hair and large, almost-black eyes, it occurred to him again for perhaps the thousandth time, that she was one of the most gorgeous women he'd ever met...and he'd made the acquaintance of quite a few. It never once occurred to him that those same genes had granted him the same good looks, altered to give him a strictly masculine appearance.

"You're looking great, Nicci," he told her fondly, truthfully.

Nicole gazed at him as if he'd hung the moon, not to mention a few million stars. Ignoring his casual attire and drinking in the sight of his handsome face, she replied, "You look pretty good yourself."

Nick's smile was slow, mocking. "You know what they say: clothes make the man."

Nicole's laughter was light, bubbly, almost a giggle. It didn't go with her haute couture image or her twenty-nine years. Her mischievous eyes noted the way the T-shirt molded the muscles in his chest. "In your case, I think the man does a lot for the clothes."

"You wanna order now?"

The intrusive question sent both Nick's and Nicole's gazes flying to the worn face of a middle-aged waitress who stood with her pad and pencil in hand.

Nick arched a questioning eyebrow at his sister. "Breakfast?"

Nicole shook her head. "You *know* I don't do breakfast, Nick," she reminded him.

"Oh. Right." He smiled at the waitress. "Just a glass of orange juice for the lady and the number three with ham, grits and gravy for me."

"Toast or biscuits?" the waitress asked.

"Biscuits," he said with a wink and a smile that caused the woman to blush. Completely flustered, she turned and walked away, making a notation on her pad. Nick gave his attention back to Nicole, who held out her hand. He took it in his.

"Flirt," she said.

"I'm not a flirt, I'm just friendly," he countered with a smile.

"You're also a liar," she teased. Then, without warning, the humor fled from her eyes and in its place was a bleak despair. She clutched his hand tightly. "I miss you, Nick," she confessed. "So much."

Nick let the love in his heart show in his eyes. "I miss you, too."

"Enough to stop cavorting around the country and come home?" she asked hopefully.

The gleam of tenderness in his dark eyes died. "Home? I don't have a home."

"You could have," Nicole said, eagerness in every line of her body. "All you have to do is make up with Keith and Daddy and—"

"Make up with Keith and Dad?" Nick exploded.

Nicole cringed. Nick knew that she hated scenes of any kind and deplored shouting, and he couldn't help noticing the way his outburst had captured the attention of several people in the café. He lowered his voice. "I'm sorry," he said, "but in case you've forgotten, between them, my father and my brother took away everything in this world that mattered to me, except you. And you want *me* to make some sort of conciliatory move?"

Nicole's face held a look of earnest entreaty. "If you want to patch things up—"

"I don't." The cold finality in his voice brooked no argument. Furious, he tried to release her hand so that he could leave, but Nicole held tight. For long seconds, he stared at the long, manicured fingers clutching his. Then he let his gaze rise until it met the pleading of hers. "Let it go, Nicci," he said softly.

She released his hand, but they both knew that he wasn't talking about her physical hold on him. "We've had this conversation before—several times the last three years as I recall," he said. "I don't want anything to do with the Logans. Not now. Not ever."

"Not even me?" she asked, the threat of tears apparent from the thickness of her voice.

Nick didn't say anything as he sat looking into the eyes of the only member of his family he cared a hoot in hell about. As twins, he and Nicole were closer even than the closest brother and sister. Though he didn't understand why she wouldn't make the break from their family, he loved her, which was why they rendezvoused somewhere every few months and caught up on what was going on in each other's lives.

His heart, tender despite the bitterness and pain filling it, contracted at the hurt in her voice. "I'm here, aren't I?"

Nicole nodded, and the waitress arrived with Nick's breakfast, thankfully saving her from the disgrace of tears.

He saw how close her emotions were to the surface, something the family had been dealing with for several years. He wanted, needed, to make her see how futile her wishes for reconciliation were, even as he desired to protect her. He reached for his coffee cup. "Nothing's changed, Nicole. And it never will. Not now. Not ever."

Her eyes, still damp with unshed tears, met his. "But it has," she said. "That's partly why I wanted to see you." When Nick only looked at her with questioning eyes, she said, "Belinda found out that Keith was having an affair with his secretary. She left."

Nick didn't even pause at he shook salt and pepper onto his eggs. Three years ago, the announcement might have moved him. But a lot of water had run under the proverbial bridge since then. He felt no emotion at hearing that the woman he'd once loved had left the brother he despised, only a sense of retribution.

"Nick?"

"What?" he said, glancing up.

"I thought you'd be interested."

"Sorry. I'm not." He gave his attention to buttering a biscuit, glad he could say the words and mean them. It had taken him almost two years to get over the woman who'd crawled into his brother's bed a week before she was to marry him.

"Keith is threatening to take the baby away from Belinda."

Nick's head came up in surprise. "Why would he do that? He didn't even want her."

"He thinks that since Belinda is so crazy about Kimmie, he can control her through the baby."

Nick's appetite fled. He swore, softly and violently, wondering as he did if the brief flash of bitterness he saw in his sister's eyes was real or imagined. He pushed his plate back and reached for the bill lying beside his saucer.

"Let's go," he said, rising.

Nicole grabbed her white straw purse and stood. Nick headed toward the exit as fast as his legs could carry him, hardly stopping as he slapped the ticket and a ten-dollar bill down next to the old-fashioned cash register. He pushed open the door and strode out into the clear September morning, Nicole close on his heels.

Reaching into his pocket for his sunglasses, Nick whipped them out and settled them on the bridge of his straight nose. Then he slung his leg over the shiny chrome and black motorcycle sitting at the curb and looked up at her, his mouth set into a grim line.

"What are you going to do?"

"I don't know what you're going to do, but I'm getting the hell as far away from here as I can."

EDEN STEPPED ONTO the brick patio Ben Calloway had built at the back of the house, a basket of peppers and tomatoes bumping against her bare leg with each step she took. It was hot, and gathering vegetables in the late afternoon was no picnic. Perspiration darkened the hair at her temples and trickled down her spine, causing the black tank top she wore to cling to her damp skin.

Inside, she set the basket onto the countertop and raked her hair away from her heated face with both hands. She headed to the refrigerator and pressed her hand against the lever in the door. A piece of ice dropped into her waiting palm. Standing beneath the draft of the slowly turning ceiling fan, she rubbed the ice over her neck and upper chest. The ice cube didn't stand a chance against the heat of her flesh, and a trickle of cool water slithered between the valley of her breasts, bare beneath the form-fitting, wash-faded fabric.

Like the touch of a practiced lover, the sensation caused her to shiver and made her nipples contract to button hardness. Eden couldn't help the moan of frustration that escaped her, but before she could do more than curse her body's obvious needs, the telephone rang, drowning out the rhythmic whirring of the fan, mercifully destroying her sensual longings. She dropped the bit of remaining ice into the sink and reached for the receiver.

"Hello?" she snapped, crossing her arms across her aching, unbound breasts.

"My, my, aren't we grumpy?"

The sweet-as-maple-syrup tones belonged to Mariah, but Eden was in no mood for her sister's frivolity. "What is it, Mariah?" she asked shortly.

There was a long pause and then Mariah said, "Is this the Calloway residence? The place my sweet, kind, long-suffering and generous sister Eden lives?"

Shame for her abruptness swept through Eden. It wasn't Mariah's fault that she was so unhappy, but by heaven she was *tired* of being sweet and kind and all those other miserably boring things everyone thought she was. She wished she was daring like Mariah. Bold like Jo. And in control like Tess. But the extent of her rebellion against thirty-three years of predictable behavior was to trade in her neat slacks for cutoffs that she should have thrown away years ago, and to leave her bra in the drawer when she'd dressed that morning. She sighed. So much for the exciting new Eden Calloway.

"Edie, are you all right?" Mariah asked, hearing the sigh filter through the phone lines.

"I'm sorry, Mariah. I'm just...hot, I guess."

"Well, why don't you turn on the air-conditioner?"

The question was one Eden grew tired of answering. She shook her head wearily. "It's on," she lied. "I've been outside in the garden."

"*That's* where you've been. I've been trying to call the last thirty minutes."

"What's wrong?" Eden asked, motherly concern surfacing, even though she hadn't needed to mother Mariah in years.

"Nothing's wrong. I just called to see how you like your new perm."

Eden brought her hand up to finger her new, shoulder-length, crinkly hairdo. How could she have forgotten her first bid for defiance against the old, plain, stick-in-the-mud Eden, especially since she'd worn her hair long and straight for so long? It *did* make her look...what? Interesting? Younger?

"Since you're not talking, I guess you don't like it," Mariah said, breaking the lengthening silence. "But I think it's really sexy. You should have done it years ago."

"I do like it," Eden hastened to assure her. "You did a good job."

"Thanks," Mariah said. "Hold on." Eden heard her talking to someone in the background. "Okay," she said at last to the invisible person, and then told Eden, "I guess he'll be there any time."

Eden frowned. She'd never get used to the way Mariah's mind flitted from one subject to the other, or the way she expected everyone to understand exactly what she was talking about. "He? Who?"

"Nick," Mariah said, as if that cleared everything up nicely, thank you. "That's why I called."

"I thought you called to ask about my perm."

"Oh, well, that, too," Mariah said breezily. "But I wanted to let you know he was coming."

"Nick?" Eden said.

"Yes. You remember Nick, don't you? He's been here a couple of times."

Vaguely, Eden did remember that some hippie biker friend of Mariah's had shown up a few times. If she remembered correctly, he was a couple of years older than Mariah. *Young.* She'd heard him referred to as the motorcycle bum. What was his name? Hogan? Grogan? "Isn't he the one who saved your life?" she said at last.

"That's him!"

"I've never set eyes on him. Somehow I've missed him whenever he's flitted through town." *Thank heaven!* Eden's voice held just a hint of disdain. A motorcycle bum, for goodness sake!

"You said you wanted to rent out the garage apartment, and he's going to be here for a while, so I told him to come out and talk to you."

"I appreciate it, Mariah, but I'm not into charity," Eden said as kindly as possible.

"He can pay," Mariah retorted. "I got him a job with Seth."

Eden sagged against the cabinets and rubbed at the headache forming in the center of her forehead as she tried to recall what her sisters had said about good ol' Phantom Nick.

*"He's handsome, no doubt about it. But he's a drifter."* Jo's words echoed through Eden's mind. Great. Just what she needed. He'd probably hang around Calloway Corners

long enough to mess the apartment up, then he'd get an itch to move on.

"Mariah, I don't think—"

"He's wonderful. You're gonna love him," Mariah interrupted, unwilling to be swayed by Eden's logic.

A sound, unmistakably a motorcycle roaring up the long lane leading to the circle drive, sent Eden's startled gaze winging toward the front of the house. "Damn," she muttered. "He's here."

"You better go, then," Mariah said. "Let me know what happens, will you?"

"Sure," Eden said, cursing her baby sister under her breath. "Talk to you later." She slammed the receiver down and started toward the front door, thoroughly put out with the world in general and Mariah in particular.

*"He's certainly is handsome . . . but trouble, with a capital T."* Tess's impression of Nick what's-his-name sauntered through Eden's whirling mind. Trouble. Sweet heaven. If he was anything like Mariah, no telling what kind of people he might drag home. And if he was handsome, there would probably be women. . . .

The motorcycle came to a halt in a flurry of grinding gravel just as Eden pushed open the front door, her mind still searching for and discarding reasons she couldn't possibly rent to him.

At the top of the steps, she stopped and thrust her hands into the back pockets of her cutoffs. From that point, her mind was a jumble of vague impressions and half-remembered opinions.

Shiny black paint. A lot of chrome.

*"He's a drifter."*

Tight jeans. Correction. Very tight jeans.

*"Handsome . . . trouble with a capital T."*

Black T-shirt. Mirror-type sunglasses.

While Eden's mind struggled to assess the situation, he got off the motorcycle and started toward the house. He'd taken no more than two long strides when he saw her standing there, poised near the steps. He stopped in his tracks and brought his hands up to rest on his narrow hips. She couldn't see his eyes for the dark glasses, but her palms grew sweaty beneath the thorough scrutiny he was giving her. The word rude flashed through her mind. And cocky.

*Say something!* But she couldn't because her mind was a blank.

He smiled then, a slow smile so perfect, so beautiful, so blatantly sexy it stole her breath. The next few seconds spun out in a surreal slow motion. He reached up with one hand and drew off the sunglasses...hooked the earpiece over the pocket of his T-shirt . . . smiled again.

"Hi. I'm Nick Logan."

*"He's wonderful."* Mariah's assessment whispered through her mind. *"You're gonna love him."*

# CHAPTER TWO

"I'M LOOKING FOR Eden Calloway," Nick said, nearing the porch.

Eden, who was still recovering from the wallop of his smile, shielded her eyes from the blinding glint of sun off shiny chrome. "I'm Eden Calloway."

Once again, Nick stopped in his tracks, his eyes making another of those head-to-toe surveys. *This* was the noticeably absent Eden Calloway? The oldest Calloway sister? This woman with the tousled, tangled mass of strawberry-blond hair that grazed her bare shoulders and formed a slightly frizzy frame for the soft innocence in her jade-green eyes? This woman's feet were bare, and she wasn't wearing a bra. This was the spinster? The do-gooder?

Somehow, Nick had gotten the impression from hearing Mariah and her sisters talk about Eden that she was prim and proper, though looking back, they'd never actually used those words. What they had said was that she was calm. Dependable. Sweet. And could be counted on in a crisis. In short, she possessed sterling attributes, but wasn't married. Nick's mind had translated the information wrongly, that those attributes equated to homely as hell.

But Eden Calloway wasn't homely at all. Oh, he wasn't going to lie to himself. She wasn't drop-dead gorgeous like Jo, or beautiful in that unique and exotic way Mariah was. And she didn't have the classic beauty of Tess. The beauty he saw in Eden Calloway was more subtle, less defined, less something he could have put into words or put his finger

on—though, he thought, as his groin tightened in the most
primitive and uncouth way—he'd like to put his fingers on
her—all ten of them.

Whatever "it" was, it was there and had something to do
with an aura of total femininity. Even though she wasn't
wearing any makeup, everything about her screamed W-O-
M-A-N. Sexy woman, he amended, and, unlike most
women, she didn't need the artifice of cosmetics to accen-
tuate the fact. She was more curvy than any of her sisters,
and the curves invited exploration—from the gentle roundness of her hips and the length of shapely thigh to the fullness of her breasts, excitingly bare beneath the dampness of
the clingy top. Even her dusty feet, with the pale peach pol-
ish adorning each toe, were pretty.

Eden grew uncomfortable again beneath the intensity of
his gaze. Mariah's drifter friend was definitely disturbing.
Young. And handsome. She understood why E.Z. had taken
an instant liking to him. They shared certain traits—a quick
smile, a sexy voice and the hint of teasing warmth in their
eyes. But she also thought she knew why Seth agreed with
Tess that he was trouble. Once wild and reckless himself,
Seth undoubtedly recognized those traits in Nick and
understood the consequences they might involve. Now that
she finally had a chance to judge for herself, Eden thought
she'd cast her vote with Ford, who never jumped to conclusions about anything or anyone. Like Ford, she preferred to
wait and see.

Arriving on the motorcycle, and dressed as he was with
the sunglasses and his slightly wavy hair a bit too long in the
back, there was definitely an untamed restlessness surrounding Nick Logan. Anyone could see that. But Eden was
learning from firsthand experience that restlessness was a
manifestation of other problems, an offshoot of inner unrest. And, while any woman worth her salt could recognize
his blatant flirtatiousness, it would take someone well ac-

quainted with despair to recognize the sadness hiding deep
in the recesses of his teasing dark eyes.

*You're fooling yourself, Eden. Face it. You just want him
to stay because you're restless. And lonely.*

That wasn't true, she argued with herself. She wasn't *that*
lonely. It was just that he looked like he needed a little care.
Someone to give him a good hot meal. A little...
mothering. But Eden was honest enough with herself to realize that it was an emotion far distanced from maternal
concern that prompted her to defend her appearance.

"I apologize for looking such a wreck, but I've been in
the garden, and Mariah just now called to let me know you
were on the way."

Wreck? Here she was, thinking she looked like a wreck
while he contemplated how her deep, throaty voice sounded
as if she'd just made hot, fast love to someone. He wondered if she always went around dressed like a wild thing
from the Louisiana swamps and if the sweet promise of her
mouth was a lie.

Nick cleared his throat and tried to clear his mind of the
disturbing thoughts. He wasn't certain when, if ever, a
woman had made such an impact on his libido. "I hope I'm
not disturbing you."

"No. Not at all," she said hurriedly.

He shifted his weight to one leg and smiled again. "Mariah said you had an apartment to rent."

*"Trouble with a capital T."* Tess's words were a reminder
from the depths of Eden's memory.

"I do, yes, but it's been vacant a long time and I haven't
really finished remodeling," Eden hedged.

"I don't need anything fancy. Just a roof over my head."

"Oh." Eden twisted her fingers together and wondered
what she could say to that. "How long would you be staying?"

He sensed her hesitation. His laughter was short, almost embarrassed. He made a sweeping gesture toward the motorcycle. "I know I travel light, but if you're worried about the money, I can give you a couple of months in advance."

"Oh, no! I mean . . . you're a friend of Mariah's."

"Which automatically makes me honest?" he asked, lifting his heavy eyebrows.

Eden couldn't help smiling at that. "No. It automatically makes you—"

"Wild? Crazy? A little flaky?" he asked, liking the way her mouth tipped up at the corners. She looked like a woman who needed a reason to smile.

"I was about to say interesting," she said. Then added, "Maybe just a little flaky."

Nick laughed, a rich, warm sound that scattered frissons of tingling awareness through her.

"Would you like to see the apartment?" she asked.

"If it's no trouble. I can come back later if you're busy," he offered.

She shook her head. "I'm not doing anything. The kids are gone for the day, and I was just going to take a shower and fix some dinner."

"Kids?"

"I keep a couple of preschoolers. I had three others, but they moved before school started." *As if he's interested, Eden. Don't bore the poor man silly. . . .*

"Why do you baby-sit?" he asked.

Eden looked surprised. "To make money, Mr. Logan."

"Nick," he corrected. "I'm too young to be Mr. Logan." Then, without waiting for her comment, he said, "I don't mean to be nosy, but I thought your family owned a timber company."

"We did. We do," Eden corrected. "But it's been hard since Daddy died. None of us really knows the business, and we've had a lot of repairs lately."

Nick's first thought was that he could help. He squashed it immediately. He wasn't about to tie himself down. "Tough," he sympathized, knowing firsthand how draining expensive maintenance could be.

Eden mistook his short answer for disinterest. "I'm sorry," she apologized. "I didn't mean to dump on you."

"You didn't," Nick assured her. "I asked."

He was... nicer that she imagined he would be, Eden thought, starting down the steps. "Let's go see the apartment."

"Don't you need to get a key?" he asked.

"Not in Calloway Corners," Eden said, as he fell into step beside her. "We seldom have thefts in the country. I lock up if I'm going to be gone a while, but otherwise, there's no need."

Side by side, they walked around the corner of the house toward the garage apartment Ben Calloway had built for the live-in help he'd hired to care for his daughters after Grace died.

She was a good height, Nick thought. Barefooted, she was just right for kissing... He pulled his thoughts up short. What was the matter with him? He'd barely set eyes on the woman, and he already had the hots for her in the worst possible way.

*So it's been a while, Logan. But that kind of thinking is stupid. Real stupid. Eden Calloway is not the kind you can love and leave. She's the two-point-five kids and station-wagon type. And worse, she's Mariah's sister, which automatically makes her out of bounds.*

He tried to ignore the way her unbound breasts bounced the slightest bit with each step she took.

"Mariah says you'll be working with Seth," Eden said to break the silence growing between them.

Nick shifted his gaze from the creamy swell of her breasts to the pure lines of her profile. What had she said? "I beg your pardon?"

She turned her head to look at him. "Mariah said you'd be working for Seth Taylor," she repeated.

"Yeah."

"Are you a carpenter, then?"

"I've worked with wood some," he told her truthfully.

"I suppose you've met Seth?"

"Once. Twice, maybe," he said thoughtfully.

"You'll like him," Eden said. "He's a nice guy, a hard worker and an excellent builder."

Nick heard the warmth in her voice. Was there something between his new boss and Mariah's sister? "It sounds as if you think a lot of him."

Eden smiled. "I do. I've known him all my life. I think he'll make Tess a good husband."

Nick couldn't hide his surprise…or his relief. "He's going to marry your sister?"

"He already has. A couple weeks ago," Eden said with a light laugh. "They're crazy in love, and I'm glad. They both deserve some happiness."

Crazy in love. Nick heard the words, words that once applied to himself and Belinda. He didn't believe in those words any more, and he felt that in a year or so, once reality set in, Eden's opinion of that elusive emotion would change, too.

Eden started up the outside stairs leading to the apartment. Nick followed a few steps behind, watching the slight sway of her slender hips in the short cutoffs. She was halfway up when she stopped suddenly, muttering, "Ouch."

Not expecting her to stop, Nick's momentum carried him right into her, so hard that he knocked her off balance. She uttered a soft cry of surprise as his arms circled her waist and he pulled her against him to keep her from falling forward. For the span of a brief second, he was aware of her breasts pressed against his arm, of the fragrance of her soft hair crushed against his face and the way the roundness of her bottom rested against the most masculine part of him.

"What's the matter?" he asked, his breath stirring the tendrils of hair near her ear.

"I got a splinter in my foot," Eden explained, acutely conscious of the strength of his arms circling her, the hard breadth of his chest and the aroma of some masculine cologne with a sharp, peppery scent.

Nick's hold on her relaxed. "Sit down and let me see."

With his hands steadying her, Eden turned on one foot and sat down on the rough wooden step, which was in dire need of a painting. Nick backed down a few feet and, cupping her heel in the palm of his hand, lifted her foot to eye level.

Eden was left staring at the top of his head and trying to ignore the warmth of his hands supporting her foot and ankle. That funny, uncomfortable feeling returned, and to help combat it, she concentrated on trying to decide what color his hair was. Not black, she thought, but dark, coffee-bean brown. She imagined she could smell the clean fragrance of his shampoo, but decided she was probably fooling herself.

"I see it," Nick said. The splinter was small, perhaps half an inch long, and imbedded in the ball of her foot just below the skin. He brought his own booted foot up a step and let her heel rest on his bent knee. Then, wedging his hand into his tight jeans pocket, he drew out a small knife and opened the blade.

"Is it so serious I need surgery?" she asked as he leaned over again.

The teasing question brought his head up in surprise. With their faces no more than a foot apart, there was no mistaking the smile dancing in her eyes. He would have never guessed from what he'd heard that Eden Calloway possessed a sense of humor. Pleased, he smiled.

"You never know," he responded with false seriousness. "I believe in being prepared."

Her lips curved into a heart-hammering smile, and Nick bent to his task once more. Sliding the blade of the knife beneath the splinter and securing the sliver of wood between the blade and his thumb, he pulled the splinter out with one quick jerk.

"Ouch!"

"Sorry," he said, angling her foot to see if there was any wood fiber left beneath the skin. "That ought to get it. I'd wash it real good and put some peroxide on it when you go in."

Eden massaged away the smarting pain in her foot. "Thanks. I will." She grasped the railing to pull herself up, and Nick automatically reached out to help her.

"Thanks," she said, hoping he didn't notice how breathless she sounded. Turning, she went up the remaining few steps and pulled open the screen door.

Nick followed her inside, easing the door closed behind him.

"This is it," she said, making a sweeping gesture with her right hand as she crossed the small kitchen to the living area. "There isn't a bedroom, but the sofa makes out into a bed, and it's a good one. As a matter of fact, it's new."

Nick's eyes swept over the big room, taking in the good quality cabinets, the new kitchen flooring and living-room carpet and the new furniture and wallpaper. "It's great," he said. "I can't imagine what would make it better."

"Curtains," Eden said, looking around the room, seeing the possibilities as only a woman can. "Or at least mini blinds." She turned back to the kitchen area. "I wanted to get some new flooring in the bathroom, and there's no table in the kitchen."

"No problem," Nick assured her. "What's the rent?"

"A hundred fifty?" she said, making it a question instead of a statement.

"Fine. I'll give you a month's deposit and a month in advance. Is that all right?"

Eden nodded. "Yes."

"Do you want me to sign some sort of lease agreement?" he asked, reaching into his pocket again.

"That won't be necessary," Eden told him as he counted out the cash. No use confessing that she hadn't even thought of having some sort of agreement made up. No use confessing that business wasn't her strong suit, that she was better at baby-sitting and making jam.

Nick offered her the money and held out his hand. "It's a deal, then," he said.

She put her hand in his for the second time, letting her hand get lost in the strength and warmth of his. His fingers were long and the nails were clean and cut short. Dark hair grew on the back of his hand. She couldn't help thinking how capable a hand it looked...not at all the hand of a motorcycle bum. With a bit of regret, she pulled her fingers free and stepped away.

"I'll go and let you get settled," she said.

Nick's sexily shaped mouth curved into another of those devastating smiles. "That shouldn't take long, since everything I own is on the bike."

"Then you'll need linens and towels. I'll bring some later."

"Great."

"The television gets good reception," she told him, heading toward the door. "But they haven't brought cable out this far yet."

"No problem. I don't watch a lot of TV anyway. I read a lot."

"Really?" she asked, an avid reader herself. "What type of books do you read?"

"Mainstream. Adventure. Stephen King. Ludlum."

Eden smiled. "We have similar tastes, then. I have a lot of books if you care to come and check them out some time."

"Thanks, I might do that," he told her. "But I imagine I'll be too tired to read most nights."

Eden smiled. "Seth is a hard taskmaster." She lifted herself to her toes and lowered her heels to the floor, knowing she should leave, but reluctant to do so. "I'll go now, but I'll bring the other things later."

"Thanks. I appreciate it."

Eden stepped outside and started down the stairs. The memory of his smile stayed with her all the way to the house.

NICOLE LOGAN'S CHARCOAL STICK moved slowly, as if she knew what she wanted to portray but wasn't certain she had the skill to do it. The evening gown she was sketching was a new idea, the lines sleek and simple and exceptionally good. Clothing design was something she always wished she could have tried her hand at. Indeed, she had studied art at school and had plans to go on to a New York art school when she had had the . . . breakdown.

The charcoal in her slender fingers snapped beneath sudden pressure, and the dark mark on the sketch of the gown ruined the perfect clarity of her design. Nicole's mind whirled with the pain of half-remembered feelings and snatches of conversation that haunted her even after eight years. Why couldn't she remember?

She had been pregnant, but because of the circumstances surrounding the baby's conception and her resulting mental instability her mother and the doctors had decided that she shouldn't have the child.

Rape. An ugly word for an ugly deed. It didn't make sense. Everyone said she had loved Lucas, and he had loved her but if they loved each other, why would he hurt her that way?

Shaking her aching head and groaning at the memories that wouldn't leave her alone, Nicole's eyes filled with tears. Her hands lifted to her ears to shut out the sound of her own voice screaming. There had been the sound of scuffling, yelling, and the sound of flesh meeting flesh. Luke had fallen...and then...

And then what? She couldn't remember. She could never remember beyond this point. Needing to escape, Nicole leaped to her feet and ran to the bathroom medicine chest, grabbing a bottle from the row on the second shelf. She shook two tablets into her hand and gulped them down with a paper cup full of water. Her eyes, wide and frightened even after all this time, stared back at her.

*Don't think about it!* she commanded herself. Think about something, anything else. She whirled away from the mirror and ran into her bedroom, the tail of her white silk robe billowing out behind her. Think about something nice...something pleasant, she thought, flinging herself across the thick down comforter of rose satin. Think about...

Nick!

Nick. She rolled to her back and covered her face with her forearm, willing the troubling memories away and forcing herself to think about Nick and how wonderful it would be when he came home for good. Where had he come from when he called her the night before? Where had her brother gone when he'd left her that morning? Remembering the tenderness of his touch and the strength emanating from him, Nicole felt the rapid beating of her heart slow to a more natural rhythm.

In a matter of minutes the tablets began to work their
particular brand of magic, and Nicole Logan was trans-
ported to a land of sleep where she was able to bask in
blessed forgetfulness.

ONE HOUR TO THE MINUTE after Eden had left her new tenant to settle in his new domain, she was ready to face him
once more. Bathed, and with her newly washed hair creating a red-gold halo around her face, she took a deep breath
and started out the backdoor, carrying a plastic trash sack
filled with items Nick would be needing while he was in
Calloway Corners. She crossed the brick patio and went
down the three steps and across the short expanse of sidewalk, which disappeared abruptly into a thick mat of St.
Augustine grass.

By the time she got to the bottom of the apartment stairs,
Nick, was coming out of the door, almost—ridiculous
thought—as if he'd been watching for her. Nick at the top,
Eden at the bottom, they stared at each other. It couldn't
have been for more than a couple of seconds, but it was long
enough for Eden to note that he'd taken off his shirt and
that, even as low as his jeans fit on his hips, there was no
telltale tan line. The natural segue of her thoughts brought
a blush to her cheeks that darkened the hint of makeup she'd
applied after her shower.

It was long enough for Nick to see that she was nervous
for some reason. Was she having second thoughts about
renting to a strange man in a place where no one locked their
doors?

She started up the stairs.

"Stay there," he said, bounding down the steps in his
socks. "I'll help you."

Used to carrying heavy loads, Eden couldn't help feeling
a rush of pleasure as well as surprise. It was nice to have
someone take over a task as small as this one, she decided.

She relinquished her burden, but the narrowness of the stairway didn't allow for her to precede him up. Instead, she followed, a witness to the way his tight jeans molded the purely masculine muscularity of his buttocks and the strength of his thighs.

At the top of the steps, he held the door open for her, following her inside and setting the bag on one end of the sofa. Eden dumped the contents out and began to restack the towels and washcloths.

"Would you like me to put the sheets on the sofa bed for you?" she asked.

He looked surprised by the offer. "I can do it, thanks."

She couldn't help smiling. "I keep forgetting that today's man isn't as helpless as my dad was."

Nick plunged the tips of his fingers into his front pockets. "Helpless?"

Eden shrugged. "Well, maybe not helpless. But they were waited on hand and foot. I'm afraid it's a habit I haven't been able to break since my father died. I still tend to pamper my sisters' husbands."

"I imagine they love it," Nick said.

"Oh, the guys love it," Eden confessed with a smile, "but it isn't endearing me to my sisters."

Nick laughed lowly. "I imagine not."

Something in the room made the sound of his low laughter intimate. To cover the rush of awareness pulsating through her, Eden picked up a bar of soap, which claimed to be one-fourth cleansing cream. "I thought you might need this."

"Thanks," he said. "I do. As a matter of fact, I'll need quite a few things."

"If you're buying a lot, I'd suggest Brookshire's on Highway 80," she said. "I try to use the local grocery stores for milk, bread, things like that."

"It's hard to buy a lot when you're bringing it home on a motorcycle," he said.

Eden smiled at the picture his words created. "I guess you're right. I can run you in one evening, or you're welcome to use the station wagon."

*Station wagon. Just as I thought.* "I might take you up on that."

Fighting off the breathlessness that resulted from another of his smiles, Eden didn't ask which offer he meant.

"Is there a fast-food place nearby?" Nick queried, his palm rubbing slow circles on the hair covering his chest. "I haven't eaten all day and I'm starving."

Eden, who had fixed and consumed three meals a day for as long as she could remember, looked shocked at the idea of someone not eating all day long. She was even more surprised to hear herself say, "I'm having leftovers, but you're welcome to join me if you like."

## CHAPTER THREE

"I HAVEN'T HAD any food this good since I was in high school and used to go home with one of my dad's foremen every now and then," Nick said, halfway through the meal. "This is great."

The praise fell on Eden's ears like a benediction. She had told Nick that she was having leftovers, when actually the purple hull peas were the only thing remaining from a previous meal. Fighting the panic that assailed her as soon as her invitation had tripped off her lips, she had rushed to the house and cut thick slices of ham to pan fry. In blatant defiance of the cholesterol warnings, she'd started potatoes crisping in a skillet of bacon drippings and quickly stirred up a batch of corn-bread muffins, which were popped into the oven. By the time Nick arrived almost thirty minutes later, she'd sliced a platter of fresh tomatoes, and everything else was close to being ready.

"Thank you," Eden said. "Some fried okra would have been good, but it takes a while to do."

"If this meal was any better I couldn't stand it," Nick said, popping a bit of buttery corn bread into his mouth.

Eden was glad she'd gone to the extra trouble. Without any false modesty, she knew she was a good cook. No, she was a great cook, one thing she had over her sisters, who could barely boil water. She actually enjoyed it, but she hadn't cooked much since her father died. It was nice to know she hadn't lost her touch, and that something she did was really appreciated.

"Why haven't I met you before?" Nick asked, spooning redeye gravy over his second helping of ham and potatoes. "I've been through here a couple of times to see Mariah."

Eden had been wondering the same thing. "I don't know. I've heard a lot about you from Mariah."

Nick grew thoughtful suddenly. When he looked up from his plate, there was seriousness in his eyes. "Is she happy?"

"Mariah?" Eden said, wondering at the twist the conversation had taken. "She's happier than I've ever known her."

"And the reverend is treating her okay?" Nick pressed.

Eden couldn't help the questions of her own that flitted through her at his subtle interrogation. Why was he so concerned about Mariah? Was he carrying a torch for her sister? Is that why he had come through the Haughton area to see her on more than one occasion?

"Ford adores her," she said, truthfully.

"He'd better."

*Oh-oh.* Eden frowned and drew in a slow, troubled breath. If Nick did still care about Mariah, she might as well nip it in the bud. The last thing her sister needed was a brokenhearted swain on her doorstep. "You aren't, " she began, "I mean, you don't...uh— Are you in love with Mariah?"

She didn't know what kind of answer she expected, but it certainly wasn't the look of total surprise that molded Nick's face, or the deep, rich laughter that filled the dining room.

"Me? In love with Mariah Calloway? Thankfully, I have better sense."

"Then why do you keep coming around?" Eden asked, puzzled.

"She's a good friend. Men and women can be friends, can't they?"

"Of course," Eden said, thinking of her own friendship with Seth. "But Mariah is hardly the type to listen to anyone's troubles, much less sympathize with them. And she's never been particularly stable. Oh, I don't mean... It's just that she's so...so—''

Nick smiled briefly. "I know. But Mariah and I never shared our troubles. Never asked each other questions we wouldn't have wanted asked of ourselves. We took each other at face value, lived each day as it came, and each of us understood the other's need to do what we did and to be what we were, even though we didn't know why.''

His eyes had grown cloudy with memories of places she'd never been, things she'd never seen. Eden watched him visibly pull himself back to the present.

"Sometimes, Eden, someone comes along and you know, I mean you *know* that that person is going to play a major part in your life. You know that the vibes, or whatever the hell they are, are right.''

He shrugged, obviously embarrassed by the depth of his observation. "Mariah and I felt that in each other. We've shared some of the most meaningful experiences in life, and neither of us would risk losing what we feel for each other by falling in love.''

Eden couldn't think of a single reply. She was surprised and impressed, both by his feelings and by his ability to vocalize them. From the image he projected, she wouldn't have thought Nick would have a serious or meaningful thought in his whole body. So much, she thought, for first impressions.

"Does that ease your mind?'' he asked, breaking the quiet growing between them.

Eden's gaze flew to his. "I beg your pardon?''

His mouth curved into a knowing smile that caused her sedate heartbeats to stumble. "Tell the truth, Eden. You were worried that I'd come back to stir up trouble in Mariah's life, to try to win her back or something like that—weren't you?''

Eden couldn't resist the smile. She returned it. "Yes."

"Well, rest your fears. I only want her to be happy." Then, as if they hadn't been talking about the past, he asked, "It's amazing how different all you sisters are. There isn't a single thing the four of you have in common."

"Yes, there is," Eden corrected. "The Calloway green eyes."

Nick laughed. "That's about it, all right. I've never seen four more different girls come from the same two parents."

"We come in sort of matched sets, though," Eden told him. "Mariah and Jo are the type to set the world on fire, and Tess and I are the type to keep the home fires burning."

"Is that why you've stayed here all your life? Because you're the homey type?"

Hearing Nick refer to her as the homey type made Eden feel like a pair of worn-out house slippers. Irritation, as it had so often of late, stirred inside her. She felt a sudden need to make him understand, perhaps to make herself understand why she'd made the choices she had, even though they weren't sitting so well with her now.

"The homey type," she repeated, and hoped he didn't notice the sarcasm. "Well, that's certainly part of it. I don't think any of us can deny our true nature for long. But it's more than that."

"Tell me," he urged. "You're a beautiful woman. If you're anything like your sisters, you're smart."

*Beautiful?* Plain vanilla Eden Calloway? The compliment tripped off his silver tongue so easily it had to be a lie. "Salutatorian," she said, reminding herself that his compliment was meaningless, only a word and an overused one at that.

"I beg your pardon?"

"I was salutatorian of my senior class."

"But you didn't go to college. Why? Why would someone with so much going for them elect to stay in a small town?"

Eden's laugh was short and tinged with uncertainty. "I've been asking myself that a lot lately, and I've come to the conclusion that it's several things."

"Like?" he prompted, spearing a bit of ham and popping it into his mouth.

"Like our mother dying when Mariah was born. As strange as it sounds, that one incident sort of . . . shaped all our lives. At least it did mine." Her eyes met Nick's. "I was the oldest and, even though we had a housekeeper, I somehow felt that I had to take care of everyone."

"How old were you?" Nick said.

"Seven." Eden's smile was both wistful and poignant. "You have to understand what I said earlier about us not being able to deny our basic natures. I've always been the serious type. When Mama left to go to the hospital, she told me to take care of Daddy and the girls while she was gone. I took her literally. When she didn't come home, I thought her instructions still stood. Of course, I couldn't do a lot at seven, but the older I got, the more I took on myself.

"By the time I was fourteen the housekeeper was gone, and for all intents and purposes, this house became mine. My sisters all came to me for comfort and advice as I took on more and more of a mother's role. It wasn't planned, and it wasn't any big sacrifice on my part, it just . . . happened. In the beginning I did it because Mama always taught us that when we started something we should see it through. Later I stayed because it was easier than going out and making a new life for myself."

Nick mulled over what she'd said. He wasn't certain that he could have made the sacrifices Eden Calloway had for her family. "Didn't it ever chafe?" he asked. "Didn't you ever wish you could leave it all…get married and move away, or just go follow the wind?''

The question shook Eden, coming so close to the feelings plaguing her of late. "Sometimes," she muttered.

The knowledge that the conversation had drifted around to things she would rather not think about made her realize that she and Nick Logan had got into a pretty heavy discussion. She hadn't imagined they would find any common ground for conversation, and here she was, spilling her heart and soul to him—a total stranger.

She pushed her chair back and leaped to her feet. "How about some coffee and peanut-butter pie?" she asked.

"Peanut-butter pie?" he asked incredulously.

"It's good. I make the best piecrust in the ArkLaTex," she boasted.

Nick laughed, a deep throaty sound that sent frissons of pleasure and longing down Eden's spine. "I'll just bet you do."

The rest of the evening was spent talking about the area— how good the fishing was on Lake Bistineau, the upcoming Red River Revel and the state fair. It was only after he'd gone, the kitchen was cleaned up and Eden lay in her solitary bed trying to banish the memory of his smile from her mind that she realized that, while Nick was an accomplished conversationalist and talk between them hadn't lagged at all, he hadn't volunteered one word about himself.

NICK STARED UP at the freshly painted ceiling of his temporary lodging. He shouldn't have had that cup of coffee, he thought, turning restlessly to his side. He needed to get to sleep if he wanted to impress Seth Taylor the next day, but he couldn't get Eden Calloway off his mind.

He could still picture her as she'd stood at the edge of the porch, the afternoon sun glinting off the red-gold of her hair, the thin cotton knit clinging to her sweat-damp body, and the way her hips and legs had looked in the short cut-offs. The impact she'd had on him was nothing short of phenomenal, since he'd met quite a few women the past three years and considered himself to be pretty jaded.

She was softness and light and the serenity of cool lily ponds, all wrapped up in a hoydenish package that under-scored her femininity instead of detracting from it. Yet her actions and the picture she painted of herself all indicated that Eden saw herself as the country mouse, scurrying around in the shadow of her more glamorous sisters.

Anyone who wasn't blind could see that she had more things going for her than she imagined. There was a warm naturalness about her that made her easy to talk to. She was a gracious hostess, anticipating his every need, from refill-ing his glass to refusing his help with the dishes. And every now and then, he got a tantalizing glimpse of a sense of hu-mor she tried to hide—or didn't know she possessed.

*Not to mention her body.*

Nick's own body responded to the memory of the thrust of her nipples against the wash-softened fabric of her tank top as his thoughts came full circle. Even though she'd been more soberly dressed in slacks and a cotton knit scoop-neck sweater at dinner, it was the picture of her long tan legs and the swell of her breasts that robbed him of his sleep. How could any woman who looked like she did possibly be con-sidered a spinster?

*And how can you possibly be thinking such erotic thoughts about Mariah Calloway's sister?*

Damn! As much as he was intrigued by her, as much as he'd like to pursue getting to know her and teaching her that she had the potential to be as exciting as her sisters, he knew he shouldn't. Too much was at stake, and for the moment, he'd run as far as he could.

Running. He'd been pursuing that pastime for three years now, ever since Belinda's betrayal. Ever since his father's act

of disloyalty. He ran from the truth of his family's perfid-
iousness, from his own feelings of insecurity and in search
of qualities he wasn't certain even existed. Integrity. Loyalty. Love.

If it weren't for the love he felt for Nicole, Nick would
have denied its existence. Belinda certainly hadn't loved him,
and familial love was a joke. His mother, Theresa, hadn't
cared enough for him to take his part and fight the injus-
tices done to him at his father's hands, and whatever emotions bound his parents, love and respect didn't appear to be
among them any more . . . if they ever had been. It was no
wonder.

At sixty, Stuart Logan, the still-handsome timber mag-
nate and sole owner of Logan Enterprises, was energetic,
ruthless and, as one of the richest men in the ArkLaTex, a
law unto himself. Which is why, even though Nick loved
every aspect of the timber industry and Keith despised it,
there had been no complaints when Stuart decided years ago
that he would make Keith vice-president.

Then, a month before the appointment was announced,
Keith had left for Europe and one final fling before he took
his place in the business world. But instead of coming home,
he had expanded his three-week vacation to one month and
then two. Word filtered back that Keith was seen skiing in
Zurich, sailing on a friend's yacht in the Caribbean and
gambling in Nice. And everywhere he went there were
women. Unsuspecting ingenues on vacation with their mid-
dle-income families. Wealthy widows. Rich playgirls who
frequented topless beaches and flaunted their femininity
with G-string bikini bottoms. Keith Logan had become the
epitome of the metropolitan playboy.

In June, after months of waiting, Stuart had come to
Nick, who had recently graduated magna cum laude from
the University of Arkansas at Fayetteville, offering him the
vice-presidency if he would agree to learn every aspect of the

timber business. Nick accepted the offer without hesitation, making the mistake of thinking the offer indicated some sort of change in his father.

For the next five years, Nick worked in every one of the various businesses that made up the Logan conglomerate. He bought timber, leased land and helped replant hundreds of square miles of cutover land. He learned to operate a skidder and ran the machinery at the plywood factory and lumber mill as well as personally going over the books for each company. At twenty-six, he was on the brink of accepting the position he'd worked so hard for and just a few scant weeks from a marriage the social columns deemed made in heaven.

Then, as plans and worlds are wont to do, his began to fall apart. Without warning, without fanfare, without so much as a postcard, Keith came home, jaded and broke and pitifully penitent. Without any apparent thought for either Nick's hard work or feelings, Stuart offered Keith, his prodigal son, the position he'd deserted five years earlier. Nick's position. A position Keith didn't hesitate to accept.

Crushed, Nick fought the fury and disappointment filling him, but in the end he'd lost the battle. He should have known better than to trust Stuart, but what really hurt was Keith's willing acceptance. It proved beyond a doubt that his brother was a true Logan.

Nurturing his battered heart, Nick looked to his upcoming marriage for hope and happiness. Two weeks later, he made an unplanned visit to Belinda's apartment and found Keith in his fiancée's bed. In a rare show of violence, Nick had beat his brother's handsome face to a pulp and left.

He spent a night wallowing in liquor. With his life and his dreams as shattered as his brother's nose, Nick fortified himself with a strong dose of bitterness and set out on a new Harley Davidson with no place to go, no destination in mind. He would run with the wind until the money left to him by his grandmother ran out, and then he'd see.

And that was exactly what he'd done. With nothing to lose, he'd sought the fast lane. Fast cars, fast planes, fast boats and fast women. His only regret had been leaving Nicole. It still was.

He could see her now, as she'd been earlier that morning, a beautiful, fragile woman standing in front of a rundown café, watching with a lost look in her eyes as he'd cranked up the bike and driven away.

That look saddened him. The Nicole who had been so full of life as they were growing up had ceased to exist somewhere along the way. He knew that the trouble with Luke Tanner and Nicole's subsequent breakdown the summer after they'd graduated from the university was the root of the problem. She had come home from the exclusive sanatorium in California where she'd spent almost two years, a changed person—no longer vivacious, rambunctious and a little wild. Yes, she functioned in the world. She even ran her own clothing boutique. But the fire of her personality had been extinguished, and in its place was a fragile, delicate, even docile person Nick hardly knew. She seldom dated and had never married.

Up until that summer, he and Nicole had shared everything, but she never talked about what had happened the night Keith had brought her home, battered and bruised, Luke Tanner's victim. The doctors said that even though she had been told what happened, she didn't remember it or the loss of her unborn child a few weeks later. In the curious way the mind has, it had banished the events to some dark corner where they might never be recalled. Like Nick, but in her own way, Nicole was running from her past.

Looking back, he was never certain when the running had stopped and the search had begun. Was it when the pain of Belinda's deception dulled? Or when he'd dragged Mariah

Calloway from the salty sea off the coast of Aruba? Nick had heard of soul mates, but he'd never believed in their existence until he met Mariah. Like him, she was running hell-for-leather toward destruction at the same time she secretly wished someone would stop her.

Mariah understood his need to race in the Grand Prix, just as he understood her need to take his place when he'd broken his leg. They were both drawn by danger, filled with restlessness and urged on by an impossible need to seek tomorrow today. He hadn't shared his past with her; she accepted that. At first, she'd been as silent about her yesterdays as he was, but gradually she began to share her feelings with him. Feelings for the father she loved so much, funny stories about her sisters and warm tales about the small Louisiana town where she'd grown up.

If anyone had asked him what he was looking for, Nick couldn't have said. But whatever it was, Mariah held the key. Maybe it was proof that the close-knit, loving family she claimed to have was real...or to prove it wasn't. Maybe that's why he'd subconsciously headed his bike in the direction of Calloway Corners when he'd left Nicole standing alone on the sidewalk that morning. Maybe in spite of everything he was still nurturing the faint hope that the very things his heart and mind now denied really did exist.

EDEN GOT UP at five-thirty and put on the coffee to brew as she did every day. But this morning was different. It had taken her hours to go to sleep the night before. Her mind had been so busy replaying every nuance of her meeting with Nick and their conversation at dinner that it had been almost an hour after midnight the last time she'd looked at the clock.

Even now, the memory of his hands on her ankle and foot tugged at the heartstrings of her femininity, making her wonder what they would feel like on other parts of her.

*Cool it, Eden. The man isn't interested. He's too young,
and very accomplished at flirting, so don't make any big
deal out of it.*

Right. She wouldn't.

Why was it that sex seemed to be on her mind so much
lately? she wondered as she laid several strips of lean bacon
into a cast-iron skillet. Though it was touted in books,
flaunted on television and served as the basis for every kind
of advertising from toothpaste to beer, sex—or the lack
thereof—had never been more than a fleeting problem.

Whenever Eden's curiosity threatened to get the best of
her and tempted her to find out for herself what all the fuss
was about, Eden reminded herself that the place she'd cho-
sen to live, the place she would probably spend the rest of
her life, had an extremely healthy grapevine. There were no
secrets in a small country town, especially if there was any
hint of gossip about any member of the elite few families
who were considered the backbone of the community.

She'd always considered indiscretion of any kind too big
a chance to take, and she had squelched her infrequent bouts
of sensual longing and filled her life with more activity.
More canning, more community projects, more kids to care
for. The strategy had worked amazingly well until lately,
when, one by one, her sisters had found the man of their
dreams. Eden realized that her chances of finding that same
fulfillment were growing slimmer every year.

*Unless you marry Dan.*

Eden placed a strip of bacon on a paper towel to drain.
She'd tried to give Dan's proposal serious consideration as
she'd lain there wide awake the night before, but somehow
her thoughts were taken up with Nick Logan and the feeling that he needed someone...some mothering, maybe.

*Get real, Eden. Mothering was the farthest thing from
your mind when you saw him getting off that bike. And it's
the last thing you think of when he smiles at you.*

Determinedly, Eden took some frozen orange concentrate from the freezer. Okay, so Nick was attractive and he made her feel attractive. There was no crime in that. He might be younger than she was, but she was only window-shopping; she wasn't planning on marrying the guy. She was thirty-three and on the shelf—not dead. The fact that she could appreciate a handsome man and the way he filled out his blue jeans only proved, thankfully, that her hormones, though packed away, were still alive and well. It meant that even though her biological clock was ticking away, it hadn't run out. But it didn't mean anything else.

It certainly didn't mean that she felt anything more for Nick Logan than her usual inclination to take care of someone. After all, she'd spent the better part of her life doing just that, and now that her father and sisters were gone, it was only natural that she try to find someone who needed looking after. As a matter of fact, Nick couldn't have come along at a more opportune time. She needed someone to take care of right now, someone or something to fill the void in her life. She'd lost three of her kids when school started, and with Molly's and Jamie's mother only working part-time, it left her with far too much time on her hands.

Eden dismissed the nagging feeling that she was fooling herself and added three cans of water to the orange concentrate.

She was stirring the juice when she saw Nick step out onto the landing. Leaving the wooden spoon in the pitcher, she crossed the hardwood floor to the back door, pushing the screen door open and heading across the patio and down the sidewalk. She stepped out onto the dew-wet grass just as Nick reached the bottom of the steps. Then, as if something drew his attention to the house, he stopped and looked in her direction.

She was barefoot again, he thought, and wearing another pair of cutoffs, but this pair was newer, less frayed. Her lightly tanned midriff was left bare by a khaki-hued, sleeveless crop top with a knit band below her full breasts. He sighed and folded the earpieces of his glasses together.

"Good morning," she said.

"Hi."

Eden couldn't help noticing that his smile was missing. "Slept badly, huh?" she asked.

"Terrible," he admitted, hooking the earpiece of the glasses into the pocket of another T-shirt.

Her nerve was failing fast. "Probably the coffee and a new bed," she said inanely.

"Probably."

*Ask him, Eden. You've come all the way out here. You have to do something besides tell him good morning.*

She locked her hands behind her back and lifted herself to her toes, then lowered her weight back slowly to her heels. "Since you don't have any groceries, I thought I'd see if you'd like breakfast—or at least some coffee."

Nick considered the invitation. Just as he'd finally drifted off to sleep, he told himself that he'd do everything in his power to stay away from Eden Calloway, for her sake and for him, yet here he was, giving serious consideration to her offer of a shared breakfast.

Why not? he asked himself. He liked being with her. He was lonely; she was lonely. And like Mariah, there was something about Eden that calmed the inner unrest that drove him from horizon to horizon.

Mariah.

She was Mariah's sister, and he didn't want to spoil that relationship, but what harm was there in spending a little time with Eden? A few meals, a little conversation and some harmless flirting never hurt anyone.

"Sure," he said.

He smiled then, the smile she'd missed seeing when he'd first walked up, a smile that went straight to her heart and made her forget that Nick was the age of her youngest sister.

"DID YOU UNPACK the new jewelry, Sandy?" Nicole asked, rubbing at her throbbing temple absently. The medicine always made her feel as if she'd indulged in a three-day drunk the morning after she'd taken it, but sometimes she had to have the stuff for her sanity.

A young woman with sleek blond hair looked up from the blouse she was buttoning onto a mannequin. "Sorry. Not yet."

Nicole gritted her teeth to keep from saying something she knew she'd regret. "You watch the front," she said. "I'm going to the back for some coffee. I'll unpack it myself."

"Okay," Sandy said, hearing the subtle reprimand in her boss's voice.

"And Sandy. Move those scarves to the front window."

"Yes, ma'am."

Nicole walked through the narrow showroom toward the stockroom and the coffeepot, her heels sinking into the luxurious carpet. Nicole's was one of the most popular and exclusive boutiques in Little Rock. Her parents had set her up in it after she'd come home from the hospital in California. Surprising everyone, Nicole had taken to the rag trade like a duck to water. She had an eye for color, a flair for fashion trends and a burning desire to be self-supporting.

And she finally was, Nicole thought with a smile. Last year she'd repaid her father every cent he'd used to finance her business. Stuart had taken the money, not, he'd told her, because he'd needed it, but to humor her.

They'd been humoring her for years. Which was why Nicole had declined their offer to buy her a house on Edgehill Road in the Heights. She lived, instead, in the once-elegant house in Little Rock's Quapaw Quarter, which had been left to her by her grandmother. Bit by bit, she was restoring it to its former beauty, and the very nature of the necessarily slow process was healing for her, in a strange way. She only wished Nick could find some way of healing the hurt inside him.

Hardly aware of its beauty, Nicole unwrapped a big, clunky necklace of brass and copper, an import from India. She understood why Nick couldn't stand to be around either her father or their brother, Keith, but she didn't understand why Nick felt the need to ride that damn motorcycle all over the world. And she didn't understand why he didn't settle down somewhere nearby and do what she'd done. She'd made it on her own. She'd proven that despite the . . . problems she'd had, she could survive in the world. She'd proven that she could overcome the past, even though its very elusiveness haunted her at times when she least expected it.

A strange unexplained sixth sense warned her that someone was watching her. Her hands stilled and Nicole lifted her head from her task. Keith stood in the doorway, his hands thrust negligently into the pockets of his expensive slacks. Nicole's eyes widened and her fingers tightened around the rough-edged disk. She took a deep breath and willed the frantic beating of her heart to a slower pace.

"Hello, Nicci," he said, sauntering into the storeroom as if he owned it. Nicole wanted to tell Keith not to call her by that name. Nicci was Nick's pet name for her. She wanted to tell Keith to leave. But she only sat there, clutching the necklace as if it were a talisman against some dreaded evil.

He stopped directly in front of her and, reaching out, tucked a lock of mink-brown hair behind her ear. Nicole fought a suffocating feeling. Jerking her head back, she swiveled the desk chair and leaped to her feet.

Keith only smiled. "So how's business?" he asked, his blue eyes roaming the clutter of the stockroom.

"It's good. Very good," she tacked on to let him know she no longer needed Logan financial support.

"That's great," he said with a million-dollar smile. "What's been going on?"

Nicole shrugged. "The same thing. Work. More work."

"And I don't suppose you've seen Nick lately?" he asked.

The bit of color in Nicole's cheeks paled.

Keith noticed. Seemingly of its own volition, his hand came up and rubbed at the bump marring the bridge of his once perfect nose...a blemish he refused to correct because it reminded him of the mutual hatred between him and his brother. He smiled again, a smile meant to invite confidences, a smile that usually worked very well, but was wasted on the woman standing before him.

"Well, where's he off to this time?" Keith asked cheerfully. "California? The Bahamas?"

"I don't know," she said, glad she could answer him truthfully. "He didn't say."

Keith's blue eyes grew icy and his smile turned brittle. The little bitch was getting too damned independent. "Oh, I think he did, but since you're so busy, I won't bother trying to get you to tell me. I'll let you get back to your work," he told her, sauntering toward the door.

Nicole watched him go, and her breathing didn't return to normal until he disappeared from sight.

"What a hunk!" The praise preceded Sandy, who burst through the door with typical twenty-year-old enthusiasm. She stopped short just inside the room. "Good grief! What happened?"

Nicole blinked away the blank look in her eyes, having no idea what Sandy was talking about. Following the direction of the younger woman's gaze, she looked down at the front of her outfit. Blood stained the toffee-hued skirt of her

silk dress. Like someone drugged, she lifted the hand still
clutching the necklace, uncurling her fingers from it to re-
veal a ragged cut where the sharp edges of the sphere had
sliced through the soft, pampered skin.

## CHAPTER FOUR

SATURDAY, NICK'S FIRST day off, rolled around. He rose early as usual, thinking how easy it had been for Eden to persuade him to join her for meals. By Friday, their routine seemed set. Breakfast at six in the morning; dinner after he'd come home and cleaned up each evening.

He had thought that a few meals, a little conversation and some harmless flirting couldn't hurt anyone. He was wrong. So much proximity to Eden Calloway was making him forget his altruistic vow to leave her alone because she was Mariah's sister. Like water dripping on a stone, the time spent with her was eroding his resolve and the layer of flint he'd shrouded his heart in.

He was learning that it was nice to be with a woman for a purpose besides the obvious—though the farfetched possibility of that particular scenario occurring with Eden held definite appeal. And time spent with Eden reaffirmed what logic told him was true: there were good women in the world.

He had watched her with Molly and Jamie. Eden was patient, gentle, loving, yet firm. He overheard snatches of conversation with her sisters and couldn't help but hear the love in her voice as she offered tidbits of advice and soothed their fears with sisterly concern. He knew that she made cookies for the youth group at Ford's church, and he listened as she made plans to visit the old folks' home in Bossier City. She took a casserole to a woman who'd lost her husband in a car accident, fried chicken for a friend who just had a new baby and offered to keep someone's kids just so the woman and her husband could drive to Jefferson, Texas, to spend their tenth anniversary at a bed-and-breakfast inn.

If anyone had told him about Eden's good works, he might have pictured her as a self-righteous do-gooder. But the picture he was forming was far from that. The simple fact was that Eden Calloway was a caring person. A person who took time out of her life for other people. No—a person whose life revolved around other people. He liked her. He liked her a whole hell of a lot. So much, in fact, that he didn't intend to stay around over the weekend for more exposure.

Eden wasn't the kind of woman a man could love and leave without destroying her...or himself...or maybe both. And he wasn't the kind to stay anyplace for long. *Don't forget that, Logan, and you'll be okay.*

He knocked on the door, but poked his head inside before Eden called for him to come in. She was at the sink peeling a banana. In the split second before she turned, his appreciative gaze tracked the way her faded jeans conformed to the slim length of her legs and her sweetly curved derriere. He tried to ignore the way his hands itched to feel that roundness against his palms.

"Good morning," he said, uncomfortably aware of the way the sunshine coming through the window gilded the coppery tints in her reddish hair and the way the brightness of her smile lightened his heart.

"Hi. Breakfast is almost ready."

"I think I'll pass this morning." He saw her smile fade a degree and could have sworn that a cloud passed over the sun. "I should have told you last night, but I...uh...just forgot. There's a battlefield in Vicksburg that's crying out to be seen, and I need to do some laundry and stuff before I head out," he told her.

"Oh." Her breasts lifted in what could have been a sigh of disappointment. "Are you sure you don't have time for a quick bite?" she pressed. "I fixed milk gravy and home-made biscuits. You said it was your favorite."

Nick wondered if his shock was evident. He couldn't re-member anyone doing anything especially for him, except maybe Nicole. "You did that for me?" he asked. "Why?"

It was Eden's turn to look surprised. "Why? Because you said you hadn't had it in years—homemade, that is. It was no trouble. I would have fixed it eventually, anyway."

How could he fight that kind of logic? And how could he refuse to eat, knowing she'd cooked the meal especially for him? Nick experienced a feeling that was a cross between what an innocent being led to the lion's den might feel and the same thrill that raced through him whenever he rode the Harley wide open. Like a man going down for the count, he murmured, "I appreciate it," and then sat down.

"I HAVE A DEAL to make with you."

Nick was finishing his second helping when Eden made the offer. "What kind of deal?" he asked a bit warily.

"You do a few things around here for me, and I'll do your laundry."

Guilt rushed through Nick. He should have offered to pay her for the meals. He laughed uncomfortably. "Damn. I'm such a jerk! Here I am, probably eating you out of house and home and not offering you a cent."

"Don't be ridiculous," Eden said, refilling both their coffee cups. "I just thought that you might be willing to work out a trade. I need some things done before winter. I'm deathly afraid of heights, and the gutters need to be cleaned out from last year, and there are a few loose shingles, things like that. I thought if you didn't mind, it could be mutually beneficial."

Nick nodded. "I don't mind at all. As a matter of fact, it sounds great. If there's anything I hate to do, it's laundry."

"It's a deal then?"

"Deal," he said.

Ten minutes later, Eden watched him disappear down the gravel road that led to the highway with a strange sense of melancholy. What would it be like to just pick up and go whenever you felt like moving on? And how long before Nick packed up his meager belongings in his Harley full-dresser and traveled down that road for the last time? She turned back toward the house, thankful that Mariah and Tess were joining her for lunch.

In their honor, and because the temperature was still hovering at the miserable eighty-eight-degree mark, Eden closed the windows and doors and turned on the air-conditioning. Because her sisters were so weight conscious, she had scooped out tomatoes and filled the ruby-red cavities with chicken salad. But she drew the line at omitting the sugar from the iced tea, even though Mariah and Tess claimed that she made it so sweet it was like syrup and that every ounce they drank earned them a pound in weight gain.

At lunch, Eden served her "syrup" in frosted glasses with a sprig of mint from her herb garden, and both sisters raved. Replete, they carried their sweating glasses into the big living room to visit. Eden chose a rocking chair, this one salvaged from the nearby dump and refurbished to its former glory by hours of painstaking work. Mariah and Tess settled into opposite corners of the sofa.

"Wonderful lunch, sister dear," Mariah said with a sigh, calling Eden by the pet name they'd teasingly given her when they were all younger.

"Thanks. It's nice to have someone around at meal-time."

Mariah smiled archly. "I figured that you'd have talked Nick into joining you by now."

Eden's cheeks burned with hot color.

Mariah chortled with glee. "Hot damn—I mean, hot dog! I just won twenty bucks from Ford."

"Do you mean that you've corrupted our local preacher by tempting him to make bets?" Tess teased.

"Honey," Mariah drawled, "you'd be surprised at how many ways I've corrupted my husband."

Tess laughed. "So how did you win the twenty?"

Mariah cast Eden an apologetic smile. "I bet him that Eden would be cooking for Nick and taking care of him the same way she does everyone in less than a week."

How well they knew her, Eden thought. "Well, he didn't have any groceries that first night," she said, determined to defend her actions. "And besides, it's lonely here with Daddy gone."

Neither Mariah nor Tess could overlook the wistful note in their older sister's voice.

"You need to get away from this house and do something different, Eden," Tess said. "Why don't you take some classes at the community college?"

"Tess," Eden warned. "Please don't start. I'm thirty-three years old. I don't want to study at night."

"Ah," Mariah said, winking at Tess. "It's the nights that are getting to you, huh?"

"If you'd get out more, you could get a date," Tess said.

"I date," Eden informed her sister in a frosty tone. "As a matter of fact, I have something to tell you."

Mariah gave Tess a this-sounds-important lift of her eyebrows. "Well," she asked, "what is it?"

Eden raised her chin. "Dan Morgan asked me to marry him."

"What?"

"Dan!"

Mariah's response was chorused with Tess's.

"Is this the same Dan Morgan you dated in high school?" Tess asked, a frown furrowing her smooth forehead.

Eden nodded. "Yes."

"The same one who married Gail what's-her-name?"

"The same," Eden said, getting the feeling that her news was being received with slightly less enthusiasm than a case of the flu. "Well?" she said at last. "Say something."

Tess looked from Mariah to Eden. "Well, it's none of my business, but I always thought he was a real jerk for breaking that date to the prom because you had to be in earlier than all the other girls did," Tess offered. "But that was a long time ago, so why should I hold it against him? It's how you feel that counts."

Eden stifled a sigh and looked at Mariah.

"I hardly remember him," her youngest sister said. "But I say forget it."

"Forget it? He might be my last chance."

"Exactly," Mariah said, with her knack for getting straight to the point without much thought for sensibilities. "Which is why I think you should examine your reasons for even considering it. Do you just want to get married because we've all taken the plunge, or do you love the guy?"

Eden was too shocked to answer. Mariah's question had hit dangerously close to the actual truth.

Despite the bluntness of her words, Mariah's eyes held love and genuine concern. "Look, Edie, if his smile doesn't curl your toes and if his kisses don't make your heart turn back flips, forget it," she advised. "Life's too short. You'll always be sorry if you marry him without really loving him."

Tess's gaze shifted from the earnestness on Mariah's face to Eden. "She's right. It's better to gamble and lose on the real thing than to settle for second best."

Eden pushed herself up from her chair and strode restlessly to the fireplace where a black and white portrait of

Grace and Ben Calloway sat. She picked it up and stared into their smiling faces. They had been so happy. Even though she didn't remember, she knew it was true, because her father had told her. She tried to superimpose her face over her mother's and Dan's face over her father's and failed. Frustration rose like a tide inside her. She wanted what they'd had, but she was so afraid she would never find it. Not here. Not at this stage of her life. Hugging the picture to her breast, she turned to face her sisters.

"I know you're right," she said, "but what are my chances of finding what all of you have found? I know all the men who live around here and, believe me, you all got the last good ones."

Mariah rose and went to Eden. She took the picture from her and set it in its place on the mantle. Then she framed Eden's face with her palms the way Eden recalled Grace Calloway doing on so many occasions. Eden's eyes filled with tears. It was seldom that she and any of her sisters swapped roles, and when they did, she always felt a little guilty.

"Don't give up, Eden," Mariah said. "You never know when your knight might come riding up on his white charger and carry you away."

Without warning, a vision of Nick astride his shiny black motorcycle flashed through Eden's mind. Before she could register anything more than mild surprise, Mariah, with the irritating way she had, picked up the conversation they'd shared on the phone the day she'd called to tell Eden that Nick was coming over. "Your hair really is very becoming."

Thoughts of Nick fled as laughter gurgled up in Eden's throat. She hugged Mariah, thankful that her often wacky sense of timing had saved the potentially heavy moment. Even Tess laughed, though she didn't exactly understand the joke. Eden and Mariah released each other. "Promise me you'll think about it a long time before you say yes," Mariah demanded.

"Yeah, all right," Eden said with a resigned nod. "I promise."

"Good." Taking for granted that the subject of Dan Morgan was finished, Mariah said, "I hate to bring this up right now, but I guess there won't be a really good time."

Eden's intuition told her that something was wrong. "What is it? The baby—"

"The baby is fine. But I talked to Ted yesterday afternoon, and he says that the hydraulic gun at the mill has just about had it."

Ted Vincent was the Calloway lumber company foreman and had been for the past twenty years. When Ben died in December, it was Ted who helped Eden as she struggled to grasp the everyday workings of the mill. It was Ted who'd explained the interaction between the loggers who cut the trees and the mill that cut the timber into the finished lumber. He'd told her how the lumber was then distributed to various companies who sold the kiln-dried product to the public. And, while Eden had done her best to understand the workings of the company her family had founded, she would be the first to admit that her knowledge was hardly more than superficial.

"I had a sneaking suspicion that this day was coming when I checked things out with Ted in February," she said with a sense of fatalism.

"Yeah, well, we're meeting production on faith and hope. Ted says the gun could go any time," Mariah told them.

"Maybe we ought to just sell out," Tess suggested.

Mariah looked aghast. "Sell out! Tess, that company has been in our family for *years*! It just wouldn't be the same if the Calloways didn't own the lumber mill."

"I understand that, but we have to be practical. Because Daddy was a died-in-the-wool chauvinist and none of us were boys, he didn't think we needed to learn anything about the business. We have to face the fact that none of us knows diddly about what's going on down there. It's only a matter of time before we have to do something."

"Tess is right, Mariah," Eden said. "We can't go on trusting in luck indefinitely."

"I don't even want to talk about it," Mariah railed. "I know that when I started answering the phone and running the discount store back in February I didn't know anything, but I'm learning every day. I can't imagine the mill not belonging to the Calloways. I want to pass that legacy on to my child."

Tess and Eden exchanged tolerant looks at the reminder of Mariah's pregnancy. They didn't want to upset her, because even though Mariah was happy about the baby, she was still battling her fear that she would die in childbirth.

"I understand how you feel," Eden said, "and you know we'll do everything possible to hold on. It's just that Daddy let things run down so badly the last few years, and with the pine beetle infestation two years running..." Eden's voice trailed away, her point made. "I've been thinking that we'll see how things go through the end of the year, and then try to get a professional consultant in to tell us where we stand. Maybe we can use the mill as collateral and borrow enough money to renovate and upgrade or something. The new thing seems to be computerized equipment. Until then, let's just sit tight and see what the economy is going to do."

Mariah smiled. "That's a good idea. You always think of something."

Eden smiled wanly.

"Well," Tess said. "Since we've solved our immediate problems, I've got to get it in gear. Seth wanted to go to a movie tonight, and I have to pick Jason up at his mother's and take him to Tony's to spend the night."

"I need to go, too," Mariah said. "The young married couples are getting together at the house and I still have to make a mountain of sandwiches."

"If you had let me know earlier, I could have done it for you," Eden said.

Mariah wore a look of mock indignation. "Eden, Eden, you can't do everything for us forever. When that knight of your comes along, he might whisk you off to some glamorous place, and if I couldn't make tuna-fish sandwiches, how would I manage?"

"You have a point," Eden conceded with a smile.

"What are you doing tonight?" Tess asked. "If you don't have any plans, you can go to the movies with us."

Eden rolled her eyes ceilingward. "No, thanks. I may be a wallflower, but you can't ever accuse me of being a fifth wheel. As a matter of fact, Dan is taking me to Firenze's for dinner."

"Firenze's?" Mariah said. "My, my, I'm impressed. Have Nick tell you about that little French place on the Riviera sometime." She stood on tiptoe and kissed Eden's cheek. "See you later, and remember—think about it."

"I will."

Tess hugged Eden, and the trio crossed the polished floor to the door. A bit sadly, Eden watched them go to their cars, then waved as they pulled out of the drive. She stood there for a moment, worrying over Mariah's comments about the mill and her assumption that things would work out.

Why was it that everyone thought she had all the answers, when she couldn't even decide what she should say to Dan? Even taking her sister's warnings to heart, Eden still wasn't sure what her answer to his proposal would be.

THE MOTORCYCLE SPED through the night, the wind tearing at Nick's hair. In defiance of the law and in keeping with some intangible inner turmoil, he often rode without a helmet reveling in the feel of the wind and the exhilaration that rose inside him.

Speed had always been an aphrodisiac, a higher high than any drug could induce and more mind-altering than any chemicals known to man. When he was racing with the wind, the lines delineating the highway were somehow mesmerizing, unrolling before the spinning wheels of the Harley and enabling him to separate his actions from the churning thoughts of his mind.

The trip to Vicksburg had done one thing: it had separated him physically from Eden. But it had failed to do what he really wanted. It hadn't kept him from thinking about her and her family and how genuine they all seemed.

*Not seemed, Logan. Are.*

Okay, so the Calloways were some of those rare creatures—actually an endangered species in this old get-even world—genuinely caring people. But they'd probably never had hard times. The depth of their caring had probably never been tested. Would they all be close if one of them tried to take the family business from the others the way Keith had done him? Would Mariah be so loving toward Eden if she found her in bed with Ford?

Memories of the past inevitably brought memories of Nicole. Memories and guilt for leaving his sister to deal with whatever secrets haunted her from the past.

The Goodwill Road exit veered off to Nick's right and, shifting to the side, he took the slight turn that led to Highway 80. It was nearing one in the morning, but Nicci wouldn't mind if he called. He pulled into a gas station, a place obviously popular with truckers.

Braking to a stop, Nick turned off the motorcycle and leaned it against its stand. Then he wedged his hand into his pocket and pulled out a fist full of change. He dropped a quarter into the pay phone, dialed the operator and gave her the long-distance number. It rang once. Twice.

"Hello?" Nicole whispered in a drowsy voice through the phone lines.

Nick smiled. "Hey, sleepyhead."

"Nick?" Nicole cried, instantly awake. "Nick, where are you? Are you here?"

"Shh, sweetie," he said. "Slow down. I'm not in Little Rock. I'm in Louisiana."

"Louisiana? Where in Louisiana? Keith came by to see if I'd heard from you, but I told him I didn't know where you were."

Nick's mouth twisted bitterly. Keith liked worming information on his whereabouts from Nicole. "Good for you. How are you?"

"I'm fine." Her laughter was thin. "It seems like longer than a few days since I've seen you."

"Why don't you let me come and get you for a while?" he said. "I've got a nice apartment in a little town."

She sighed heavily. "I can't, Nick. The boutique—"

"Oh, right," he said with a smile. "I keep forgetting that you're a big businesswoman these days."

"You'd better have a smile on your face when you say that," Nicole warned.

"I do, I do." Nick looked up at the star-spangled sky and felt more lonely than he had in a long time. How had it come to this? he wondered. Why was he separated from the only person in the world he loved? It wasn't fair, but until she saw fit to leave, there was nothing he could do about it. "Look, Nicole, I'm at this truck stop," he said, "and someone wants to use the phone. I'll call you in a few days, okay?"

"Okay. I love you, Nick."

"I love you, too. Bye." He cradled the receiver and got back on the Harley, anxious to get home, his mind centered on the relative peace he'd felt since he'd been in Calloway Corners and the woman who was chiefly responsible for it. He pulled out onto the road and made the right-hand turn onto Highway 80. Was Eden asleep in her solitary bed? Did she think of him as often as he thought of her? He smiled into the night.

Now why would he imagine that Eden would be interested in him? She thought he was exactly what he appeared to be—a no-account biker who couldn't hold a job and wanted no responsibilities. She was thirty-three and single, and he'd bet his Harley that she hadn't stayed single so long for lack of offers. No, the lady obviously liked her freedom, and it was the height of arrogance and presumptuousness for him to even think that she would be interested in him.

He saw the Doyline road ahead and geared down to make the turn. Just a few more miles and he'd be there. Just a few more miles and he'd be home....

EDEN WOULD BE GLAD when they got home. Dinner had been nice, and the comedian at Jody's Comedy Shop had been funny, but she knew that once Dan pulled into the driveway, the preliminaries would be over and they would get down to the real purpose of the date—her answer to his proposal.

What would she say? Mariah said she shouldn't marry him if she didn't love him. And Eden did love him, although she grudgingly admitted that it wasn't the wild kind of crazy, she-couldn't-live-without-him love; it was a safe, I-like-being-taken-care-of kind of feeling. The problem was that even though she'd never experienced the former, and was fairly certain at this point in her life that she never would, was it fair to Dan to marry him when she didn't feel the same depth of emotion for him as he did for her? Was she settling for second best? And would she be giving Dan second best?

She closed her eyes and leaned her head against the headrest. As seemed to happen frequently of late, a picture of Nick sauntered through her mind. Nick, wearing his skin-tight jeans, his T-shirt and sunglasses, running his strong tanned fingers through his wind-tousled hair.

Nick. Mariah's friend. Too young to be anything more than her friend. And why would she think that he wanted to be more? He was worldly, handsome, and he'd been around. She was a country girl born and bred. She didn't belong in his fast-paced world any more than he belonged in the slow, easy world of hers.

The car came to a halt, and Dan shut off the engine. Reluctantly, Eden opened her eyes. Dan turned toward her, his left arm hooked over the steering wheel, his right draped across the back of the seat. His short blond hair glittered in the moonlight, and his eyes, blue and hidden in shadow, regarded her with tenderness, the same tenderness that molded the curve of his lips. He was handsome, she thought—not a dashing, reckless sort of handsome like Nick, but a quiet, even-featured attractiveness.

"You've been quiet all evening," he said, the hand near her head brushing the hair away from her face.

"I think I'm just tired," she said. And she was. Tired of the sameness of her life. Tired of doing the same thing, seeing the same people.

"I won't keep you, then," he said, leaning down to brush his lips across her cheek.

Eden reached up and placed her hand against his smoothly shaven face, and Dan's mouth moved to hers. There was gentleness in his kiss, and love, and an underlying hunger that told her he wished she would ask him in. She'd thought about it several times, but somehow, she just couldn't, even though they had been dating several months.

Eden enjoyed his kisses and caresses—it never occurred to her that most men would have considered her a tease—and she even wondered what it would be like to feel his naked body next to hers. She wondered, but not enough to risk finding out.

Dan's tongue broached the barrier of her lips, and he pulled her closer. There was something different about him tonight, an aura of intensity usually lacking in his manner. She could feel it in the demanding way he kissed her and in the masterful way he brought his hands to her breasts. Taken by surprise, Eden didn't object. It was nice, she thought, judging his kisses from an objective viewpoint. Very pleasant. But not earth-shattering.

His mouth deserted hers, and he trailed a string of kisses down her neck, inching inevitably toward the swell of her breasts. But before he reached her collarbone, the unmistakable sound of an approaching motorcycle rent the still of the night.

Nick! Eden froze. She couldn't stop the rush of guilt that coursed through her. The gleam of the single headlight sliced through the night, illuminating the interior of the car. Dan straightened with a curse.

"Who the hell...?" he grumbled, turning toward the approaching sound.

"It's my new tenant," Eden explained, torn between gladness that Nick was back and embarrassment because he'd ridden up while she was necking with Dan in the front seat of the car.

"Well, his timing is lousy."

Maybe it was, and then again maybe it wasn't, Eden thought as the Harley flashed past, down the drive leading to the garage apartment. She wondered if he'd had a good day, if the battlefield had met his expectations and if he'd missed being with her for dinner.

"You could ask me in, and we could continue this in more pleasant surroundings," Dan suggested, his voice intruding on her wayward thoughts.

Her gaze moved from the shadowy form of the garage apartment to Dan's face. She felt another flicker of guilt. "I'm very tired," she hedged.

Dan's sigh underscored his irritation, yet he'd known what her answer would be. "And have you made up your mind about marrying me?" he asked, almost as if he knew the answer to that, too.

Eden shook her head. "I'm sorry. I know you're anxious for an answer, but I don't want to rush into a decision as important as this one. There are a lot of things to consider, Dan. I've been single for a long time. I'm set in my ways. You have two daughters, one of whom isn't crazy about the idea of your marrying anyone. It will be extremely hard on all of us to find a common ground."

"Michelle will come around," he said.

"I hope so. But I still want to be certain that what I decide will be the best for us all," Eden said adamantly. "And that includes Marla and Michelle."

"So the answer is no." There was no mistaking the disappointment in his voice.

"I don't have an answer. I need more time."

Dan drew in a deep breath and pulled her close. He held her tightly for a long time, and then planting a chaste kiss on her lips, released her. "You've got it."

Eden smiled in relief. "Thank you."

He opened the car door and helped her out from his side. Hand in hand, they walked up to the front porch. He unlocked her door and, with another brief kiss, left her standing there while he drove off into the night.

Eden couldn't help the guilt and sadness that washed over her. Why had she prolonged it? Why hadn't she just told him no?

*Because you didn't want to hurt him.*

She turned off the porch light, leaned over and took off her shoes and started toward the bedroom. The high-heeled beige pumps were tossed in the general direction of the open closet door. She hadn't lied to Dan. She *was* tired, but in a strange way she was keyed up. When she thought of Dan touching her, Eden grew hot with embarrassment—not for letting him do so, but for the reasons she'd allowed it. Oh, they'd had a lot of fairly steamy kissing sessions, but she'd never thought much about his kisses except that they were tolerable, pleasant, even. Tonight had been a deliberate experiment. She'd wanted to see if his kisses...what was it Mariah had said? She wanted to see if his kisses made her heart turn back flips. And she'd found out.

They didn't. Neither did his touch.

Darn! she thought silently, going to the bed and doing a belly flop on it. She was a thirty-three-year-old virgin—though there wasn't a person in the state who would believe it—looking to rectify that status quo, but somehow she couldn't...or wouldn't. Eden rested her chin on her palms. Why hadn't she ever plunged into the sexual seas of the new morality? Was there something wrong with her?

Restlessness, her constant companion lately, drove her to her feet and out to the front porch. The night air cooled the heat of her indignation, even though the breeze was warm and the humidity was high. It was a gorgeous night, the kind that hints of autumn even while holding on to the last heat of summer. She sighed. Autumn had always been her favorite season, but somehow, this year she hated to see the summer go.

With no regard for her new pantyhose, she crossed the peeling front porch and stepped out onto the dew-wet grass. Rounding the house, she headed toward the Oriental bridge that spanned the narrow creek that meandered across the expanse of lawn between the house and the grove of woods beyond the yard.

She was almost there when she noticed the shadow-shrouded figure standing at the top of the bridge's arch. Gasping in surprise and bringing her hand up to her pounding heart, Eden stopped dead still.

"Hi," a deep voice said, just before she saw the flare of his cigarette lighter.

Eden gasped. "Nick?" she squeaked.

His laugh was as warm and mellow as the night. "Who else?"

"You scared the daylights out of me," she confessed as her heart rate slowed to normal. "What are you doing out here?"

"I could ask the same of you. I thought you went in."

A hot blush warmed her face. Eden wondered if he had seen Dan kissing her. "I did," she said, going to stand beside him. "I wasn't sleepy."

"Me, either."

She leaned against the railing behind her and turned to look at him in the moonlight. The silvery glow of the moon gilded his wind-tousled hair and the bold planes of his rakish features, driving shadows into the hollows... interesting shadows that made him look handsome and exciting and just a little dangerous. Her heart sprinted forward once more. "How was Vicksburg?" she asked, wanting to break the growing silence.

He took a deep drag off the cigarette and blew the smoke toward the sky. Then he turned his head and smiled.

Eden's heart somersaulted in her breast.

*Never marry anyone until their kiss makes your heart turn back flips.* Mariah's words of wisdom sauntered through Eden's mind and meshed with the exhilaration unfurling through her. Kiss? she thought, in a dazed sort of wonder.

Her heart turned flips when he smiled at her, for crying out loud! What would happen if he kissed her?

"Vicksburg was good," he said, but she was so wrapped up in her thoughts she didn't hear him.

Eden knew now why she was so indecisive about Dan. It had nothing to do with his daughter's feelings and very little to do with her own feelings. Her inability to give him the answer he wanted had more to do with the man standing beside her, the man who had brought a breath of something new and invigorating into her life.

"What did you do today?" he asked, when she didn't respond.

Even though she was still reeling with the feelings surfacing inside her, Eden was able to respond to his question. She shook her head. "Nothing much. Mariah and Tess came over for lunch. I had a date tonight."

"I noticed. Anyone special?"

What could she say? She couldn't tell him that Dan had been pretty special until a drifter called Nick Logan had ridden into her life a few days before and turned it topsyturvy. She couldn't tell him that the unexpected and forbidden had happened, that in the span of a few short days she was feeling things for a stranger she was beginning to think she'd never feel. She couldn't tell him that she was drawn to him in a more intimate way than she'd been letting on even to herself... even though he was younger than she was.

"Are you asleep?" Nick asked, his voice sounding a thousand miles away. "Eden?"

"What?" she said in a dreamy voice, turning toward him and inclining her head to look up at him. It was a mistake, she realized too late. Looking into his eyes in the moonlight was tantamount to drowning in a warm sea of sensuality.

"Is he special?" Nick repeated, his voice soft and filled with...what?

"I've known him a long time," she said evasively. "Since high school."

"Oh," was all he said. Then he smiled again. "In that case, I have a suggestion to help you unwind."

His smile, she thought randomly, should come with a message from the surgeon general: *Warning. This smile hazardous to your heart.* "What do you mean—in that case?" she asked, unable to follow his thinking.

"I don't like to horn in on someone's else's woman."

For an instant, she literally stopped breathing. The implications of his simple statement couldn't be misconstrued. The words held infinite possibilities. And Eden wanted to explore each one. "And if I'm not...someone else's woman?" she asked, hardly able to speak for the breathless anticipation filling her.

"Then I'd ask you to go for a ride with me," he said, taking another pull off the cigarette.

"A ride?" she echoed, her eyes widening.

He nodded.

"On your bike?" *With my arms around you?*

"On my bike."

Eden thought about it a moment. But only a moment. The idea frightened her. Thrilled her. She'd never ridden a motorcycle before...after midnight...with a handsome drifter...a total stranger, but it sounded exactly like the kind of thing that had been missing in her life, and she was more than ready for something different. She shrugged with false nonchalance.

"Why not?" she said, tossing thirty-three years of caution to the wind. "It sounds like fun."

Her answer surprised Nick. And pleased him. He flicked his cigarette into the creek. "Then let's do it."

## CHAPTER FIVE

"WATCH OUT FOR THE exhaust," Nick warned a few minutes later as he rolled the Harley out into the moonlight. "It's probably still hot."

Eden didn't give her new paisley skirt a thought as she leaned down and grasped the back hem. She drew the garment up between her legs and tucked it into the waistband in the front, giving the skirt a Sumo-wrestler look. She smiled at her own ingenuity and climbed onto the seat, exposing a generous portion of creamy thigh. Nick was reminded again of what great legs she had.

He handed her his helmet. "Put this on," he urged Eden huskily.

Eden lifted the helmet to her head. It was heavier than she'd expected, and she would rather not wear it. She'd prefer to feel the wind in her hair, but law was law. With a resigned sigh, she fumbled to hook the straps beneath her chin. "What about you?"

"I hardly ever use it," he told her, reaching out to help. Their hands touched, warmth to warmth, but instead of drawing hers away as instinct dictated, Eden curled her fingers around his, stopping him.

"Then I don't want to wear it, either," she told him.

He looked deeply into her eyes. It might have been a trick of the moonlight, but he thought he saw pleading there...and something near desperation. He nodded and unfastened the chin strap. Then he helped her get situated on the seat, got on himself and started the engine. He turned and looked over his shoulder at her; their faces were mere inches apart.

Excitement and anticipation shone in her eyes. He watched her tongue peek out to bathe her lips with moisture in a move that was as unstudied as it was sexy. Nick's heart slammed into high gear. It was all he could do to keep from leaning over and taking her lips with his.

"Just hang on to me," he said over the sound of the engine instead, while he damned the fact that Eden was Mariah's sister.

She nodded and put her hands on either side of his waist. Even with the frail barrier of knit separating her hands from his flesh she could feel how hard and fit and warm he was. How would his skin feel to her touch? she wondered. Then, realizing the turn of her thoughts, a tormented sigh escaped from her. It promised to be a long ride.

Putting the bike into gear, Nick started the motorcycle rolling down the driveway, turning onto the gravel road that led to the highway and picking up speed with every second. The bike sailed up the slight incline of the railroad track and bucked as its well-sprung tires hit the steel rails. Eden yelped in surprise and grabbed him more tightly. She thought she heard him laugh.

Her arms circled his lean, hard waist and her breasts and cheek were pressed against the firm musculature of his back. He smelled like warm, virile man, she thought, imagining that she could hear his heart beating beneath her ear. A silly idea, considering that hearing anything over the powerful roar of the Harley's engine was almost impossible. What she thought was the pounding of his heart was more than likely the sound of her own.

While Eden fought the heady feelings generated by Nick's nearness, he turned toward town, the Harley hurtling through the night. Gradually, she began to relax. They passed through a residential section, and then the high

school loomed up on the right. Eden grinned. She wondered what her former principal would think if he could see
prim, proper Eden Calloway with her skirts hiked up, sitting astride a motorcycle.

Nick made a left at the corner, and then in the span of
half a block another right, and they were in the town proper,
which consisted of two grocery stores, a car wash, a feed
store nestled near the railroad tracks and a pulpwood company. Another series of snakelike curves brought them to the
parish library and a new video store and gift shop housed in
the old post-office building. Funny that she could remember when it was new.

The building of Louisiana Downs racetrack on the east
side of Bossier City a few years ago had contributed to the
residential and commercial growth in the other part of town
which, strangely, was located several miles away on Highway 80. That growth had necessitated the construction of a
modern new post office, which had been built on the last
vacant corner where McKinley and Highway 157 intersected. The intersection was a landmark of sorts...the only
red light in her hometown.

Her hometown. Home. Despite the restlessness and the
feelings she'd had of late, Eden was reminded that this was
the place all her sisters—like pigeons coming to roost—had
migrated to, the place she herself had never been able to
leave despite her occasional bouts of discontent...the same
discontent that had prompted her to take Nick up on his
offer of a midnight ride in the moonlight. A ride that was
miraculously soothing that discontent and easing the burden of her mind.

Time ceased to exist as the interstate unfurled before
them. Problems—what to do with her staid life, her petty
jealousy over her sisters' happiness, her possible attraction
to the man sitting in front of her—all faded beneath the roar

of the Harley's engine and the whisper of the wind through her hair.

Once, she'd thrown her head back to look up into the heavens and was astonished at the sudden finite feeling that swept through her. This was it, she thought, with something akin to panic. This was her life. Not a dress rehearsal. She was suddenly glad she'd accepted Nick's offer. Glad she hadn't missed this opportunity to savor the beauty of the September night with someone else...glad she'd had the opportunity to enjoy it with Nick, even though they hadn't spoken a word since he had filled the tank with gas at the Circle K before they'd headed for the Interstate.

Content with the moment, satisfied that she had done the right thing by accepting his offer, Eden laid her cheek against Nick's broad back, unaware that she tightened her hold on his waist the merest fraction. Unaware of the look of peace on her face that only the night witnessed.

It was approaching four in the morning when Nick let her off in front of the Calloway house. With the engine idling and staying astride himself, he helped her dismount. Still holding the hand he'd used to steady her, he took in the wild tangle of hair around her face and the unmistakable look of pleasure in her eyes.

"Well?" he asked, fighting the impulse to reach up and draw her head down for a kiss.

"I loved it," she said simply. "I'd like to go again some time."

One corner of his mouth formed a half smile. "I'm sure that can be arranged."

"Great," she told him. Then, rising up on tiptoe and lowering her heels back to the ground, she drew her hand free. "I'd better get to bed."

"Yeah. Me, too."

"Breakfast tomorrow?" she asked.

"Don't you go to church?"

"Yes, but—"

"I think I'll sleep in. I can pick up something at McDonald's later on," he told her.

Disappointment flooded her. She nodded. "I'll see you some time tomorrow, then."

"Sure. Good night."

"Good night."

Eden watched as Nick put the motorcycle in gear and headed toward the garage apartment at a leisurely speed. She was aware that she had been rather presumptuous to assume that he would want to have breakfast with her even on weekends. She was also aware that she didn't care. At some time during the ride she'd come to a decision...a vow that she would be more assertive, more aggressive about the things she wanted. She would live the rest of her life to the fullest, and the devil take the hindmost.

WHEN EDEN TOOK her usual pew in the Methodist church where she'd attended services for most of her life, she was aware of the low trill of hushed conversation that followed her. She was late, inexcusable behavior for Eden Calloway. But the night had taken its toll, and she'd been so relaxed when she'd finally got to bed that when the alarm had sounded, she'd slammed the off button down and promptly rolled over and gone back to sleep.

Thank goodness Mariah and Ford were cooking hamburgers after church, she thought, discreetly covering a yawn. At the thought of Ford and Mariah, a shaft of guilt shot through her for what she was coming to think of as a long string of mini problems in her life. She was torn between thirty years of loyalty to the congregation where she'd grown up and a feeling of disloyalty for not supporting Ford in his ministry. After all, Ford *had* been a pillar of strength during Ben Calloway's last illness, and Ford had delivered a moving message at her father's funeral. For a while, Eden had been a regular attendee of Ford's, but somehow she hadn't been able to give up her childhood Methodist ties. Thankfully, the sermon started before her mind could launch a full-scale inner battle over the problem, and by the time the service was over an hour later, Eden had forgotten it.

She was making her way slowly through the crowded aisles to the foyer when a familiar voice said, "Car trouble, Eden?"

Eden turned to see Jessamine Hardy, the self-appointed congregational conscience, standing behind her, a look of righteous concern on her bright-eyed face. Eden fought back a retort as sharp as Jessie Hardy's features and forced a pleasant smile to her lips. "No, Jessie. I'm afraid I overslept."

Jessamine tsk-tsked and shook her head. "You're working too hard, my dear, what with cooking for that young man staying with you and all."

Eden's eyes widened a fraction. How on earth had Jessamine Hardy found out that Nick was sharing meals with her? And how dare she insinuate that there might be something shady going on? Knowing Jessamine as she did, Eden knew she hadn't misconstrued the older woman's sly comment that Nick was "staying" with her.

Determined not to let the gossipy old biddy get the best of her, Eden showed her teeth in a grim smile. "Actually, Jessie, it's been lonely since Daddy died. I'm enjoying having someone to cook for again. And Nick seems to need some looking after."

"Commendable, Eden," Jessamine said, knowing that Eden had her number but not willing yet to let go of the topic of conversation. "Absolutely commendable. We'd expect no less of Ben Calloway's daughter. But you watch yourself with that young man."

"I don't know what you mean, Jessie," Eden said evenly, thinking that if Jessie called Nick "that young man" one more time, she would scream. "Nick is an old friend of Mariah's—"

"Exactly," Jessie interrupted.

Eden gave the nosy woman a frosty look. "I beg your pardon?" she said in matching tones.

Jessamine knew that she'd overstepped unspoken boundaries at last. She smiled ingratiatingly. "No offense, dear, but we all know that Mariah was a wild little thing before she married that preacher fellow. Her friends might not be...well, you know what I mean. And sometimes when women get to be your age, they get lonely and do foolish, desperate things."

Eden felt another of those guilty feelings wash through her, perhaps because Jessamine Hardy was so close to the truth. Is that what was happening to her? Was her agreement to go with Nick on the motorcycle last night an act of foolishness? And heaven help her, was she *desperate*?

Clutching her purse against her breast, Eden forced another smile. "I appreciate your concern, Jessie. Really. But I'm not prone to acting foolishly."

Jessamine nodded in seeming total agreement. "That's what I told Ned when he said he saw you on the back of that boy's motorcycle at the Circle K last night."

Eden's face blanched and her heart nosedived to the tips of her toes.

"Ned had the heartburn real bad and had to go get some stomach tablets," Jessie explained, mollified by the shocked look on Eden's face. "I told him it couldn't be you when he said the woman had her skirt all hiked up around her hips and...Eden? Eden?" The last words were flung at Eden's departing back, as she hurried toward the exit.

"I'm sorry, Jessie," Eden fabricated, throwing a panicked, apologetic look over her shoulder, "but I'm having
lunch with Mariah and Ford, and I'm going to be late."

Not waiting for Jessie's answer, Eden pushed her way
through the last lingering members and fled the church
building as if the hounds of hell were nipping at her heels.

Despite her need to get away, it took Eden five minutes to
make her escape with people asking her how she liked her
new renter and what it was like being a landlady to a young,
handsome drifter. Did he belong to the Hell's Angels? Had
he really saved Mariah's life? Was he working for Seth
Taylor? And did he really have a tattoo on his stomach? She
had driven away from church feeling like a gladiator who'd
just faced a coliseum full of hungry lions. One thing for
certain, the Haughton grapevine was in perfect working order.

By the time she went home and changed into her jeans
and shirt, Eden was in a thorough frenzy about what to do.
Should she do as she'd always done and conform to everyone's opinion of her, or should she stick to the promises
she'd made to herself the night before and live her life the
way she wanted? She hadn't shown any more leg with her
skirt pulled up than she would have in a pair of shorts and—

No, she'd made up her mind! She hadn't done anything
wrong by going with Nick, and she was darned if she was
going to let a bunch of narrow-minded old fogies dictate
how she should live her life!

THE FIRST THING Eden saw when she pulled into the driveway of Mariah's and Ford's newly finished house just off
Oliver Road was Nick's shiny chrome and black Harley. Her
firm resolve melted the slightest bit.

"Wonderful!" she muttered beneath her breath. "More
fuel for the fire."

She crammed the gearshift into park and grabbed her purse and the plastic container of oatmeal cookies from the seat, telling herself all the while to calm down. Everything was fine. Surely the grapevine wouldn't reach all the way to her sister's house.

The car door opened unexpectedly, and Eden looked up with a gasp. Nick smiled down at her.

"Hi," he said in a sexy tone that sent shivers down her spine despite Jessie Hardy's warnings. "Need any help?"

"No, thanks," she said, her tone a bit stilted. "I can handle it." She got out of the station wagon; Nick closed the door behind her. "I didn't know you were coming over," she told him. *If I'd known, I wouldn't have come.*

"I didn't, either," he confessed. "I was trying to decide which of Bossier City's fast-food places to have lunch at when Seth came over and told me Mariah wanted me to join you all." He smiled, and the crinkles in the corners of his eyes deepened.

Eden's heart did a cartwheel, and she thought again of Mariah's comment about hearts doing back flips.

"I'll take a charcoal-grilled hamburger over eating out any day of the week," Nick told her, unaware of her discomfort as he let her precede him up the steps and onto the porch.

He opened the door for her, and Eden paused in the doorway. Sounds of madness and mayhem assaulted their ears...the Calloway clan in top form. An unwatched television sat blaring forth a Sunday afternoon movie and Ford, Seth and his son, Jason, sat around a card table, playing a game of blackjack. Tess and Mariah were absent, probably in the kitchen, Eden thought. She was filled suddenly with an incredible sense of warmth and home that had nothing to do with Mariah's new house or decorating skills and everything to do with the people bantering lightly back and forth.

"Make those patties nice and thick, honey," Ford called out, his brow furrowed in concentration as he studied his hand.

"Stuff it, Rev," Mariah yelled back, "or I'll make you come in here and do it yourself!"

Ford might as well not have heard for all the impact her threat had on him. "And don't forget to warm the beans in the microwave." He eased the edge of his cards down onto the table and looked at Jason, who was dealing. "Hit me," he said, "but not too hard."

"Baked beans?" Tess sang out, loudly enough for all to hear. "Are they safe to eat? Who made them?"

"I did!" Ford and Mariah said simultaneously from their different vantage points in the house.

Eden cast a mirthful look at Nick, whose own eyes held a glimmer of laughter.

"Like hell," Seth drawled. "Oops! Pardon me, Preach. I brought those beans back from McClards Barbecue in Hot Springs when I went up for that load of rock." He spied Eden and Nick in the doorway, and his blue eyes lit with pleasure. "Hey! Come on in."

There was a round of welcomes, and Ford challenged Nick to try his hand at twenty-one while Eden excused herself and escaped to the relative quiet of the kitchen.

"Hello, sis," Mariah said, glancing up as Eden entered the kitchen. "What's in the container?"

"Oatmeal cookies."

"Mmm, good!" Tess said from her place at the sink where she was slicing onions and tomatoes. She tossed a smug smile over her shoulder. "The way to a man's heart is through his stomach, they say. And if that doesn't work, there's always a midnight motorcycle ride—right, Eden?"

Eden's mouth fell open. She couldn't have been more shocked if Tess had told her what color underwear she'd put on that morning.

"Come on, sis," Tess urged, her eyes alight with mischief, "Tell us about it. Where did you go?"

"Tess..." Mariah cautioned warily.

"I don't believe this," Eden said with a shake of her head. "What?"

"That everyone in town—maybe even all of Bossier and Webster parishes—knows I went for a ride with Nick. How? Who told you?"

Tess shrugged. "Seth said Glen Holiday told him. I didn't mean to upset you. I just wanted to rag you a little bit. Why? Has someone else said something about it?"

"Only half the Methodist church," Eden said, her voice thick with sarcasm. "Jessie Hardy cornered me and said that Ned thought he saw us at the Circle K."

"Well?" Tess asked.

"Well, what?"

"Did he see you with Nick?"

Eden threw her hands up in disgust and plopped down in a wicker chair near the dining table. Propping her elbows on the glass top of the table, she buried her face in her hands. "All right. Yes. Yes, he did. I did go for a ride on Nick's motorcycle last night. Barefooted, and with my skirt tucked up." She raised her head and pinned a challenging look on Tess. "Do you have a problem with that?"

Tess was familiar with that fiery light in her oldest sister's eyes. Through the years, they'd all learned that Eden had three moods: sweet affection, pouty brooding or total fury. Thankfully, the better side of her nature was also the side most often seen, and Tess certainly didn't want to stir Eden up. "I don't have a problem with it at all," she said, backing down from her teasing. "I *like* Nick."

Eden turned the look on Mariah, who leaned negligently against the cabinets, her arms crossed beneath her breasts, her face wearing a thoughtful expression.

"What about you, Mariah?" Eden taunted. "Do you have a problem with the fact that I went for a late-night joyride with your friend, even though he's your age?"

"More to the point," Mariah shot back gently, "do you?"

The question knocked Eden off stride. "What do you mean?"

Mariah shrugged. "You and Nick are both single. You don't have to ask anyone's permission to see him—least of all mine. But you brought up his age. Do you have a problem going out with a younger man?"

Eden considered Mariah's question. The fact that she was seven years older than Nick was a fact that caused her considerable worry... not to mention his rootlessness and his earthy handsomeness. There were at least a dozen other things about Nick Logan that cautioned Eden to be very careful in her dealings with him.

While Eden was still considering Mariah's query, the younger woman spoke. "Rest your fears, Edie. You aren't old enough to be his mother. He *is* younger than you, but he's three years older than I am—twenty-nine."

Eden made a quick calculation and exhaled a sigh of relief. She was only four years older than Nick.

"You like him, don't you?" Mariah said.

This question, too, caught Eden off guard. "What's not to like?" she tossed back flippantly.

Mariah smiled. "You're right. He's a nice guy. I'd trust him with my life, or— Good grief, you're blushing, Eden!"

Was she? The hated habit of blushing was a sure sign that Eden was telling a lie. "I am not!"

"He's sexy as all get out, isn't he?" Mariah probed.

Eden lifted her slim shoulders in a brief shrug. "How can I deny the obvious? Yes, he's sexy."

"I think you should go for it," Mariah said, surprising Eden with her unexpected blessing. Then she qualified her bold statement. "Go out with him. Have a good time. Nick is a lot of fun and he's a wonderful companion. He knows how to make the most of a moment."

Eden remembered the ride through the autumn night and how they had hardly spoken a word . . . how he had seemed to know that words weren't needed.

"Just don't fall in love with him," Mariah cautioned.

*Love!* Eden pushed aside a niggling feeling of unease. While she knew she was attracted to Nick—strongly attracted—she certainly hadn't thought of her feelings as anything approaching love. But now, with the possibility presented, she felt an inexplicable sadness. It was very possible that Mariah's warning had come one moonlit ride too late.

Eden's smile was wistful, like that of a little girl looking through the toy-store window at a ten-speed bike when all she could afford was a tricycle. She looked at Mariah. "Not even if his smile makes my heart do back flips?"

A look closely akin to fear—fear for Eden—crossed Mariah's striking features. "If you can stop it, don't let it happen, Eden. There's something inside Nick that won't let him stay in one place for long. He told me one time that he follows the sun. I don't know what drives him to keep packing up and moving on, but I know you shouldn't count on him staying. He never does."

Eden forced a smile to her lips. "Don't worry, Mariah. If I haven't fallen head over heels by now, I doubt Nick Logan could cause me to."

Tess's troubled eyes met Mariah's. The look in them said that she doubted there was anything Nick Logan couldn't cause a woman to do if he set his mind to it. Mariah agreed. She was going to have to give Nick a good talking to. Friendship was one thing. But blood, as they say, was thicker than water.

They had a good time laughing and conversing over the meal, which was eaten outside, on the redwood deck. The beans were wonderful, and the hamburgers were done to perfection. They had just finished playing a desultory game of cards and were contemplating drawing straws for naps on the sofa when an afternoon news brief came on, giving the effect of a new drop in oil prices on the economy.

Seth rose and turned the volume up. "I want to see if this is expected to hurt building in the Shreveport area."

Ford nodded. Nick yawned and stretched and then laid his head on the table while he waited for Eden to return with his cold drink, hardly aware of the news, and at the moment not caring.

"Closer to home," came the crisp no-nonsense voice of the newscaster, "Stuart Logan, a name that had been synonymous with the timber industry for four decades, is currently under investigation for wrongdoing connected with the July purchase of the Anderson plywood factory in southern Missouri."

Nick's head lifted; he focused his attention on the television screen. He wasn't even aware that Eden had returned.

"...An unidentified source says that several thousand dollars was exchanged as payment for a series of incidents that now look as if they were more likely sabotage than mere accident. Several other takeovers are also under investigation."

"Any kin to you?" Seth asked, turning to Nick with a smile that said he knew his question was ridiculous.

Nick's gaze held a thoughtful quality as he turned to look at him. "Pardon?"

Seth laughed. "I asked if you were related to those Logans. I was only trying to give you a hard time."

"There are a lot of Logans around," Nick said shortly.

He stood and turned, almost running into Eden, who was holding his glass. She was looking at him with concern etched on her features. A groundless fear and a nameless panic invaded him. He urged a smile to his lips and took the proffered glass, wondering how long it would be before he could make his escape.

"KEITH? DID YOU HEAR the news?" The feminine voice, coming through miles of phone cable, was filled with concern.

"Of course I heard the news, Mother." Keith Logan picked up the desk phone with one hand and strode as far as the cord would allow, his agitation apparent. "The police have been snooping around for the past two days."

"Well?" she snapped. "Are they going to find anything?"

Keith smiled grimly. "Let's just say that if the informer is who I think it is, there's a good chance that the allegations can be chalked off as nothing more than revenge for being fired."

A slow chuckle filtered through the phone lines. "Very good, Keith. What does Stuart say?"

"Don't worry about Dad. He isn't worried, because he doesn't know anything's up."

The woman laughed again. "Ignorance is bliss, huh?"

"So they say." Keith paused and looked out at the dreary September day. He rubbed at his aching temples. He'd never thought it would come to this. "I think you'd better take it easy down there. As a matter of fact, why don't you back off and let well enough alone for a while? We have to move easy on this one. Especially now. What you have done should start reaping benefits before long, wouldn't you say?"

"It should," Keith's mother agreed.

"Then we're okay."

"Keith, will you keep in touch?"

"Of course I will."

"And Keith," she said. "I always knew you'd come through for me."

He smiled, filled with a sense of accomplishment. "Thanks, Mother."


THE PHONE BOOTH outside the Country Corners grocery store was empty when Nick pulled the Harley to a stop. Straightening his leg and wedging his fingers into the front pocket of his tight jeans, he curled his fingers around some loose change, drawing it out and placing it on the booth's ledge. He put in a quarter and punched in Nicole's apartment number.

She answered on the third ring. "Nicole Logan."

Nick heard the assurance in her voice and wondered why, in contrast to her voice, she seemed so fragile.

"Hey, Nicci," he said, smiling even though she couldn't see him. "How's it going?"

"Nick! Hi. Are you here?"

Nick sighed. He hated hearing the eager, hopeful note in her voice. "No, baby. I'm still in Louisiana."

"Where in Louisiana?" she asked.

"A small town near Shreveport," he told her automatically. "Look, Nicole, I heard something on the news about—"

"The supposed sabotage of the Anderson plywood factory," she supplied.

Nick was surprised again. Fragile or not, there wasn't much that got by her. "Yes. Is it true? What do you know about it?"

"I can't say whether or not it's true. But you and I both know that through the years, Logan Enterprises has taken over a dozen places like Anderson's."

Nick's heated curse should have blistered the phone cable. The news didn't surprise him. If the truth were known, the Logans had probably been gobbling up small, independent companies even while Nick was working for his dad.

"So what are you doing?" Nicole asked, as if the subject of their family was closed. "You mentioned that you had an apartment."

"I do. I have a job working for a contractor."

"Nick Logan pounding nails?" she asked incredulous.

"You'd be surprised what I've done to earn a buck since I left Arkansas," he told her, turning to see a burly guy with a Mötley Crüe T-shirt and a greasy-looking ponytail waiting to use the phone.

"I doubt it. I know what lengths we'll both go to have our independence."

"Yeah." He sighed again, wishing he could find out more about the allegations against his father, but not liking the look on the waiting man's face. "I'd better go, Nicole. I'll talk to you in a few days."

"All right," she said grudgingly. "I love you, Nick."

"I love you, too."

Nick cradled the receiver and relinquished the phone. He made his way back to the Harley, his forehead drawn into a frown. He didn't know why he'd called Nicole. It only made things worse for them both, and he might have known she would know little more than he did. Come to think of it, he wasn't certain why he felt the need to know all the disgusting details. He guessed it was just that strange human weakness and fascination for horror. And he wondered if he would ever grow beyond it.

He recalled the feeling that had swept through him when Seth had asked him if he was related to the Logans who'd been spotlighted on the news. Fear, sharp and pungent, had filled him. Fear that he would be connected with his family and the peace and contentment he'd felt since coming to Calloway Corners would be snatched away from him with the same callousness as everything else he'd wanted in his life.

And fear that if Eden knew that his family was less sterling than hers, she wouldn't give him the time of day.

# CHAPTER SIX

THE NEXT TEN DAYS passed quickly, and October arrived as September departed—hot and sultry. Dove and quail gorged on the fat pods of goat weed growing along the roadways and in the fields, and the pasture grasses dried in the heat of the Indian summer sun. The sumac had turned scarlet, the color of the maple leaves ranged from yellow to salmon to crimson, and the hue of the sweet gums ran the gamut from bright red to deep purple, offering contrast to the plentiful oaks, which dropped their dull brown leaves desultorily or, as some species did, clung to them until the new leaves pushed them off in the spring.

There was a heavy, waiting quality to the autumn days that Eden found unnerving. She had a feeling that something was going to happen, though she couldn't imagine what, since nothing except the deaths of her parents had disturbed the even tempo of her life in thirty-three years.

In keeping with their agreement, Nick repaid Eden for her home-cooked meals and the laundry she did for him by emptying last year's leaves from the gutters on the house and cleaning out the chimney. He fixed some loose shingles, scraped and repainted the peeling front porch and fixed her garbage disposal when it went on the fritz. It was a mutually beneficial pact.

Not so beneficial were the considering looks she received from the Haughton residents who had known her all her life, nor the realization that she felt a growing attraction for Nick. Eden sighed. He seemed to be trying to put some distance between them since the Sunday afternoon they'd spent at Ford's and Mariah's.

Eden knew that something was bothering him, but she had the feeling that he would carry whatever it was to the grave. It often occurred to her how little any of them knew about Nick Logan. Still, that lack of knowledge didn't stop her from craving his smile or—despite Mariah's warning about falling for him—fantasizing about whether his sexily shaped mouth could drive her to distraction, the way she had the feeling it could.

Fantasizing. Eden shook her head, trying to rid herself of the memory of the incident more than a week ago that had triggered her first full-fledged fantasy. It had been on Monday morning, the day after they'd cooked out at Mariah's and Ford's. Nick had gone to work without breakfast because he'd overslept. She had gone to get his laundry as she had every few days since he moved in, and when she picked up the dirty, sweat-dampened jeans he'd worn the day before she had heard a dull thud as something fell to the floor.

Glancing down, Eden saw an expensive-looking, partially opened billfold on the kitchen tiles. She smiled, remembering how many times she'd washed her dad's billfold—money and all—because she'd neglected to check his pockets and he'd forgotten to turn them out . . . as Nick had. She reached down and picked up the leather square, but when she did, something fell to the floor, something small and square and covered in foil. Her fingers closed around it before she realized what it was.

*I like to be prepared.*

Nick's words, which had nothing to do with the present situation, spun through her mind, and the realization of what the object was dawned so quickly that she dropped the package again.

A condom.

Stooping once more, Eden gingerly picked up the foil pack, turning it over in her fingers. The breath trickled from her in a long, shuddering sigh. She didn't know why the thought of Nick carrying protection around should be so disturbing, since television, books and articles stressed the need for safe sex.

It shouldn't have bothered her, but it did. It proved beyond a doubt that Nick might be younger than she was, but that he wasn't a boy. He was a man with a man's needs. It meant that Nick had a sex life—not of course, that she hadn't supposed he did, as handsome and sexy as he was. But finding that condom put an end to supposition. This was proof positive that Nick had a lover, or more than one.

She put the condom in the billfold and laid it on the kitchen table. She hoped he would never know that she'd found it. It wouldn't bother him, of that Eden was sure, but *she* would be embarrassed if she even suspected that he knew.

It was much later, after she'd gone to bed, that she thought about it again. And with the thought of Nick making love to someone came the thought of him making love to her. She closed her eyes and imagined that he was kissing her...that gorgeous mouth of his was urging her lips to part, that his tongue was mating with hers while his hands covered her breasts....

With a sigh, Eden dragged her thoughts back to the present. She didn't seem to be able to help herself. After that day, the fantasies had become progressively graphic, progressively exciting...for all the good they did her. Nick was polite when he came for meals, nothing more.

Her gaze drifted to the kitchen window, which overlooked the garage apartment. The door was open, so she wasn't running the air-conditioning. Nick liked the house open when possible, too.

She loaded the last piece of flatware into the dishwasher and wondered why he hadn't come to breakfast. It was Saturday, a day he generally got off, but Seth's crew had been working overtime and on weekends to complete the renovations on a club on the once infamous, now fading, Bossier strip. Maybe they'd finished.

As she stood gazing at the apartment, the screen door opened and Nick stepped out onto the landing. Tucking in his shirt as he went, he bounded down the stairs.

Eden whirled away from the window before he saw her standing there like some lovesick teenager waiting to catch a glimpse of the boy she had a crush on...the same boy who didn't even know she was alive. A wry smile tugged at her lips. The analogy pretty well summed up the situation.

She had to get hold of herself. She knew from Mariah's warnings that Nick had no intention of getting serious about any woman—or about settling down in one place, for that matter. And if the way he'd been treating her was any indication, he wasn't even interested in one of those brief, torrid affairs the townsfolk seemed afraid she'd fall into. She might as well content herself with the fact that any interest he showed her was strictly because she represented home-cooked meals and a laundry ticket.

A knock sounded at the door. The sluggish feeling of disappointment vanished, along with the frown furrowing her smooth forehead. Pivoting on the ball of her foot, she called, "Come in!"

The door opened and Nick stepped inside. The freshly starched shirt he'd been tucking into his new jeans was familiar. She had ironed it.

"Good morning," he said, offering her a tentative smile. She smiled back, a smile that rivaled the October sunshine in brightness. Nick's hard-won resolve faltered.

"Good morning. I didn't know you were coming for breakfast. I'll have to fix you something." She started for the pantry, wondering why, despite the chasm widening between them, she felt compelled to explain herself to him.

"Don't bother. I'm not very hungry."

She stopped in midstride. "Oh . . . fine, then," she said. "You aren't working today?" she queried, making a vague gesture toward his clothes.

Nick shook his head and shifted his weight to one hip. He hooked his thumbs in the belt loops of his jeans. "We finished last night. We don't start a new job until Monday."

She smiled, a half smile. Her wistfulness reminded him of Nicole. "I bet you're ready for some time off."

"More than ready," he agreed. "That's why I stopped by."

"I beg your pardon," she said.

"I was planning on going to the races this afternoon. I thought I'd see if you'd like to go with me."

The races. Though Louisiana Downs had been a local attraction for several years, Eden had never gone, never placed the first bet. It wasn't that she was fanatically opposed to gambling, it was just that she had better uses for her money. But this was different. Nick was asking her to go with him. She didn't have to bet; she could just go and watch the horses run and enjoy her time with him. After all, who knew how much longer he would be around?

"Come on," he urged, sensing her hesitation. "It'll be fun. Besides, the Pick Six is up to a hundred and forty thousand today.

"It is?" Her eyes brightened. She knew what the Pick Six was. For a two-dollar ticket, you could pick six horses you thought would win six consecutive races. If they all came in, you won...sometimes a little, sometimes a lot. It was a lure that drew fans to the windows in droves, even though the chance of winning was about as slim as the chance of Nick settling down in Calloway Corners.

Eden looked at him, wanting more than anything to say yes. Despite the warning ringing in her ears she was unable to think of why she shouldn't. "Okay," she said. "I'll go. But I warn you, I don't know anything about gambling."

One corner of Nick's mouth crawled up in a lazy smile. "Don't worry about it. I know enough for us both."

As usual on a Saturday, Louisiana Downs was swarming with people hoping their horse would cross the finish line first. Eden chose two names she liked for the daily double, and she and Nick split the two-dollar bet. He assured her that her method of choosing a horse was as good as any.

"Did she win?" Eden asked as the first four numbers of the second race flashed up on the tote board.

"Unless there's an objection," he explained. "But I didn't see anything questionable happen. Talk about beginner's luck!"

In a matter of minutes, the results became official. Smiling, Nick turned to Eden. "We won."

"We did?" She glanced at the tote board and saw that their two-dollar ticket would pay three hundred fourteen dollars. She gave a squeal of delight and grabbed Nick around the neck in an enthusiastic hug he returned in kind.

Nick held her close and thought about the vibrant impulsiveness sheltered inside her, an impulsiveness guarded by traditions and upbringing, an impulsiveness only seldom given free rein. Her usually opaque, jade-green eyes sparkled like shimmering facets of emerald, and her voice took on the excitement and pleasure of a teenaged girl granted her first kiss.

Kiss. The thought of kissing Eden was never far from his mind, and standing there with her arms locked around his neck, the need to taste her mouth seemed mandatory. Only the press of the crowd stopped him.

Eden must have seen something of that need in his eyes, because she was suddenly aware of how secure and warm his hands felt through the thin cotton of her blouse. She was aware of how her breasts were crushed against his chest and of how well her feminine curves fit against the masculine contours of his. Aware and frightened of how good, how right it felt. She disengaged herself slowly, but couldn't drag her gaze away from his.

Nick was shaken, too. Striving for normalcy, and still holding on to her upper arms, he asked, "What are you going to do with your winnings?"

Eden had no intention of cutting her happiness short. Just when she thought Nick was determined to push her away, he had asked her out, and she intended to make the most of it.

"I'm going to give you your half, and then I'm going to bet the rest. I'm playing with their money now."

She did just that. When they left several hours later, Eden was considerably ahead. She wasn't sure when she'd had such a good time and was smart enough to realize that beginner's luck had a lot to do with the wad of money crammed into her purse. She was also aware that her betting partner had a lot to do with how good a time she'd had.

"Well," Nick asked as she preceded him through the back door, "what did you think?"

"It's fun," Eden said over her shoulder, but it wasn't the excitement of the race or money she'd won that she was thinking about. It was the way her heart had pounded every time she and Nick put their heads together, and the way her pulse raced when he smiled.

"It's fun as long as there isn't a lot of money involved," she added for clarification, turning toward him. It was an unfortunate move, because Nick was right on her heels. He literally ran into her, knocking her off balance. He reached out to steady her, his warm hands curling around her upper arms.

Eden's breath caught in her throat. High on the happiness of the day and tipsy on the excitement of his nearness, she tilted her head back to look up at him, her lashes lifting in slow seductive increments. She knew she was flirting...with Nick...with trouble. She didn't care.

He looked down at her, fully aware of what she was doing, fully aware that his teasing words were as calculated as her actions. "Careful with your money, are you?"

Eden lifted her shoulders in a half shrug. "Careful with everything that's mine."

Nick didn't doubt it. She was generous to a fault with anything that had to do with giving—time, help, energy—but she was guarded with her emotions and reactions and stingy with her laughter. Her complexity was one reason he was so strongly attracted to her. He wanted to see her blossom into a fully giving woman—his woman—and friendships be damned.

He let his gaze drift from her eyes to her mouth, randomly charting the line of her upper lip, naked now of the bronze lipstick she'd worn earlier. Without any logical reason, he remembered seeing her in the car with Dan.

Jealousy—unexpected and unwarranted—reared its ugly green head. Nick vowed that Dan Morgan would never taste her lips again...not until he'd had his fill of their ripeness.

Eden saw the light of determination in his brown eyes and her insides began to quiver with awareness. His gaze was like a touch. She could almost feel his lips on hers. Almost. Almost...

"Are you careful with your kisses, too?" he asked, his voice a low thrum of need.

The desire in his eyes was blatant and intense. Eden's tongue peeked out and skimmed over her lips, leaving them shiny wet with moisture. "Especially my kisses."

Stifling a groan, Nick pulled her closer. She saw his eyes close, saw his head tilt to one side. And then she didn't see anything else, because her eyes were closed, too. Breath and thought fled beneath the heady anticipation filling her. The touch of his mouth was feather-light, whisper-soft and packed the wallop of a ton of TNT. The pent-up breath Eden had been holding escaped the tightness of her throat and soughed against Nick's mouth in the guise of a breathless whimper.

Taking the sound as acquiescence, he pulled her deeper into his embrace while he urged her lips apart with tiny nuzzling kisses and the barest touch of his tongue.

Eden refused him admittance. It was almost as if she knew that if she gave him that part of her, her body wouldn't be long in following, and where her body went, her heart went, too. Placing her hands against his chest, she pushed gently, drawing away.

Nick's hold on her shoulders loosened, but before she pulled completely away, before the warmth of her lips left his, he took two final sips from them. Then, holding her at arm's length, he regarded her through lazily narrowed eyes. "Wow."

Yes. Wow. A classic understatement. Eden knew he was a man who'd been around, knew his answers were as likely to be as calculated for a positive response as his moves undoubtedly were. But she also knew she was thinking the same thing. "Nick, I—" she began, only to be interrupted by the shrill ringing of the telephone.

She disentangled her gaze from his and frowned at the offending instrument. Nick let his hands drop to his sides, and Eden felt suddenly bereft. She crossed the room to the phone, her hips, in the snug jeans she wore, swaying gently. Pulling off her clip earring, she nestled the phone against her ear. "Hello."

"Where have you been?" Mariah said without preamble. "I've been trying to call for hours."

Eden fought back a feeling of annoyance. Why did her sisters think she should let them know her every move?

She'd been doing fine without checking in with anyone for years. "Nick took me to the races. Is something wrong?"

Even through the phone lines, Eden discerned the disgust in Mariah's tone. "It's the hydraulic gun again. It stopped working this morning, and when I called the people in Baton Rouge they said it would be the middle of next week before they would have anyone free to come up and check it out. In the meantime, we're losing money hand over fist."

Eden's heart sank. Just what they needed. She had the feeling that the mill finances weren't in great shape as it was. "Can't Ted fix it?" she asked, flicking a worried glance toward Nick.

Indicating that he'd be outside, Nick turned toward the back door. Eden appreciated his courtesy in giving her privacy for her telephone conversation.

"He says he can't," Mariah said. "Tess sent Seth over to take a look, but as he says—he's a carpenter, not a mechanic." She laughed, a laugh that sounded as if it might hold a hint of tears. "I don't know why I called you, except that we usually do when things go wrong."

"Sorry, but off hand, I don't know what to do. Do you have any other ideas?" Eden asked.

"No," Mariah replied and sighed deeply. "Except to shut down production until we can get it fixed."

The thought of shutting down the mill filled Eden with trepidation. With a few rare exceptions, the Calloway lumber mill had run in full swing as long as she could remember. Besides the fact that thoughts of shutting it down—even temporarily—seemed like some sort of sacrilege, Eden couldn't nudge aside the nagging feeling that if the doors shut this time they'd never open again.

"It's truly amazing," Mariah said, the sound of her voice intruding on Eden's thoughts.

"What?"

"About Ted and Frannie," Mariah said, as if that explained everything.

Ted, the middle-aged foreman, had been with the mill for years, and Frannie Glidden was the bookkeeper who had been hired shortly after Ben Calloway's death. Neither of them had anything to do with faulty equipment, so Eden figured that Mariah was right in the middle of one of her pick-up-in-midstream conversations.

"What do Ted and Frannie have to do with the machinery breaking down?"

"Nothing," Mariah said. "But of all the people in the world, I would never have put Ted with Frannie."

"Mariah," Eden said patiently, not really caring, "do you mind starting at the beginning?"

"Oh, sorry. Ted and Frannie have a *thing* for each other."

Eden was shocked. To her knowledge, Ted hadn't dated anyone since his wife of thirty-four years had died. "You're kidding!"

"Nope," Mariah said with a giggle. "I walked in and caught them right in the middle of a big, juicy kiss."

So? Eden thought. Ted was a nice-looking man for his age. Maybe he couldn't fix the hydraulic gun because he had other things on his mind. "Well, as Seth would say, 'Whatever melts your butter.' Ted's a grown man and he deserves to be happy."

"Yes, he does."

"Look, Mariah, let me give this some thought," Eden told her. "I'll see if I can round up someone to come take a look. Meanwhile, you stop worrying. Stay at home and prop up your feet and let Ford take care of you and that niece or nephew of mine—okay?"

"Okay."

"I'll call," Eden promised, and then hung up the phone. Clipping the earring back on, she made her way to the back patio, a frown marring her features.

Something was wrong, Nick thought as he left the room. Outside, he settled himself at the patio table and stared at the woods fringing the well-manicured lawn. He had seen it in Eden's eyes when she'd met his gaze. He had heard it in her voice as she talked to Mariah.

"Hi."

Tess Calloway rounded the corner of the house and started up the sidewalk to the patio. Nick had been so worried about Eden's telephone conversation that he hadn't even heard Tess drive up. He smiled at Eden's sister. "Hi."

"Where's Eden?" Tess asked, sitting down across from him.

"Inside," Nick said shortly. He didn't want to talk. He wanted to listen, to see if he could figure out what was going on. "She got a phone call. Mariah, I think."

*"Can't Ted fix it?"* Memory of the question Eden had asked before he came outside slipped into his mind in spite of Tess's intrusive presence. Something must be wrong at the mill.

"Where has she been all day?" Tess asked with a frown. "We really needed to get hold of her."

"We went to the races," Nick explained.

A second later he heard Eden's voice, filtered through the open screen door, asking, "Do you have any other ideas?"

"The races?" Tess said with raised eyebrows. "That's got to be a first for Eden. How did you do?"

Nick's eyes strayed toward the open door and the sound of Eden's voice.

"What do Ted and Frannie have to do with the machinery breaking down?"

*Definitely the mill,* Nick thought, Eden's despair crystal clear to him. But what? "We did good," he said, realizing that Tess was waiting for an answer. "Real good."

Tess couldn't help noticing the way Nick's eyes strayed to her sister's shadowy figure beyond the screened door. "Beginner's luck, huh? I can't believe Eden has changed so much lately.''

"Changed?'' The statement drew Nick's attention away from the telephone conversation at last.

"Yes. This time last year Eden would never have dreamed of going to the racetrack, much less placing a bet...or going for a motorcycle ride with a stranger.''

Despite the lightness of Tess's tone, Nick sensed her worry. She was afraid that he'd get involved with Eden and then pull a disappearing act. He smiled the smile that was designed to set hearts aflutter and pulses racing. It wasn't a smile that Tess found encouraging.

"I'm hardly a stranger, Tess,'' he argued. "Mariah and I have known each other for a long time.''

"Tess! What are you doing here?'' Eden's voice preceded her through the doorway, her presence precluding any further discussion of her relationship with Nick.

"We've been trying to get hold of you all afternoon, and I thought I'd drive by and see if you were working in the yard or something,'' Tess said with a smile.

"Nick and I went to the races.''

Tess's glance strayed to Nick. "That's what he said.''

"That was Mariah on the phone,'' Eden explained. "She told me what happened at the mill.''

"She was beside herself,'' Tess told them. "Do you know anyone else who might be able to fix it?''

"Would I be considered nosy if I asked what's the matter?'' Nick asked, looking from Tess to Eden.

"Of course not,'' Eden assured him. "Our equipment is not only outdated, it's in bad repair. We've been having trouble with the hydraulic gun for several months now, but our foreman has always been able to patch it up. Something happened today that's beyond his field of expertise. The repairman from Baton Rouge can't get there until some time next week, so we're up a creek until then.''

"Do you want me to look at it?" Nick offered.

"You?" Eden asked.

Nick's smile was a wry twist of his lips. "Yeah, me. If the truth were known, I'm a lot better with machinery than I am with a nail gun."

Eden and Tess exchanged a what-have-we-got-to-lose look. Then Eden shifted her gaze to Nick. "Why not?"

EDEN OPENED HER EYES slowly, turned her head and looked at the bedside clock. Nine forty-five. Too late to get ready for church. She stretched, thinking how refreshed she felt after a night of sound sleep. She always slept like a rock when it rained. She could hardly believe it when she had awakened during the night to the sound of thunder rumbling through the house and rattling the panes in the wooden windows.

She had burrowed deeper beneath the sheet and bedspread, thinking, in that funny half-awake-half-asleep way people do, that the welcome wetness would probably usher in weather that was more autumnlike. It had been a dry fall, and she was thankful that the rain the weatherman had been predicting for days had finally arrived.

Now, she lay snuggled beneath the covers, wishing the fan was off and wondering if Nick had enough blankets to keep warm. When she had gone to bed the night before—after he had successfully patched up the hydraulic gun at the mill— it had been with a feeling of intense relief that they'd been spared shutting down, at least temporarily. She was thankful and relieved that they had been spared putting dozens of men out of work.

Nick had verified Ted's opinion by telling them that the machinery needed replacing, but that they could probably buy some time by replacing the worn hydraulic pump. Tess, Mariah and Eden had thanked him, and Eden promised that she'd have Frannie order the pump first thing Monday morning.

Frannie. And Ted. Eden covered a yawn and a smile and folded her arms beneath her head. It was unbelievable that Ted was involved with someone like Frannie. He was calm, staid and dependable, and Fran was vivacious and loud and just a little rough around the edges. Eden wondered how two such different people had drawn together.

*For the same reason you're drawn to Nick. Opposites attract.* Eden could imagine that Ted might like a little more...uninhibited woman this time around. Oh, well, she thought. There was no fool like an old fool.

Swinging her feet off the bed, Eden raked her hair away from her face while the phrase marched through her mind. *There's no fool like an old fool. No fool...old fool.*

Was she a fool? she asked herself, shivering in the cool air and reaching for her robe. She thrust her arms through the sleeves, letting the memory of Nick's kiss wash over her. Mariah had phoned before she and Nick could talk about their kiss and what was happening between them, and on the heels of that, Tess had shown up. Then they'd spent the better part of the night at the mill. Nick, his brow furrowed in concentration and perspiration dripping off his face despite the navy bandanna he'd tied around his forehead, had worked for hours at the mill trying to get the machine that carried the logs to the saw in working order again.

It was after midnight when they got home, and Eden was so physically wrung out that she'd fallen into her bed with nothing more than a cursory good-night to Nick. Until this moment, she hadn't had time to dwell on the impact of his kiss and what it made her feel—or what it meant, if anything.

It had been heaven. And hell. Like a jolt of electricity, the touch of his mouth to hers had streaked throughout her body, sizzling her nerve endings with tingling awareness and generating a hot, melting heaviness in the lower part of her body. Her breasts had grown heavy, aching for a touch—his touch.

Eden covered the fullness of her breasts with her palms, pressing against them as if that firm pressure could stay the feelings still simmering inside her. Even hours after his kiss, she could recall the firm softness of his lips and the way they teased and sipped as they nuzzled and nibbled at hers.

What about Nick? Had it affected him the same way?

*"Wow."*

Memory of his voice, thick with emotion, drifted warmly into the uncertainty of her thoughts. She smiled and wondered what the day would bring. Whatever it was, she was ready to welcome it with open arms.

The sound of the Harley starting dissipated her happiness like the popping of a soap bubble. Her bare feet skimmed across the hardwood floor of the bedroom. Raking back the lacy curtains, she watched as the black bike sped down the driveway toward the highway.

It was Sunday. He didn't have to go to work. Where was he going so early? Why hadn't he come for breakfast? she wondered. Even from a distance, a bright shaft of sunlight glinted off the shiny chrome of the motorcycle as Nick headed left toward Haughton. She let the curtain fall back into place and turned toward the empty room.

More to the point, was he coming back?

NICK HEADED TOWARD Haughton and the cup of coffee he knew would be ready at the Country Corner grocery store. Eden had been exhausted when they got home in the wee hours of the morning. Figuring she might want to sleep in, he had decided to go in to town for his coffee and his weekend call to Nicole.

He hadn't slept well at all. Like Eden, he'd been tired when they returned from the mill, but his mind wouldn't let him rest. He replayed every nuance of the day—the fun he and Eden had shared at the races, the heady sweetness of her mouth and the way her kiss had put all the kisses he'd tasted in the past to shame. And the more he had thought about that kiss and the way it made him feel, the more worried he had become.

What was it about Eden that threatened to make him forget Keith's betrayal with Belinda? How and why was Eden accomplishing what dozens of other women hadn't been able to do? What magic did she wield that wiped away the bitter memories and the subsequent years of pain he'd suffered?

Was it the sweet serenity of her smile? The aura of pure femininity that radiated from her like sunbeams from a summer sky? Or the goodness he saw manifested in her a dozen times a day, in a dozen different ways? Whatever it was, it was extremely potent and dangerous. Falling for anyone—especially Eden Calloway—wasn't in his plans. And if he knew what was good for him, he'd keep riding the Harley straight through the light up ahead, and on toward the horizon.

Instead, he turned into the grocery store's parking lot, pulling right up to the outside phones.

He knew what he should do, but he also knew that he couldn't leave because of an unshakable feeling that unless something was done in a hurry the Calloway lumber operation was headed for trouble. He wasn't certain what he could do, but if it was nothing more than keep the equipment from going completely, he needed to stay and do it. He lit a cigarette and dialed Nicole's number.

"Hello?" Nicole's sleep-husky tones scattered his thoughts.

"Good morning," he said, a fond smile curving his lips.

"Nick!" Nicole said, her sleepiness vanishing at the sound of his voice. "Are you—"

"No," Nick interrupted, leaning against the phone booth and squinting in the sunshine, which seemed doubly bright after the storm. "I'm not in Arkansas. I'm still in Louisiana. I just thought I'd give you a call while the rates were cheaper."

"Are you low on money?" Nicole asked, her voice suddenly filled with worry.

He laughed and took a deep drag off his cigarette, exhaling before he spoke. "No. Unless I go a little crazy the money Grandma left me should last a long time."

"So what have you been doing? How's the...carpentering?"

"It's fine. We finished remodeling one of the old juke joints on the Bossier strip the other day."

"You're in Bossier City?"

Nick sighed. Keith was always wanting to know where he was, and though it wasn't a very mature attitude, Nick gained a perverse sort of pleasure from keeping his whereabouts secret from him.

"Near there," he said, flipping the half-smoked cigarette into the parking lot. "What's going on up there?"

"Keith is still trying to prove that Belinda is an unfit mother. Mama is the same. Oh! I forgot to tell you something the other day. We heard that Ellie Tanner died."

Nick's heart ached in sudden sympathy for Gil, Ellie's husband. As a kid, he and Gil's son, Luke, had followed Gil around listening and watching—learning the timber business. Gil had given Nick the attention his own father denied him. After the incident with Luke and Nicole, Stuart had given the Tanners a choice: leave or have their son charged with rape. When they had gone, Nick had missed both Luke and Gil terribly. He could have used Gil's expertise in learning the business after Keith abdicated.

Ellie had been tops, too, everything he had always wished his own mother could be. And, unlike the living arrangements at the Logan mansion, the feelings Gil and Ellie shared in their three-bedroom tract house had been obvious and sincere. To this day, it was hard to believe that Luke had hurt Nicole, and despite that, Nick had always felt the utmost respect for the elder Tanners.

"Ellie Tanner?"

"Yes. She'd been sick a long time. Some sort of blood disease."

"I hate to hear that," Nick said, and then asked the question he'd called to ask. "What about the investigation?"

"Nothing new. They haven't hauled Daddy or Keith to jail yet. They're fighting like cats and dogs, though. I don't know what about."

Suddenly the sunshine didn't seem so bright. Nick wanted, no, *needed* to get back to Eden, to let her smile warm his heart. As usual, he wanted to hear the news, to make contact with his family. As usual, he couldn't stand it when he did. "I've got to go, Nicole," he told her. "I'll call you soon."

"All right, Nick. Take care."

Nick hung up and climbed onto the Harley, setting the sunglasses onto the strong bridge of his nose. He pulled out onto the street and headed toward Calloway Corners, thinking of the ongoing investigation of the Logans' purchase of the Anderson company. He knew that his family had bought out failing timber operations in the past, but he hadn't suspected that they helped them along the way to financial ruin.

He prayed that Nicole would forget what he'd said about where he was staying, because someone could probably finagle the information from her. He had a sneaking suspicion that the Calloway mill was in a little financial trouble, and if Keith found out where he was and started checking

around, he might get wind of it. If the allegations against his
family were true—and he had no reason to doubt them—the
Calloway mill was just the type of target Stuart and Keith
liked to hit on.

# CHAPTER SEVEN

THE COFFEE HAD JUST finished perking when Eden heard the motorcycle coming up the drive. Outwardly calm, she filled two mugs with the fragrant brew and tried to ignore the frantic beating of her heart. Through the window, she saw Nick stop the Harley near the back patio instead of pulling it into the shelter of the garage, as he usually did.

Her hungry gaze devoured him. He was wearing black acid-washed jeans that sheathed his superbly muscled thighs with the same loving fit of a fine leather glove. Due to the cooler temperatures brought on by the rainfall, he had swapped his customary T-shirt for a plain gray crew-neck sweatshirt.

He neared the house, striding up the shallow steps and across the patio with sure, determined strides. Eden picked up the coffee as his knock shattered the stillness in the room.

"Come in!" Was that reedy sounding voice hers?

The door opened and he stepped inside, filling the aperture and her heart with his presence. He stood with his hand on the knob, his eyes making a slow, thorough survey of her from the top of her shining strawberry-blond head to the tips of her toes, which were encased in battered tennis shoes.

She looked fantastic, he thought. The lower temperature had caused her to give up her shorts—at least for a day—for very old, excitingly tight jeans. A plaid shirt of dark blue, white and rust was tucked into the waistband. She had rolled up the sleeves to the elbow and the top buttons were undone, revealing a vee of deliciously tanned skin and the delicate hollow of her throat.

Nick wanted to press his lips to that hollow, wanted to plant a row of kisses along her collarbone. He wanted to see if the flesh of her full breasts was any softer than that of her mouth. Instead, he dragged his wandering gaze back to her face. As if she had divined the turn of his thoughts, a soft rose blush climbed to the crest of her cheekbones.

"Good morning," he said solemnly, shutting the door behind him.

"Good morning."

He crossed the room and indicated the coffee she held. "Is one of those mine?"

She held a cup out for him wordlessly. His fingers curled around hers, trapping her hand between the heat of the cup and the heat of his touch.

"I didn't expect you," she said. "I thought I heard you leave." *For good.*

*I tried to leave you, Eden. I couldn't.*

"How did you know I'd be back?"

"I didn't," she told him simply.

She relinquished the cup, but his eyes still held hers. Both of them knew that the conversation was being conducted on two levels—the verbal one whose answers satisfied the stilted, necessary conversation, and the answers and feeling that were clearly readable in each other's eyes.

"You aren't going to church?" he asked, pulling out a chair and sitting down.

She shook her head. "I overslept. I thought I'd work out in the yard . . . rake up the leaves the storm blew in."

"I'll help you."

Eden couldn't hide her surprise. "You don't have to do that."

"I know I don't. I want to." ... *to spend some time with you*. He smiled. "I think I owe you some sort of chores for doing my laundry."

Memory of the condom flashed through her mind, followed by the memory of his kiss...and a forbidden thrill of excitement. She shrugged. "I have to do mine, anyway."

"But it was a deal," he reminded her. "You do my laundry; I help you out. So today, we rake leaves."

THE SUNDAY-MORNING SUN gathered strength as the morning progressed, climbing the cobalt sky and banishing the cooler temperatures. Rays of warmth penetrated the leafy openings of the trees and danced on the leaf-strewn lawn while limber branches dipped and swayed with every breath of the capricious breeze. If the temperature kept rising long sleeves and sweatshirts wouldn't be necessary by noon, and by midafternoon they would probably think summertime had returned, Eden thought, blotting her perspiring face on the upper sleeve of her shirt.

She and Nick had worked side by side all morning, raking the damp leaves into huge piles that she would burn when they dried out. They hadn't talked much, but his kiss was still uppermost on Eden's mind...and his too, if the contemplative, sidelong looks she occasionally intercepted could be trusted. As she had ever since he had come, Eden felt as if something was about to happen, but since she didn't know what that something was, all she could do was sit and wait.

Her stomach growled suddenly, reminding her that neither she nor Nick had eaten breakfast and that all they'd had for lunch was a haphazardly thrown together sandwich. She was dying for a cup of fresh coffee and a slice of the coconut cake she'd baked the day before.

Shielding her eyes against the sun, she spotted Nick several yards away, bare-handedly attacking the tenacious vines entwined among the branches of a white oak. Eden had given up on eradicating them years ago. Obviously he was taking the yard work seriously. Besides raking, he had reset some loose bricks along the flower beds and trimmed the hedges bordering the house. She surveyed the huge yard with a sigh. It would be nice if it would stay clean when they finished, but she knew from the lessons of a lifetime that in a few days it would have to be done all over again.

*"If God didn't want those leaves on the ground he wouldn't have made them fall."*

Eden smiled as one of her mother's favorite sayings drifted sweetly through her mind. Grace had never been one for working in the yard, and at the moment, neither was her oldest daughter. Propping her leaf rake against the trunk of the pine that grew on the east side of the house, she went toward Nick.

Hearing the rustle of her footsteps, he glanced over his shoulder and smiled. Eden's heart tripped over itself. Slowly and deliberately, she drew off the cotton work gloves she was wearing and shoved them into her back pocket. "How about a break?"

"Sounds great," he said, yanking on a particularly stubborn vine. "Let me finish this up first."

But Eden was tired of work, and she didn't want him working a single second more. She wanted to talk to him. Wanted to see if he'd bring up the subject of their kiss. Longed to see if he'd do it again. It was a glorious autumn day, and they were wasting it by raking leaves.

"It can wait." She spoke to his broad back.

"I'm almost finished," he said, without turning around.

The hidden, daring side of her began to surface as it had the night she'd gone with him on the motorcycle. The teasing side of her—the side that only her family saw—joined forces. Impulsively she whirled and went to a large pile of leaves Nick had raked up. Grabbing a double handful, she threw them in the general direction of his head and, without missing a step, sprinted toward the front yard, laughing at him over her shoulder as she went.

Shock molded the features of Nick's handsome face for just an instant. He planted his hands on his hips and regarded her with a narrowed, considering look. Eden stopped beneath the outflung arms of the huge live oak. Bending over, she propped her hands on her knees. Her teasing smile rivaled the brightness of the afternoon sun.

She was gorgeous! he thought, moving toward her as if drawn by some magical, invisible thread. He smiled back, a slow, sensuous curving of his mouth, and pointed his forefinger at her in warning. "You're asking for it."

Eden straightened. "Me?" she asked with feigned innocence, glancing around as if looking for the real culprit.

Nick stopped and made a big display of pushing up the sleeves of his sweatshirt. He took another step toward her. "You."

She crossed her arms across her breasts and shifted her weight to one leg in a cocky, daring stance. "What did I do?"

"What did I do?" he mimicked, nearing her with long, ground-eating strides. "You, Ms Calloway, threw a handful of wet leaves at me."

Eden saw the reckoning in his eyes. She uncrossed her arms and stepped backward, retreating one step for every two he took toward her. Then, mesmerized by the look in his eyes, she stopped completely and held her arms straight out in front of her as if to block his approach. "Now, Nick," she said. "Don't do anything rash—anything you'll regret."

He stopped within arms's reach of her.

"I never do anything rash, Eden," he told her. "I always think things through very carefully." Reaching out, he grasped her wrists in a gentle hold and, step by slow step, pulled her nearer. He guided her arms around his back until they were anchored at his waist and they stood breast to chest. Then he brought his right hand up and fit her chin in the angle created by his fingers and thumb. The pads of his callused fingers whispered along the curve of her jaw.

He lowered his head toward hers. ''And I don't think there's a chance in hell that either of us is going to regret this.''

Before Eden could do more than realize that he was going to kiss her, his mouth met hers. Her eyes drifted shut in sublime contentment. She arched her back and locked her arms more tightly around him in an instinctive gesture as old as Eve.

His kiss was everything she remembered. More. Before, his kisses had been tentative, searching. This kiss was slow and easy, deep and drugging, and his open mouth worked against her lips with a slow, grinding movement.

She relaxed against him and felt his other arm go around her shoulders. She was glad for the support since her knees refused to lock and her bones had turned to rubber. Her mouth opened and was instantly filled with the erotic probing of his tongue. She closed herself around it greedily, accepting the intrusion with a willingness born of deprivation and anticipation.

A sweet heaviness filled the virgin emptiness of her lower body. A longing for fulfillment to ease the empty feelings gnawing away at her usual serenity. An emptiness that needed to be assuaged. An emptiness that she now believed could only be satisfied by this man. A virtual stranger.

His kisses affected her senses so strongly, her head was spinning so rapidly, that Eden was only marginally aware that he had lowered her to the ground until the crackling rustle of leaves alerted her to the fact.

She opened her eyes.

Above her head, the brilliant rays of light darted through the perpetually green leaves of the live oak, playing hide and seek with the shadows that brushed the ruggedly masculine planes of his face, which was bent low over hers. Their eyes meshed, mated.

Eden couldn't recall feeling more alive in her entire life. For the span of a few heartbeats all her senses were focused, fine-tuned to the sensations he was drawing from her. She could hear the faraway cry of a dove. Could smell the damp scent of the ground mingled with the faintest aroma of Nick's cologne.

Slowly Eden became aware of other things: her shirt had come loose from the waistband of her jeans, and the leaves beneath her tickled her back; one of Nick's legs was wedged between hers, and his thigh pressed intimately against the mound of her womanhood; her breasts, straining against the flimsy barrier of lace and satin, were full and heavy, aching for a touch . . . Nick's touch. Her tongue skimmed over her lips. They tasted like Nick.

A slumbrous smile lurked in the depths of her eyes. She reached up and trailed the tips of her fingers along the dark brush of his eyebrow. Nick turned his head slightly and feathered a kiss along the inside of her forearm, his tongue tracing a lazy pattern.

Like a blind person longing to discover a person's looks, her fingers traced his eyelashes, the bold slash of his nose and the hard contours of his cheeks and jawline. When her finger gently tugged at the sensual fullness of his bottom lip, Nick ducked his head and nibbled at her finger, drawing it into his mouth with a slow, stroking suction that tugged at the heart of her womanhood. She wanted him to fill the void his touch created. Raising up on her elbows, Eden fastened her mouth to Nick's with hungry ardor.

A sound, a cross between a groan and a growl, rumbled up from Nick's throat. He threaded his hand through her

hair, cupping the back of her head in his outspread palm
and lowering her to the cushion of leaves while Eden's arms
crawled up the solid wall of his chest and around his neck.

She had never encountered anyone who could kiss so
well . . . not, at least in her limited experience. She felt as if
she were drowning in sensation as his open mouth drank
deeply from hers. Her hips moved upward, pushing against
the hardness of his thigh in a restless gesture. She couldn't
get close enough, couldn't *feel* enough to satisfy the craving incited by his rapacious mouth. Her tongue dueled with
his in blatant need as she pressed closer, closer . . . arching her
back in an effort to meld her body with his.

His hand moved from her head, and it was only a matter
of seconds before she felt its warmth against the bareness of
her back as he pulled her shirt from the waistband of her
jeans. Eden dragged her lips from his and buried her face
against his shoulder.

His hands bracketed her waist, his splayed fingers sliding
up her rib cage until his thumbs brushed the undersides of
her breasts. Hot lips bestowed random kisses over her temple and cheek, and his thumbs were just making a tentative
foray beneath the elastic of her bra when the unmistakable
sound of a car coming up the driveway penetrated the
thunderous waves of desire towing Eden under.

A car. Someone was coming. She went suddenly still in his
arms.

Attuned to every nuance of her behavior as he'd never
been to a woman before, Nick sensed her sudden with-
drawal. He lifted his head and looked down at her, his dark
eyes filled with passion.

"Eden?" he queried softly as she strained to see beyond
his shoulder.

"S . . ." she began, the effort to talk almost beyond her.
"Someone's coming."

Nick turned his head and looked over his shoulder. Sure enough, a car had just come over the railroad tracks and was slowly making its way toward the house. Dan's car. Nick swore. And got to his feet. He reached down a hand to help her up, even as her gaze moved from his face to the driveway.

*Dan!* She took Nick's hand automatically. He pulled her to her feet with a smooth, easy motion, and then, without another word, he turned and started around the house.

"Nick!" Eden cried. "Where are you going?"

His smile was cynical. His voice was several degrees cooler than normal. "I thought I'd let you explain to Dan why you and I were rolling around on the ground. I hate to be ungentlemanly, but as you can see, I have problems of my own."

Eden's eyes followed his hand as he gestured toward the masculine bulge straining against the placket of his jeans. Her face was flaming as her gaze went to his once more. Nick didn't notice. He was already halfway to the apartment.

NICK SWORE SILENTLY as he made his way across the leaf-strewn lawn. He was furious. At Eden. At himself. Furious and uncertain whether to be thankful for or to curse Dan Morgan's untimely arrival. A few more minutes and...

Eden Calloway would have been his.

He'd *never* met a woman so eager, yet at the same time so apparently innocent. Apparently. That was the operative word, he thought, with a trace of his old bitterness. While it was true that Eden's life had been somewhat sheltered, her sisters were definitely eighties ladies. And he had to face the fact that while she did live in a small country town, it was hardly the boondocks by any stretch of the imagination. She was a twenty-minute drive from a city with a quarter of a million people. She was bound to know the score.

Still, her level of experience aside, he couldn't remember ever responding to a woman the way he did to Eden. Though her mouth had seemed untried, and her kisses were hesitant at first, when the barriers were down, she was all woman...all warm, giving, hungry woman. And if there was anything that turned him on, it was a woman who made him feel supremely male.

If he was the kind of person who believed in fate or karma or whatever else it was called, he could almost convince himself that meeting Eden Calloway had been in the cards from the moment he'd pulled Mariah to safety on the sandy shores of Aruba. But he didn't believe that any more than he believed that things were wonderful between the Calloway women one hundred percent of the time.

He did believe in his own instinct. And right now the red lights were flashing and warning bells were going off inside his head...all telling him that he was getting in too deep, telling him that if he had an ounce of sense, he'd get on his Harley and ride.

"Was that the Logan fellow I saw crossing the yard as I drove up?"

The car door was barely shut behind him when Dan asked the loaded question. *So much for the hope for a brief reprieve,* Eden thought. "Yes," she said, meeting his questioningly gaze squarely, "it was."

"And what were you doing?" Dan asked gently, the answer to the question obvious as he looked at Eden. Leaves were stuck to the back of her hair. Her shirt was partially out of her jeans, her lips were bruised from Nick's kisses, and her tender cheeks showed unmistakable signs of whisker burn.

Besides all that, there was the dazed look still lingering in the depths of her eyes, a look that wordlessly said that she'd experienced something wonderful, something she still couldn't quite believe, a look Dan didn't recall ever seeing in her eyes.

"Doing?" Eden repeated. "We were...raking the leaves." She noticed the way Dan's eyes strayed to her shirt...her untucked shirt...and her hair. "We were scuffling around, and I—"

Eden's explanation was cut short by Dan's palm covering her mouth. Her eyes met his. There was complete understanding there...and sadness.

"Don't," he said. "I'm not sure I want to hear it."

Eden felt his sorrow. It was closely related to her own. Losing Dan as a suitor was one thing. Losing his respect was quite another. She reached up with both hands and took his hand in hers, moving it to lay against her cheek. "He just...kissed me, Dan. That's all. You've got to believe that."

His smile was strained. "I do."

Feeling as if she'd just kicked the stray cat who turned up every morning for scraps, Eden sighed. "Come with me."

"Where?"

"To the wisteria arbor."

FROM HIS VANTAGE POINT beside the living-room window of the apartment, Nick saw Eden take Dan's hand and cradle it to her face. Pain knotted his gut, and jealousy—an emotion completely foreign to him after Belinda's betrayal but still easily recognizable by the misery that accompanied it— ripped at his heart. He remembered suddenly why he never allowed himself to get too close to a woman, why he sought out only the kind who had no interest in a long-term relationship, and why he refused to settle down in one place and take the chance on caring for anyone. Caring brought agony as well as pleasure. And he had suffered all he wanted at the hands of love.

Pain was the reward for caring.

His throat worked with the emotion clawing its way up it. And when he thought his hurt had reached its zenith, he saw Eden lead Dan Morgan into the wisteria arbor.

THE WISTERIA ARBOR was a long, tunnel-shaped retreat with a cement bench on either inside, which Ben Calloway had built for Grace the first year they were married. Originally constructed of four-by-fours and lattice panels, the years had thickened the wisteria vines into small trunks and heavier branches that intertwined with one another until the lattice was all but covered up. It should have rotted years before, but miraculously the arbor seemed as strong as it ever was. Ben had maintained that it was built from love, for love, and that love was what kept it together.

Eden believed it. As it had for her mother, its cool shady walls provided a sanctuary from the problems of the world. She listened to the sound of Dan's car fading into the distance and prayed that she'd made the right choice.

Their confrontation hadn't been pretty. He was hurt and so was she—in a different way. He was angry; she was sorry. But unchanging.

*"You're having an affair with him."* Memory of Dan's accusation still stung.

"I'm not," she protested again aloud.

*"I heard the rumor about you going off with him in the middle of the night . . . after I'd brought you home. I didn't believe it, then, but . . ."*

"It was a ride, Dan. Nothing more."

He hadn't looked convinced.

*"I love you, Eden. Doesn't that mean anything?"*

Everything, she assured him. It was special, just as the love she felt for him was special. She loved him like a friend. A good and valued friend, and those kind of relationships were far more rare than those tagged as romantic love.

Eden wiped away a stray tear, one of many that had fallen since he'd gone.

*"He'll hurt you, Eden. You know that, don't you? He'll wake up one day and ride off to who knows where, and you'll never hear of Nick Logan again."*

"I know, Dan," she whispered. "I know."

But she hadn't had a choice. Not really. She had fallen in love with Nick. Stranger. Drifter. Womanizer. He aroused her as no man had ever done. He made her happy, really happy for the first time in years. Her heart had overridden her intellect, and had taken a tumble for Nick despite the odds....

"Eden! Where are you?" The sound of Mariah's voice sent Eden to her feet. Wonderful! The last thing she needed was another well-meaning person giving her advice.

"I...I'm in the arbor!" she called, wondering how Mariah had driven up without her hearing the car.

Wearing jeans and a baggy shirt, her wild blond hair scooped up into a frizzy ponytail on one side of her head, Mariah stepped through the arched entrance of the wisteria arbor.

"Hey," she said, coming toward Eden with a smile and blinking at the sudden shade that rendered her momentarily sightless. "Are you okay? We missed you at church. I told Ford you probably went to the other one, but he said that today was your day to be with us, and I—"

Mariah stopped a few feet from Eden. Her eyes had adjusted to the lesser light and she saw the unmistakable signs of her sister's distress.

"Eden? What is it? What's the matter?"

The tender concern in Mariah's voice was Eden's undoing.

"I broke off with Dan," she said as two tears escaped the tight control she had on them and rolled down her cheeks.

She brushed them away, but they were already being followed by more. The next thing she knew, Eden was being held close in Mariah's arms. Mariah rocked her back and forth the way Eden had rocked her so many times in the past, smoothing Eden's hair and murmuring all the trite and meaningless phrases that somehow always brought about a sense that things would be all right. Eden submitted. She and her baby sister had switched roles again.

When the tears were reduced to an occasional sniffle and a soggy tissue, Mariah asked, "If it upset you so much, why did you break up with Dan? I hope it wasn't anything I said."

Eden offered her a wan smile. "Of course not. I just realized that I didn't love him enough."

Mariah's smile was understanding. "I really didn't think you did. What made you decide?"

Eden forced her gaze unflinchingly to Mariah's. "Nick," she said softly.

"Nick?" Mariah said. "Oh, Edie, you didn't?"

"I haven't done anything!" Eden said, suddenly defensive.

Mariah's pouty-looking lips twisted into a wry smile. "Nothing but fall in love with him," she stated. Seeing the truth of her statement reflected in Eden's eyes, she sighed. "Oh, Eden, how could you?"

Eden's eyes filled again. "How could I not?"

SUNDAY AFTERNOON FOUND Stuart Logan ensconced in the maroon leather chair in his office. It was on the first floor of the Georgian mansion sitting smack dab in the center of his timber empire. Weather permitting, most days since Keith had taken over the company were spent at the golf course or fishing on Lake Ouachita, and Sunday was the day he went through the personal mail that was delivered to the house. He stared at the pile of letters and circulars laying atop the massive mahogany desk and sighed.

Resting his elbows on the desktop, he put his aching head in his hands. This investigation business was getting him down. It was frightening to think that everything he had worked so hard for might be taken from him. And more frightening to think, as he was beginning to, that Keith was the reason for it all.

It had been a mistake to put him in charge, he saw that now. Better to have let Nick run things. Ah, well, it was no one's fault but his own. Nick had happened to catch the fallout from his fight with Theresa.

Lifting his head, Stuart stared at the pile of mail once more. There was no way to get it done but to start. His eyes strayed to a small padded envelope with a label from Coker, Davenport and Coker, a law firm in Tennessee. Stuart frowned. It wasn't a company he was familiar with, much less one he dealt with.

Curious, he ripped the envelope open and reached inside, drawing out a cheap dime-store diary. *What the hell?* He turned the small, battered ledger over in his hands, reluctant to open it, yet not knowing why. A small key hung from a string that was tied around the strap holding it closed. Taking the key in his smooth, manicured fingers, Stuart inserted it into the lock and turned. It gave a soft metallic click, and the strap fell away.

His heart began to beat slowly, heavily as he opened the book to the first page. Round, feminine, unfamiliar handwriting spelled a name that leaped out at him.

*Ellie Tanner.*

Surprise rendered him completely still, and his eyes blurred as he read the address, the same address where she'd lived until the incident with Luke and Nicole and he'd forced the Tanners to move away.

Ellie Tanner. Gil Tanner's pretty, quiet wife. Ellie. One of his many indiscretions, a short-lived affair that had taken place while Theresa was in California one year and Gil was overseas.

Thinking about it brought a bad taste to Stuart's mouth. As an affair it had lacked a certain something. He supposed that it was the circumstances surrounding it. Ellie hadn't pretended to love him. In fact, she had loathed him. But he had wanted her...and anything Stuart Logan wanted, he got.

He had manipulated Ellie, telling her that if she didn't come to him willingly Gil's job wouldn't be waiting for him when he got home. He had threatened that he would call the note due on their house, and that even though she was innocent of an affair with him, Gil would be told several juicy tales to the contrary.

In the end, amid tears and pleading, she had capitulated. But the victory was hollow. For a few short weeks Ellie had granted him use of her body, but never once was it an enjoyable experience. Stymied for the first time in his life by her ability to rise above the situation, he decided to end it. And the end had been a profound relief.

He had taken her, but she'd never really been his.

Now, thumbing through the brittle yellow pages, he felt the frustration that had gripped him so long ago all over again. A name—his name—leaped from the page. A vein in his temple began to throb in synchronization with his pounding head. The entry was March 10, 1955. It outlined, in vivid detail, the terms of his threats to Ellie, finishing with her decision.

*I have to do it. I don't know of any way to fight him.*

He read page after page, seeing his actions with crystal clarity, seeing himself through the eyes of one of his victims. The pain in his head increased insidiously with every word, as did his loathing of what he'd done. When he reached an entry dated May 21, Stuart's head came up in surprise. His eyes widened . . . filled with tears. He gasped and clutched his splitting head. The expensive leather chair swiveled slightly as his body slid to the floor with a dull thud.

Keith found him thirty minutes later.

Defeated by the words of a dead woman.

NICK DIDN'T TURN ON the television at all Sunday night. From his place at the window, he had watched Mariah's arrival, saw her car meet and pass Dan's as he left. He saw her go into the wisteria arbor and stay for a long time. Comforting Eden? he wondered. Later, Eden walked Mariah to the white sports car, their arms around each other's waists. After Mariah's car disappeared, he had waited for Eden to come to him . . . to pick up where they'd left off.

But she hadn't come.

She had gone into the house, and as far as he could tell she hadn't come out at all. Deep in his heart, he'd known she wouldn't. No doubt Dan's arrival had brought her to her senses and made her realize what she was jeopardizing by fooling around with a stranger in the front yard.

Nick couldn't bring himself to join her for dinner as he usually did. Instead he sat in the darkening apartment, his head resting on the back of the sofa, smoking and thinking, and not liking his conclusions at all.

Dan was offering her stability. A permanent relationship. Nick Logan was offering her a tumble in the leaves and an autumn full of heartache. It was the only thing he could offer her. Only a fool would make the wrong choice. And Eden Calloway was certainly no fool.

AFTER MARIAH LEFT, Eden went inside. She cleaned up the lunch dishes and put on some stew for dinner. Then she took a shower, put on makeup and waited for Nick to come. He didn't. He didn't come to take up where they'd left off; he didn't come to dinner. At eight o'clock she put the congealed stew and stone-cold biscuits in the refrigerator and put on the Taurus nightshirt Mariah had brought her several years before. Then she turned out the lights and went to bed.

Why hadn't he come? she wondered. Hadn't she pleased him? Was he used to women more uninhibited than she was? Was he sorry that he'd kissed her? She recalled his face when he'd said—callously said?—that he'd let her explain to Dan. Was he grateful that Dan had come along and got him out of a sticky situation? He was a young man, footloose and fancy-free. She was older, a spinster, for goodness' sake! He was probably embarrassed by her actions. He probably thought that she'd been trying to act young and playful to get his attention.

But she hadn't. The truth was, when she was with Nick she felt young and playful. And desirable. For the first time in a long time, she felt like a woman, and she only wished that she had made him feel more a man. But wishes, as she'd learned the hard way, didn't always come true.

EDEN WOKE UP SCRATCHING, her nails raking her abdomen through the soft cotton of her nightshirt. Drowsily she rolled over and tried to go back to sleep. Ten minutes later she gave up and turned on the bedside light. Lifting the tail of the shirt, she looked at her midriff. It was covered with a rash of fine red bumps already oozing clear liquid.

"Oh, no!" she moaned, "poison ivy." Highly allergic to the troublesome vine, she knew intuitively what it was, but for a moment, Eden couldn't imagine how she'd got it. She reached up and scratched absently at her cheek.

The memory of Nick's hand cradling her face flashed through her mind, quickly followed by the recollection of him pulling vines from the tree with his bare hands. Bare hands that had touched her middle...

She leaped from the bed and ran into the bathroom, flipping on the light as she went. Just as she suspected, the left side of her face was riddled with bumps and had already started to swell unattractively. She had to get to the doctor. The sooner she got a shot, the better. Past experience had taught her that if left unattended, things could get serious.

A loud pounding at the door sent her spinning around in surprise. Who on earth could be knocking at this time of the night?

"Eden? It's me. Open the door!"

The sound of Nick's voice calling her name was accompanied by another round of window-rattling pounding. Relief, sweet and heady, swept through her. She headed toward the front door, her bare feet skimming over the hardwood floors. Shooting back the night bolt, she flung open the door.

Nick stood there, clad in jeans and moonlight, his arms braced on either side of the door frame. His shoulders were broad; his waist was narrow. The curly pelt of hair covering his chest sprawled across the flatness of his belly to the hidden forbidden territory beyond the waistband of his low-slung jeans.

Eden's mouth went as dry as the Louisiana ground before the rain the night before. "What's the matter?" she asked, finding her voice at last.

"That's what I came to ask you," he said, taking a step closer and propelling her inside. "I saw your light and—good grief! What happened to you?"

Eden's hand went automatically to her face. Dull color rushed upward. "I guess some of the vines you were pulling down were poison ivy."

Nick nodded. "Yeah. It was. I'm not allergic to it, so I didn't think a thing of it."

"I guess it was on your hands," she explained, "and everywhere you touched me . . . I got it."

## CHAPTER EIGHT

THE SOUND OF A CAR DOOR slamming shut brought Nick to sudden wakefulness. Leaping to his feet, he glanced quickly around the unfamiliar room, absorbing a series of impressions. Frilly curtains. Pale yellow walls. And Eden still sleeping, despite the fact that someone was knocking on the door.

He was in Eden's room.

Memories of the night came back in vivid detail. Nick went to the window and pushed the curtains back to look outside. There was a car in the driveway, and a little girl was slowly meandering up the sidewalk. His heart sank. Today was Eden's day to keep Molly and Jamie Davis. Only Eden was too sick.

Someone had to break the news to their mother, who would undoubtedly wonder what he was doing inside Eden's house at this time of the morning. With little doubt as to who the lucky person was, Nick tucked in his shirt and went to the front door, clicking the night bolt and opening it with an apologetic—and hopefully innocent—smile on his face.

The woman was definitely surprised, he thought. It was obvious that she wasn't accustomed to a man answering Eden's door at six in the morning. Nick couldn't decide whether to defend Eden's innocence or tell Mrs. Davis that what Eden did when she wasn't keeping her kids was her own business.

"Who are you?"

Nick looked down at a little girl of four or five who was staring up at him, a glimmer of curiosity in her serious brown eyes. "I'm Nick," he said, recognizing from Eden's description that the child was Jamie.

"Where's Eden?" Jamie's mother, a tall brunette, asked, looking beyond his shoulder as if she hoped to catch a glimpse of Eden somewhere behind him.

"She's still asleep," he explained. "I'm afraid she can't keep the girls today. She's sick."

The woman looked skeptical. "Sick?"

Nick could almost see her conjuring up some kind of kinky bedroom scene in her mind—with him and Eden as the main attraction.

"Why didn't she call? This isn't like Eden at all. She's never let me down this way before."

"Good morning, Pat."

The sound of Eden's voice halted the heated defense hovering on Nick's lips. Turning in surprise, he saw her standing behind him, clad in her nightshirt and jeans.

"My goodness!" Pat Davis said. "What happened to you?" The swelling and rash on Eden's cheek validated Nick's story.

Eden's eyes strayed briefly to Nick's. She shrugged. "I was working in the yard yesterday and got into some poison ivy. Thankfully Nick was here to take me to the emergency room last night."

Nick knew the casual explanation was as much to clear him with Pat Davis as it was an explanation.

"Are you going to be all right?"

"I'm fine," Eden assured her. "I just don't look so good. I can keep the girls. No problem."

"You're not baby-sitting today." The sound of his voice issuing the ultimatum surprised everyone—even Nick.

Eden's gaze flew to his. "But Pat doesn't have anyone to keep the girls on such short notice."

"The doctor said those pills would make you sleepy. You need to be in bed," he said adamantly. "And you for sure don't need to be touching Molly and Jamie and giving that stuff to them."

Eden met the stolidness of his gaze and then looked at Pat. "I'm sorry, but he's right."

Nick thrust his hands into his back pockets and took a fortifying breath, knowing that he was going to hate himself for what he was about to do.

"I know you don't know me from Adam, but if you'd like me to watch the girls, I'd be glad to. I know they aren't used to me, but Eden will be here if anything comes up I can't handle."

Pat Davis looked at Eden as if to ask, "Can I trust him?" Nick didn't know if something in Eden's eyes reassured her or if Pat agreed because she had no choice. She nodded. "All right."

"What about your work?" Eden asked Nick.

"I'll call Seth. I'm sure that if I explain the circumstances, he can do without me for a day."

"Are you sure you can handle them?" Pat Davis asked.

Nick flashed her his most devastating smile. "Piece of cake."


"C'MON, MOLLY, take a bite for Uncle Nick...pretty please."

He'd had the girls barely forty minutes and was already having second thoughts. Eden had gone back to bed. Molly was either shy or afraid of him, and Jamie had about talked him to death. Deciding that he would take things one at a time, he had fixed bacon, scrambled eggs and made toast.

So far, Molly hadn't touched any of it. She peeked at him through her fingers and shook her head. "Don't want any."

"Molly don't like eggs," Jamie informed him loftily. "She likes cereal."

Nick propped his chin in his hand and looked at the five-year-old, who was scooping up a large bite of scrambled egg for herself. A wry smile lifted the corners of his lips. *Why didn't one of you tell me that when I asked you what you wanted for breakfast?* Nick was thankful that Jamie couldn't see the edge to the smile . . . or read minds.

"I want Auntie Eden," Molly said, popping her forefinger into her mouth.

"You can see Auntie Eden later," Nick promised. "She's sleeping right now."

"Why?" she asked, speaking around her finger.

"She's sick," he explained patiently as he held up a small triangle of toast with strawberry jam.

Molly shook her head again. Looking at him with blue eyes that promised to deal a lot of misery to unsuspecting males in about fourteen years, she took her finger out of her pretty bow-shaped mouth and asked again, "Why?"

"Because she got into some poison ivy."

"Oh," Molly said, apparently satisfied.

Nick breathed a sigh of relief.

"What's poison ibee?" she asked as an afterthought.

Nick counted to ten. "It's a real itchy rash," he said, shoving his chair back from the table and swinging Molly up into his arms. "Come on. If you're not going to eat, let's go turn on cartoons."

From Molly's happy chortle of laughter, he assumed he'd made a correct decision at last. He found the early morning cartoons and left the girls glued to the television while he went to check on Eden.

She was still sleeping. He closed the door quietly and went to clean up the kitchen, recalling how worried he'd been the night before.

After he'd knocked on her door and found out that he'd given the poison ivy to her, he insisted on taking her to the Bossier Medical Center emergency room. He was glad he had. She was itching like crazy and her face was swelling. Though the situation wasn't life-threatening, he knew she had to be in misery and that they had to get the itching under control.

The doctor on duty had given her a shot, something to make her sleep, lotion and tablets to help dry the rash up. By the time Nick pulled her station wagon into the driveway around four o'clock, Eden was sound asleep, rousing only a little as he had carried her inside and stripped off her jeans.

Then, tired from the long night and the lack of sleep but fearing that she might need him, he had stretched out on the bed beside her and fallen instantly asleep.

His loins tightened now as he recalled how he could see through the wispy peach-tinted panties she had been wearing. She hadn't worn a bra, either.

He closed the dishwasher with a thud and turned it on. If Dan hadn't come and interrupted them, he might have known firsthand if the body he'd glimpsed the night before was as exciting as he had a feeling it was. He pushed away the thought that he might never know.

"HOW ARE YOU FEELING?" It was almost lunchtime, and Nick wasn't sure what to fix.

Eden scooted up against the headboard of the bed. "Better. How are the girls?"

"We're going to make it," he assured her.

A smile danced at the corners of her mouth. "Are you sure?"

"Well," he said, his smile matching hers, "they will, anyway. They're playing outside."

They both laughed. Eden forgot how Dan's arrival the day before had interrupted the stolen moments with Nick on the front lawn, forgot that she had expected him to make some sort of move toward furthering the feelings they had for each other. And then she remembered.

How she'd responded so uninhibitedly to his kisses.

How she'd waited and he hadn't come.

She sobered abruptly.

Nick wondered what happened. "Did you want me to call anyone for you...tell them what's going on?" he asked. *Do you want me to call Dan?*

"No," she said with a shake of her head. "I'll check in with them later."

"Okay," he agreed. "So how about some lunch? I do a great Campbell's soup. And the things I can do with bologna are not to be believed."

In spite of herself, Eden found her smile returning. "There's some stew in the refrigerator. I made it for our supper last night." *But you never came.* As soon as the words were spoken, Eden wished she could bring them back. She wasn't well versed in the games between men and women. Now he would know that she'd waited for him.

Nick tried to hide his surprise. Had he misinterpreted everything that happened after Dan's arrival? Had she wanted him to come to the house after Dan had gone? Had she wanted him to finish what she'd started?

"Stew sounds great," he said. "I'll warm it up. What about the girls?"

"Open them a can of spaghetti. They love it."

He made a face and started to leave.

"Nick!"

He turned, a question puckering his brow. "Yeah?"

"Why did you come to check on me last night?" she asked. "How did you know something was wrong?"

"I saw you turn on your light and figured something wasn't right," he explained.

"Oh."

Nick left the room, intent on fixing lunch. It was only later that he realized what he'd done. He cursed as he dumped the stew into a pan. By saying that he'd seen her light go on, he'd all but admitted that he had been sitting at the window all night, staring at her room like a lovesick fool.

Eden didn't catch the implication of his words until after she'd finished her lunch and was just starting to doze off again.

*"I saw you turn on your light."*

Why hadn't he been asleep at that time of the morning? she wondered. And was it too far-fetched to think that he'd been awake . . . thinking about her?

MOLLY, JAMIE AND EDEN were taking naps, and Nick, who had stooped to watching soap operas, was dozing on the couch when a news bulletin came on between series. Eyes closed, he listened with half an ear to the latest Washington political brouhaha that switched without warning to an ArkLaTex news update.

"In Little Rock, an interview with Keith Logan—" the newscaster's voice sent Nick's eyes flying open and his gaze to the television screen "—heir to Logan Enterprises in northern Arkansas, revealed that there has been little change in his father's condition. Stuart Logan, still in intensive care, suffered a severe stroke in his home late yesterday evening. Logan Enterprises is currently under investigation for allegedly bringing about the downfall of several small timber companies and then buying them at below market value."

Still staring in disbelief at the pretty blond woman who was signing off, Nick pushed himself to a sitting position. A stroke? Stuart? Shock rendered him quiet for several moments as he tried to digest the news. Stuart Logan brought low by a stroke when he appeared to be the epitome of good health and vitality?

Nicole hadn't said anything about Stuart being ill yesterday. Frowning, Nick rose and went to the kitchen. Why was he feeling the need to call and see how their father was doing? Stuart didn't mean anything to him, did he?

THE WEEK PROGRESSED NICELY. The rain on Saturday had made the October temperatures a bit more amenable. Mariah was feeling wonderful, and the hydraulic gun had been working just fine ever since Nick put the new pump on. Since Tess had minored in math, Mariah and Eden had asked her to go over the books to see if there was any money they could divert to replace recent expenses. But with adjusting to a new teaching position, a new husband and stepson, Tess hadn't been able to get to it. Coming from a close-knit family, everyone understood. Grumbling that she had barely passed business math, Mariah decided to give the books a look herself . . . which would no doubt take a while.

Thanks to the miracle of modern medicine, Eden was all but well by Friday. After letting Nick keep the girls on Monday, Pat made arrangements for them to stay at a local day care the rest of the week, and Nick, strangely silent, had gone back to work.

It was life as usual. Shreveport-Bossier were gearing up for the Red River Revel, an annual celebration of the arts. Everyone was going...including Eden, who was going with Nick, even though she wasn't certain how it had happened. One minute everyone was talking about going; the next minute Mariah had somehow paired the two of them up. There was no way Nick could have declined without seeming churlish.

Eden could have strangled her younger sister on the spot. As much as she liked the setup, she wasn't sure how Nick felt about it. Though things seemed normal between them since she'd been out of commission with the poison ivy, she could almost feel the undercurrents of emotion flowing between them. The problem was, she wasn't certain what the emotion was.

Eden prepared for the evening, not certain what to expect. The Revel took place on the riverfront, and she wanted to be comfortable. She also wanted to go on the Harley. Olive-green pleated slacks, a khaki-hued shirt and low-heeled shoes seemed appropriate. She took particular care with her makeup and blew her freshly washed hair into wild disarray. She wasn't certain why she was taking so many pains with the way she looked—Nick had been so preoccupied lately, he probably wouldn't even notice.

NICK SHOWERED AND DRESSED for his date with Eden, humming a popular song by Heart under his breath. For the first time since he had heard the news about Stuart, Nick felt good about his father's recovery. An early morning phone call to his sister—a daily deed since the stroke—had yielded the information that Stuart had been moved to a private room the day before. Nicole said the doctors were optimistic that with time, he would regain use of his paralyzed left side and his speech. Nick had hung up, his heart lighter than it had been in days.

He didn't understand why Stuart should still matter to him after everything his father had done to him, but he did, maybe because Nick had realized this past week that Stuart was to be pitied, not hated. His father had mistakenly equated his lust for money and power with happiness. Stuart had been extremely partial to Keith, the son born of his first marriage to a woman he had been totally infatuated with. Stuart had given Keith everything he desired in a bid to gain his love and respect, and in doing so had denied himself the love and companionship of not only his second wife, but of his and Theresa's two children, as well. With the advantage of adulthood, Nick understood Theresa's bitterness and her discreet affairs better.

He wished he could share his new assessment of his father and his feelings with someone, but Nicole was too fragile, and Eden was...

What? Too important to him? She was, and he knew it. The time he spent with her was both heaven and hell, which meant that he had violated his rule not to get involved. He was getting entangled not only with Eden's family, but with their affairs as well. It was none of his business. He had stayed in Calloway Corners far too long.

Because he was concerned over the plight of the mill, Nick had been asking questions about its part in the local economy. He found out that it *was* the local economy. Without it, the Calloway Corners area would have several families joining the burgeoning ranks of the unemployed and the increasingly long food-stamp lines. Nick hated to see that happen to the town...and especially to the Calloway women.

He forced himself to think of something more pleasant—like Eden.

In a Rod Stewartlike voice, he sang a few bars of the song he'd been humming earlier. When he realized the lyrics were about wanting someone so bad, he stopped singing with comical abruptness.

*Freudian, Logan.* The song summed up his feelings for Eden very nicely.

No doubt about it, he thought, as he tucked a clean shirt into the waistband of his pants, he was caring for her too much. It was time to move on before he got in any deeper, or they found out who he was. If any of the Calloways or their husbands found out about his cautious questioning or got a hint that he was connected to the Arkansas Logans, he would never be able to talk his way out of the trouble he would be in.

With the ongoing investigation into his family's business dealings, they would never believe that he had come to Calloway Corners to find a little of the peace and contentment Mariah seemed to find here. There was no way they would believe that he hadn't come to check their situation out and turn over news of their trouble to his family. It was time to go—the sooner the better.

NICK'S RESOLVE VANISHED as soon as Eden opened the door. Her hair, bright and stylishly curled, brushed the shoulders of a plain khaki shirt. Her eyes were shadowed with olive, gold and peach, a subtle blending of color that enhanced the jade green of her eyes. A hint of worry lurked in their depths along with a quiet joy that said she was glad to see him.

Whenever he looked into those incredible eyes, he could feel himself drowning in the peace that filled him. When he was with Eden, he felt as if he'd come home . . . a place that had been only a word before.

It came to him quietly that despite the pain inflicted by Belinda, despite his years of running from commitment, despite his vows never to let it happen again, he had fallen in love with Eden Calloway . . . and Nick wasn't sure that it hadn't happened that first moment he'd seen her standing on the porch. Heaven knew he'd wanted her since then.

Recognition of his love brought out a whole set of insecurities and worries that spread through him like wildfire. Would Eden feel that he was too young? She thought he was a drifter—a man without a home, without prospects, without a future, and if he told her the truth, told her who he was, would she want to be tied to a man whose family was under investigation?

She offered him a tentative smile. "Hi."

His lips curved upward in a passable imitation. "Hi. Are you ready?"

Eden nodded. Something was wrong, she thought. Nick had been acting strangely all week, and she didn't like the worry she saw in his dark brown eyes. Maybe he didn't want to take her to the Revel. "You know you don't have to do this," she said, offering him a way out.

He frowned. "Do what?"

"Take me to the Revel." Her shoulders lifted in a self-conscious shrug. "I mean, we both know how Mariah is. You were railroaded into this date." She turned away, unsettled by the intensity of his gaze.

Nick reached out and grasped her shoulder, turning her toward him. "I want to take you to the Revel," he said solemnly. "Very much."

Eden searched for the truth in his eyes and found it. He smiled then, the smile that set her heart to beating faster, the smile she'd fallen in love with.

"I want to take you," he said again, "that is, if you don't mind if we go in your station wagon."

Eden couldn't hide her disappointment. "Of course I don't mind," she said, "but I wore slacks because I wanted to ride the motorcycle."

Nick's surprise quickly dissolved into pleasure. "You do?"

She smiled and nodded. "I love it. It makes me feel free. I don't think I ever felt free until the night you took me riding."

Nick saw the sincerity in her eyes. *And I don't think I felt free until I came to Calloway Corners.*

"Then by all means," he said, "let's take the Harley."

THE STREETS along the Red River were crowded. There were booths with artists from various parts of the country, crafts of all kinds, ethnic food and a variety of entertainment on stages scattered throughout the designated area. Dance teams danced, singers sang, and bands played. People stopped to listen, snacked until they were stuffed and spent a ton of money on the artistic offerings that were showcased.

Eden and Nick parked the Harley and met her sisters and their husbands at a predetermined spot. For the next three hours, they wandered from booth to booth. Ford bought Mariah a hand-crocheted baby afghan in lime-green and apricot. Seth bought Tess a silver and abalone necklace. Nick insisted that Eden sit for an artist who did a pastel portrait of her in the span of twenty minutes. He wanted the picture for later... when he was gone.

At a display of quilts, Eden spied one done in tints of pink and green, the very colors she was considering using when she redid her room in the spring. Part appliqué, part embroidery, it was an exquisite piece of workmanship. Eden had pieced quilts, but she'd never had any patience with embroidery, always hurrying to get finished instead of enjoying it the way she was supposed to. Telling herself that the price was too exorbitant, she longingly traced her fingertip over the tiny, even stitches—the mark of good quilting—and moved on.

They ate gyros and tacos and funnel cakes and when it got dark they sat and listened to the Shreveport Choral Ensemble's presentation. Halfway through, Nick excused himself.

With a sinking heart, Eden watched him disappear into the throng of milling people. She wondered where he was going and if he would leave her life the same way—no warning, no explanation. And he would leave. It was a foregone conclusion, a fact that she had known since the day he'd pulled up in her driveway and taken control of her thoughts and her heart. It was a fact that was brought sharply home every time he got on the Harley and left. She didn't know when he would go, but there was something different about Nick this week. Ever since Sunday and their kiss, he had been more quiet than usual. Eden could only surmise that the time was drawing closer.

She didn't hear him come back, didn't know he was any-where around until he sat down next to her and placed a large plastic bag on her lap. His eyes were smiling, the crin-kles at the corners fanning out attractively.

"What is it?" she asked. The contents felt fairly heavy on her legs, but at the same time the burden was soft.

"A thank-you," he said.

"A thank-you?" she queried. "For what?"

"For being you," he said. "Open it."

Eden didn't understand what he meant, but she com-plied. Reaching inside, she pulled out the quilt she'd been looking at earlier. Her first thought was pleasure. She hadn't said a word about wanting it or liking it, but Nick had been sensitive enough to see her interest. And he'd cared enough to buy it for her. Her pleasure faded a bit at that thought. The quilt was expensive, and she knew he couldn't have a lot of money if he traveled around the country doing odd jobs.

"I wish you hadn't bought it," she told him.

He looked puzzled. And hurt. "I thought you liked it."

"I do!" she hastened to tell him. "But it was so expen-sive, and you—"

"If you're worried about whether or not I can afford it— don't. I wanted to give it to you. All you're supposed to do is say thank you."

Eden looked at him, torn between her pleasure and her guilt for accepting it when she imagined he could use the money to a better purpose. But, she thought, it would be a way to remember him . . . after he'd gone.

She smiled at him, a dazzling smile that was thanks enough in itself. Then she leaned over and pressed her lips to his cheek. "Thank you, Nick," she whispered. "I love it."

*And you.*

They went home soon after that, declining the invitation from the others to join them somewhere for a late dinner.

Though the days were still warm, riding the motorcycle in the night air was chilly once the sun had set. Nick told her to wrap up in the quilt and hang on. She did. Eden indulged in a bit of fancy, imagining that it was like being wrapped in Nick's arms, Nick's love.

The Country Corner grocery store was doing a booming just-before-closing business as they sped by. Everything else was quiet and dark. There were few cars on McKinley, but someone was taking advantage of the car wash. Just as the day was drawing to an end, so was her date with Nick, and Eden wasn't ready for that yet.

By the time he pulled into the long lane that led to the house, Eden had made a decision. She was going to find out one way or the other just how interested he was in her. After all, hadn't she decided to take control of her life from now on? Wasn't she going for broke this time around?

Nick pulled into the driveway and stopped the Harley in front of the white picket gate. Without speaking, he helped her take off the helmet and offered her his hand to dismount. Since she still had the quilt wrapped around her, he opened the gate, his obvious intention to walk her to the door and leave her.

Which was exactly his plan. At the bottom of the porch steps, Nick reached out and grasped the edges of the quilt, as he would lapels of a jacket. A brief good-night was in his plan, too. One kiss and then he was going to the apartment and to bed. Tomorrow he'd give Seth a few days' notice.

Incandescence from the security light spilled over the front yard, partially illuminating Eden's face. Nick felt his throat tighten at the thought of leaving and never seeing her again. "I had a good time," he said huskily. "Thanks."

"So did I," Eden told him, moving imperceptibly nearer. She leaned her head to the side and lifted her shoulder, rubbing her cheek against the fabric of the quilt. "I love the quilt. Thanks for buying it for me."

"Sure." Then, because he wasn't the kind of person to be deliberately unkind and he wanted to prepare her for his leaving, he added, "You can think about me when you use it."

The slight reference to his leaving wasn't lost on Eden. He was only corroborating what she'd thought earlier. He was going to leave. Soon. But not, she vowed, before she had more than a quilt to remember him by.

A fragment of a conversation she'd had with Mariah several months before drifted through Eden's mind. She had been lamenting over what to do if you thought you found the right man but he didn't ask you to marry him. Mariah's comment had been, "Then you ask him."

The memory strengthened Eden's resolve. Once in her life, she was going to do exactly what she wanted instead of what everyone expected. She would have this night with no strings attached. She had saved herself for years, never knowing why. But now she knew that she had been waiting for Nick. He might not be her husband, but he was the other half of her soul.

Jo would call her crazy for what she was about to do.

Tess would agree.

But Mariah would understand.

Happy with her decision, Eden laughed softly and raised up on tiptoe to press a gentle kiss to Nick's lips. He responded briefly to the pressure of her mouth before she drew away. "Come on," she said.

Without waiting for a reply, she clutched the edge of the quilt and spread her arms wide, running down the short flight of steps and out onto the grass with the quilt billowing out behind her like a cape. Stopping at the edge of the live oak's shadow, she swung the covering around and spread it on the moon-dappled lawn. If she expected Nick to object, she was disappointed. Like a man in a dream, he followed her.

By the time he reached her she had already kicked off her shoes and was lying on her back, propped up on her elbows. She tipped her head back and looked at the ebony, star-sprinkled sky. "Do you like stars?" she asked.

Nick, who was shedding his loafers, was slightly taken aback. He didn't know what he expected, but it certainly wasn't a stint of star gazing. He planted his hands on his hips. "Yeah. I guess I do," he said, tilting his head back and looking upward. "Astronomy used to be one of my favorite things to study in school, but I hadn't thought much about it lately."

"For shame, Nick Logan," Eden chastised as the moonlight sought out the teasing lights in her eyes. "There's a whole world of dreams there. All we have to do is reach up and take one."

Nick was more than willing to play her game. "You think so?" he asked, smiling down at her.

Resting on one elbow again, Eden reached up and held out her hand. This time there was no mistaking what was happening, he thought. Eden was making moves that Nick was very familiar with. And frankly, he was tired of fighting his feelings for her, tired of fighting what seemed like the most natural thing in the world. He reached out slowly and put his hand in hers, letting her draw him down, down into the invisible web of her love.

With a sigh, he stretched out on his side facing her, propping his head on his hand. His free hand brushed her attractively untidy hair from her face. Like a feline seeking more contact, she turned her cheek into his palm. Starshine and moonlight spilled through the lacy branches of the tree, turning her red-gold hair to molten copper. Nick placed his finger beneath her chin and tipped her head back until he could look into her eyes. "You're beautiful."

The words went to her head like strong drink. She'd never thought she was beautiful. While she knew she was attractive enough, she'd always thought she was the plain sister compared to the other Calloways. But Nick made her feel beautiful and feminine and every inch a woman. And Eden wanted to experience the ultimate in all those things...with him.

"Make love to me."

She spoke the words so softly that for the span of a heartbeat Nick wondered if they were the whisper of the wind. But when he looked into Eden's eyes he saw the longing and hunger there.

It was what she wanted.

What he wanted.

But for some reason, he felt an obligation to remind her of the facts. "You hardly know me."

A less desperate woman might have taken the statement as a rejection. But the light of the moon illuminated the inner struggle reflected in his eyes. She didn't argue. "I want you," she said again.

For a moment, he didn't answer. His past taunted him, calling him a fool for believing her woman's words, her woman's trickery. Hadn't he been taken in by those words before? What made him think that Eden Calloway was any different? Then slowly, so slowly that he thought he was imagining his own actions, he raised his hand to her cheek once more. He might be reluctant, but he wasn't stupid, and he'd be a fool to deny them what they both wanted.

"How much do you want me?" he asked, recklessly, unable to believe what was happening between them.

*Enough to let you drive out of my life afterward with no questions asked.*

"So badly that if you don't kiss me soon, I swear I'm going to die," she whispered.

The honesty throbbing in her voice was Nick's undoing. The breath he'd been holding trickled from him in slow release. Without a word, his hand trailed down her cheek to her chin. His hand was trembling. His thumb brushed her bottom lip, pulling it down slightly and skimming her teeth. Eden's tongue touched it tentatively.

An indrawn breath hissed through his clenched teeth. Without waiting any longer, Nick cupped the back of her head with his hand and took her mouth in a bruising kiss. Eden melted beneath the onslaught of his kiss, falling back onto the quilt in a surrender so complete that it drove Nick crazy with wanting. The soft, kittenish sounds issuing from her throat drove him wild. He wasn't certain if Eden Calloway was the genteel Southern lady everyone thought she was, or a backwater-bayou witch with her own particular brand of love potion. He only knew that he had to have her...soon.

Nick felt her hands moving between their bodies and realized that her fingers were slipping the buttons of his shirt from their moorings with the accomplishment of a pro. Then he felt the light brush of her palms against his bare chest, felt her fingers skim the hard buttons of his nipples. With her help, he ripped his shirt from his jeans.

Her mouth was hot and hungry and the unexpected aggressive thrusts of her tongue—combined with the restless movements of her hips—turned him on as much as her former surrender. Eden tore her mouth from his for an instant and breathed a single word. "Wait."

Complying, Nick directed his kisses to her throat and ear. Her hands were at work between them again, and then he felt the indescribable softness of her bare breasts against his chest.

Nick went completely still. Then, driven by the need that had consumed him ever since the first day he'd seen her, he cupped one breast in his palm and drew back to look at her. His fantasies weren't nearly as good as reality. Her breasts—fuller than her sisters'—were firm, softly rounded and centered with dusky, rose-tipped aureoles. His thumb skimmed one aching bud. It puckered in instant response, and Eden arched upward with a gasp. Nick lowered his head and took aching flesh into his mouth.

"Ah, Nick, please . . . please," she groaned, winding her fingers through his hair.

"I will, baby," he growled, his voice a gentle vapor against her flesh. "I will."

The next few minutes—hours?—were nothing but a haze of pleasure, a maelstrom of desire.

Nerve endings she had never been aware of sizzled with awareness and clamored with want. Her breasts were sensitive to his every touch, and her lower body was hollow and aching with a need that only Nick could fill.

The scent of him invaded Eden's nostrils. The taste of his mouth as she ate hungrily at it was as sweet as ambrosia, a feast worthy of any goddess. And for the first time in her life she felt like a goddess. For the first time in her life she was in touch with her feminine power . . . and she used that power to the utmost, wringing low groans and husky moans from Nick.

Soft chantings of need mingled with the rustle of clothing and melded with the breeze whispering through the branches of the live oak as shirts were tossed carelessly to the ground. Her hands touched him, skimming over the muscles of his back and chest as she explored his bare torso with the care of a master cartographer. When she reached the barrier of his jeans, she boldly slipped her fingers inside and unfastened the button.

Nick's mouth left hers and he held his breath as the downward grind of the zipper filled the night. Then she touched him and he was afraid he might go spinning off the face of the earth.

"Eden, Eden . . ." he rasped into her ear.

"Take me, Nick. Now," she pleaded.

And Nick knew there was no turning back. Not now. Not ever. She was in his blood, in his heart, in his soul.

"Yes," he said softly. "Yes."

Jeans joined their shirts. Eden saw Nick open his billfold and closed her eyes to block out a sudden flurry of indecision and fear. Was she crazy? She hardly knew this man. But her heart knew him, and her heart had never lied to her before.

She felt Nick nudge her knees apart and felt the heat of his body as he lowered himself against her. Lifting leaden lashes, she opened her eyes and looked up at him. He smoothed her hair away from her face and smiled.

"Last chance to stop," he said. His voice was teasing, unsteady, but she knew he was serious. He would stop now if that's what she wanted.

"I don't want to stop."

"Good, because I've wanted this," he confessed as his hand covered her and his finger unerringly targeted the heart of her desire, "wanted you, since the first second I laid eyes on you."

Eden's breath collapsed and her heart swelled with love and thankfulness as she moved against his stroking fingers.

"It seems like I've waited so long for this to happen," he said, carefully watching the ever-changing faces of desire that molded her features. "So long."

*Forever. A lifetime.*

"I know," she whispered. "Don't wait any more."

Moving over her, Nick slid slowly into her. She was tight. So very tight. Fully sheathed, he stopped, letting the magnitude of the emotions sweeping through him soak into his very soul. Strangely he didn't know whether to laugh for the pure happiness he felt or to cry for the supreme peace spreading throughout him.

He wished he had time to sort through the myriad feelings, but Eden was impatient. She instigated a slow, sinuous movement and reached up to loop her arms around his neck, drawing his mouth down to hers.

Heartbeats melded and pounded out a pagan beat as, mouth to mouth, heart to heart, they danced to a rhythm as old as time and a song that spoke of love and need and no more lonely tomorrows.

And when the song was done and Eden lay spent in Nick's arms, with the aftershocks of their passion still shuddering through them both, she knew without a doubt that thirty-three years was worth the wait.

# CHAPTER NINE

EDEN LAY WITH HER EYES CLOSED, replaying the last few moments in her mind while the earth gradually shifted back into place. Was she dreaming? No. It was no dream. Her arms were still wrapped around Nick, and the flesh beneath her caressing fingertips was warm and real, as was the delicious burden of his weight pressing her against the hard ground.

His face was buried in the curve where her shoulder and neck met, and he still chanted her name as if it was the most beautiful sound in the world. Eden knew that the moment was indelibly etched into her mind, a memory that would offer her solace as well as pain in the years to come. A smile curved her lips while, inexplicably, tears stung beneath her eyelids.

After long moments, Nick lifted his head and looked down at her, wonder in his eyes. "Did anyone ever tell you that you are one hell of a lover?" he asked in a husky, awe-filled voice.

She moved her head back and forth against the quilt. "No."

Nick's eyes were smiling as he said, "Well, then, let me be the first, because, lady, you are."

"Thank you—I think."

His soft laughter drifted away on the breeze and was soon lost in the night. Serious then, he cradled her cheek in his hand and trailed his thumb over the contour of her bottom lip before taking her lips in a gentle kiss. "Did I hurt you?"

he asked, nuzzling his mouth against hers as he sipped at her lips.

His consideration filled her with happiness. She shook her head again. "No."

"Good." He blew a wisp of hair away from her ear. "I could tell it had been a long time for you."

Eden reached up and traced the bold sweep of a dark eyebrow. "About thirty-three years."

Nick's mouth stopped its random wanderings and he pulled back a bit to look into her eyes. "You're kidding—right?"

"No."

If the experience of making love with Eden hadn't already left Nick feeling awed and humbled, her confession would have. He drew in a shaky breath and rolled away from her to gaze up at the starlit sky. "Whew! I don't know what to say."

Eden couldn't help noticing how beautifully he was made—from the breadth of his shoulders to the strong length of his thighs and the bold proof of his sex. She placed her hand in the center of his chest. He turned his head to look at her. "Don't say anything."

"Yeah, but I feel—"

"Please," she pleaded. "Don't start feeling guilty. For both our sakes. What happened between us was something I wanted, so you certainly don't need to feel guilty." She laughed, and to Nick it sounded just a bit embarrassed. "As a matter of fact, I believe I instigated the whole thing."

He grinned suddenly. "Yeah," he said, "I believe you did." He propped his head on his elbow. "How does a woman stay a virgin until she's thirty-three in this day and age?" he asked, and then added with a wicked smile, "Are you *really* thirty-three?"

The honesty of his response brought a sudden heat to Eden's cheeks. "I guess the right man never came along to tempt me, and yes, I am thirty-three."

"I can't believe it," Nick said with a shake of his head.

"What?"

"I can't believe that you're that age, *or* that I was the right man."

"Does it bother you?" Eden asked, worried that he might think she was too old for him.

"That I was the guy you chose?" he asked completely deadpan. "It was tough, but I'll get over it."

Eden laughed at his teasing and reached out to give him a shove. Nick rolled onto his back once more, and she sprawled on top of him. Her eyes were serious. "I mean it. Does it matter that I'm older than you?"

"Does it matter that I'm younger?" he countered.

"No."

"That I don't have a job—"

"You have a job."

"—or even a car to take you out in," he finished.

"I love the Harley."

"Well, I'm selfish enough to love the fact that I was the first for you."

"Chauvinist," she chided.

"Not chauvinist," he corrected with a shake of his head, drawing her head down and whispering something in her ear.

She looked surprised. "So soon?"

"I'm a young man, remember?"

Eden's happy laughter gurgled up from her throat. She planted a string of three kisses across his chest. "Yeah?"

"Yeah. See if you can keep up," he dared.

"What did you say?" she asked incredulously. "Keep up? Keep up? By morning, we'll see who can keep it up."

"Tacky and crude, Ms Calloway," he said, his hands kneading her back as she resumed her kissing of his chest. "Very cru—ah, Eden, what are you doing? Eden...."

EDEN WOKE UP in her own bed, naked and loosely wrapped in the quilt. She opened her eyes and promptly closed them against the brightness of the saucy sunshine streaming through the windows. Stretching her bare limbs, she smiled. The night hadn't been a dream. The soreness between her thighs and the tenderness of her breasts was mute testimony that it had really happened.

Hazy memories of Nick carrying her inside after they'd made love the second time drifted through her mind. Wrapped in each other's arms, they'd slept a while, and just before dawn she had awakened to his kisses and he had made love to her again before he showered and left for work.

He would be back. She knew it. The doubts in her mind had dissipated like a morning fog on the bayou the instant she faced her feelings for him, feelings that, after the night they'd spent together, she dared to hope he felt for her, too. Was she being naive to think that because he had made wonderful, glorious love to her he cared? She knew that men didn't have to feel anything for a woman but the urge, but Nick was different, wasn't he?

With only the barest hint of a shadow to blight her otherwise bright day, Eden got up and headed for the shower, a song on her lips.

NICK COULD HARDLY WAIT for the day's end. He wanted to see Eden. He knew that what had happened between them had been the height of foolishness on his part, and he could enumerate the reasons: She was Mariah's sister. He was a man without any kind of stability in his life. And his family wasn't the sort that anyone of the Calloway caliber would want to tie themselves to for life.

The reasons didn't change his feelings. He loved her. The instant he had plunged into the haven of her body, Nick knew he had found what he had been looking for. Peace. Home. A biding place for his heart. No more running. No more hate and bitterness eating away at him. Eden was his sanctuary from the past, a bridge to his future.

The past. Funny how neither his father's defection nor Belinda's infidelity seemed important any more. But that still didn't change who he was, what kind of family he came from. He and Eden needed time to get to know each other a little better, time to get used to what had happened between them. Then he would tell her about his family.

*Face it, Logan, you don't want to tell her because you're afraid it will make a difference in how she feels about you. You're afraid she'll drop you and you'll have to go back to wandering again.*

Nick denied the accusations of his mind. But deep down, a nagging voice taunted him that there might be some truth to his fears.

"WHAT IS HE trying to say?" The fashionably dressed, dark-haired woman looked helplessly down at the man lying in the pristine white bed. Thankfully the drapes in the hospital room were pulled, blocking out the autumn sunshine and partially disguising how the left side of Stuart Logan's once-handsome face was drawn grotesquely downward.

Nicole looked at her mother. "I don't know." Never one to hold grudges—especially for things in the distant past—she took his hand. "What is it, Daddy?" she asked.

Stuart Logan's mouth twisted even more as he struggled to get his brain and his mouth to work together. Sweat popped out on his pale forehead. "Nnk . . . lllkss . . ."

"I think he wants Keith," Nicole said. "Is that it, Daddy? Do you want us to call Keith to come and see you?"

Stuart made a feeble attempt to shake his head. Filled with frustration, Nicole frowned. "I don't know what you want, Daddy, I'm sorry."

"Well, how's our patient today?" The words were accompanied by a nurse with a brisk, no-nonsense attitude. Without waiting for an answer, she swept into the room and headed straight to the windows. She yanked the drapes back and flashed Stuart a smile. "There. Isn't that better?"

He closed his eyes.

The R.N. cradled the chart she carried against her side. "Do you mind stepping outside for a few seconds?" she asked. "The doctor is here to make his rounds."

"Of course," Nicole said.

Obediently, she and Theresa filed from the room and made their way to the waiting area at the end of the corridor. Recalling the look in Stuart's eyes as he'd tried to make his wishes known, Nicole turned on her mother angrily. "I think it's shameful that Keith hasn't been here to see Daddy since he got sick."

"I know. But what can I do? Keith hardly acknowledges my existence," Theresa said. She lit a slender cigarette with quick, nervous movements. "What about Nick? Is he planning on coming back?"

*"When hell freezes over or you're dead—one or the other. That's when I'll be back."*

The taunting memory of Nick's parting shot at his father flashed through Nicole's mind. "I don't think so," she confessed. "He calls to check on him, but you know Nick. That streak of stubbornness he inherited from Daddy is a mile wide. I'm not sure if either of them will ever make a move toward a reconciliation."

Theresa took a short pull from her cigarette and went to stand at the window. The hand secreted in the pocket of her skirt curled into a tight fist as she leaned wearily against the window frame. She fought the urge to cry, fought the urge to rail at the fates that had brought them to this. For despite everything Stuart had put her through, she prayed that he would be all right. A wry smile tugged at her perfectly outlined lips, lips so much like Nicole's. Maybe she should amend that, she thought, to what they had put each other through.

Nicole was right. Nick had inherited a stubborn streak from his father...the same way Nicole had inherited her forgiving nature from him. The only thing was that Stuart had nothing to do with passing on either trait.

FOR A WEEK AND A HALF, as October climbed to the middle of the month and then eased into its third week, Eden lived on top of the world. She and Nick watched TV together, rode the Harley together, slept together and made love nearly every night. The discovery of her sexuality was a wonderful thing for Eden, and she told Nick she had a lot of catching up to do. When he told her—with a hint of laughter in his eyes—that she didn't have to catch up by the end of the month, she asked if he was complaining.

He said, "No way."

As she'd known he would be, Nick was a careful and considerate lover, fully willing to take the responsibility for their lovemaking himself. It only made Eden love him more, though she knew that if he stayed, if their affair—dear heaven, how she hated that word—continued, she would offer to accept the burden of protection herself.

Love. The word had never been mentioned between them, even though the emotion was the catalyst for her lovemaking. Nick acted as if he loved her, but she would never press him to say it. And she would never tell him first.

He was a wanderer by nature. She didn't want to drive him away, and she didn't want to hold him to her by putting any kind of guilt or pressure on him to make their arrangement permanent. She believed in the popular premise that if you let something go and it truly belonged to you, it would come back—and if it didn't, then it wasn't yours to start with. So every day she packed his lunch, kissed him goodbye and let him drive off on the Harley, never knowing whether or not he would leave his meager belongings behind and just keep riding.

So far, she had been lucky. But she couldn't help wondering when the dream and the luck would come to an end.

NICK LOOKED AT THE LEDGERS spread out before him. As he suspected, the Calloway mill was in deep financial trouble. As a matter of fact, it was only a matter of time before they would be forced to shut down the entire operation.

"Well?"

The sound of Mariah's voice pulled his gaze from the neat rows of figures to her emerald-green eyes. The haunted pre-Ford look he remembered so well was back. Nick hated to confirm her suspicions, but he had no choice. He raked his hand through his thick, dark hair. "It doesn't look good."

Mariah began to pace the small office. "That's what I thought. I can't figure out what's happened. I mean, I know Daddy didn't keep things up these last few years, but for things to be this bad . . . I just can't believe it."

"It looks to me as if it was more than mismanagement, Mariah," Nick said.

"What do you mean?"

"I mean that it looks as if someone has been juggling the books . . . for several months at least."

Mariah's mouth dropped open in shock. "Someone has been *stealing* from us?" Then, when she realized that the someone must be the bookkeeper, she shook her head in disbelief. "Frannie? No, Nick. Not Frannie."

Nick rolled the chair back from the desk. "Then who else?" he asked, fatalistically.

Mariah turned and stared out the window at the activity in the lumber yard. Nick went to stand behind her, sliding both arms around her and pulling her against him in a gesture of solace. Mariah let her head fall back against his chest. She sighed. "She was so well qualified."

"The better to shaft you, my dear," he said, in his best bad-wolf-Red-Riding-Hood voice.

The attempt at lightness fell flat. She sighed again. "Yeah." Mariah tipped her head back to look at him, and he saw that her eyes were swimming with tears. "I want to show this to Tess and see what she thinks before we tell Eden."

"Good idea."

Mariah turned in his embrace. "Will you go with me?"

Nick pulled her close and dropped a kiss to the top of her shining platinum hair. "Sure."

"WHAT!" EDEN'S SHOCK was soul-deep. Her eyes moved from Mariah to Tess as if she hoped one of them would deny the accusation Nick had just made.

"It's true, Eden," Mariah said. "I thought things looked a little off, so I had Nick and Tess take a look."

Shaken by the news, Eden sank down into a corner of the sofa. She lifted her disbelieving gaze to her sisters. "I can't believe that Fran would steal from us."

"I know." Mariah sat down beside Eden. "What should we do?"

Eden looked at Nick, who stared solemnly back at her. He wished he could keep all the ugly things away from her, wished she never had to know any kind of pain. He knew only too well how ugliness changed a person. "Call the police," he suggested.

"Police?" Eden shook her head. "No, not yet. Let's see if we can find anything concrete tonight, and if we do, we can call the police later."

Nick nodded. "It's your company."

"I'm sorry, Nick," Eden said, "but I don't want to accuse her falsely. I do think we have to tell Ted, though."

A frown drew Tess's brows together. "Ted? Why?"

"Because Ted and Fran are—"

"—in love," Mariah finished for her. She looked at Tess apologetically. "I guess I forgot to tell you that Ted and Fran have a thing going. Lordy! Ted is going to die. First Barbara and now this. Eden, you or Tess will have to tell him. I can't do it."

Eden's eyes drifted shut, as if by blocking out the room she could block out the entire incident. Still, no matter how badly she hated dealing with it, it had to be done, and years of taking charge made her the logical person to tackle the job. "Hand me the phone."

"You aren't going to do it *now*?" Mariah asked.

Once again, Eden looked to Nick for guidance. "It isn't something to put off," he said.

Without another word of argument, Mariah handed her the phone.

"THANKS FOR COMING," Eden said to Ted a few hours later.

"No problem," Ted assured her, answering her welcoming smile with one of his own.

Ushering him in, Eden regarded the man who had been foreman of the Calloway mill for the past thirty years. Ted Vincent was a tall man in his late fifties who looked no older than many men did at forty-five. His steel-gray hair was thick and well-groomed and his physique—the result of a lot of hard work—would make most younger men envious. He was a man she had always liked and respected.

She led the way to the living room, her heart aching for him. Fran Glidden was the only woman Ted had dated since his wife had died three years ago, and now they were about to tell him the woman he loved was a liar and a thief. It didn't promise to be a good evening.

Mariah and Tess sat on the sofa, while Nick lounged against the fireplace. "Do you know Nick?" Eden asked as they entered the living room. The two men shook hands and introduced themselves, and then Eden indicated her father's recliner. "Sit down, Ted. Would you like something to drink? Coffee? Tea?"

"Coffee sounds good, if it's made."

"It is," she assured him. "I won't be but a minute." She returned a short time later carrying coffee and a soda for Nick on a tray. She dispensed the drinks and sat down in the wing chair where she could face Ted. Clasping her hands tightly together in her lap, she looked askance at Tess and Mariah before beginning. "I really don't know where to start."

Ted wriggled in his chair and shifted his gaze from Eden to her sisters. With an uncomfortable smile on his lips, he asked, "I didn't do anything wrong, did I?"

"No!" Eden and Mariah said in unison.

Eden cleared her throat. "You haven't done anything, but I'm afraid Fran has."

Ted choked on his coffee. He wiped his mouth on the napkin Eden had provided. "Fran?"

"Yes. Mariah was going over the books to see if we could divert some money from one area to another to replace the hydraulic gun," Eden said. "She couldn't make heads nor tails of the bookkeeping, so she asked Nick to take a look. Somebody has been diverting money, and Fran is the only person who has daily contact with the books."

The color in Ted's face had fled. "I can't believe it," he said, looking into his coffee cup as if it held the answers to the problem. He lifted his head and met Eden's sympathetic gaze. "Have you called the police?"

She shook her head. "Not yet. We know that you and Frannie have been...well, seeing each other, and we sort of wanted to see what you thought, or if you have any other ideas about who it could be."

"No," he said with a shake of his head.

"We're going to give the books a good going over tonight, and if we find what we expect to find, we'll have to confront Fran in the morning."

Ted nodded in understanding. He set his cup down, obviously ready to leave.

"I know this is hard to take," Eden said. "I mean, when you care for someone, it's hard to believe they could do anything wrong."

"Yeah," Ted agreed, a stunned look on his face. "It is." He rose to leave.

"We'd appreciate it if you'd keep this under your hat until the morning," Nick said.

"Oh, well sure," Ted said, but he didn't meet Nick's eyes.

Nick smiled. "No sense saying anything to Fran and getting her upset in case Tess and I don't know what we're talking about."

Ted nodded. "Right."

"Besides," Eden said with an encouraging smile, "anyone can make a couple of mistakes. I'm sure Fran can explain everything to our satisfaction in the morning."

"Yeah. I sure hope so."

"So do I," Eden said. *So do I.*


THANKFULLY, THE DOOR to the trailer opened to Ted's knocking almost instantly. Fran stood there, dressed in a robe he hadn't seen before. A gold chain with a ruby pendant nestled between her ample breasts.

"What's the matter?" she asked, stepping aside for him to enter.

The exotic scent of the pricey perfume she was wearing failed to trigger his libido as it usually did, as did the sight of her bare breasts swaying beneath the satin.

"They found out you've been tampering with the books," he said, his voice dull, flat.

She shrugged. "It had to happen sooner or later."

"What are you going to do?"

"Do?" Fran laughed bitterly. "Well, I'm sure as hell not going to stick around and let them put me in jail. I'm leaving." She tossed the sweater she was holding into an open suitcase.

Ted looked around in surprise, taking in the signs of her packing with total disbelief. "You can't leave. You have to make it right. If you talk to Eden and tell her it was for your mother's medicine and treatments, she'll understand. She's fair." Even as he said it, Ted tried to block the suspicions from his mind.

Fran laughed again, a hard sound that grated on his jangling nerves. "My mother has been dead for twelve years."

"What? Then why—"

"Don't be so naive," she interrupted. "Where do you think the money for that new stereo equipment I gave you on your birthday and the clothes I bought for you these last few months came from? I sure couldn't swing it on my salary from the Calloway mill."

Ted couldn't believe what he was hearing. He had known that Fran "borrowed" money from the mill from time to time, supposedly to help out during her mother's lengthy bout with cancer. But she had sworn that she'd paid back every cent. He wondered how she'd managed to dress so well and how she had been able to afford both a new trailer and a new car, but he had assumed that, like most of America, she was buying on credit and charged to the hilt.

Unfortunately love couldn't be turned on and off at will, and the truth didn't change what he felt for her. There had to be some mistake.

"Tell me where you're going," he said. "I'll give Eden my notice and meet you in a week or so."

"No."

The rejection was flat, emphatic, and shook Ted's love to its foundations. "What?" he said, uncertain that he had heard correctly.

"I don't want you to meet me." She sighed heavily, as if explanations were a bother. "Look, Ted, I don't know what you thought was happening between us, but you may as well hear this straight. I used you." The shocked look on his face didn't even cause her to falter. "I wanted you to be so involved with me that you wouldn't pay any attention to what was going on at the mill. And it worked."

Ted's face was a pasty gray color. He swallowed the tightness in his throat. "What do you mean?"

"The breakdowns, Ted. Sure, the hydraulic gun is old and worn out. But you were so eager to be the big man that you never stopped to wonder why I was so interested in that damned piece of machinery...or why I asked so many questions about how it ran. And you were so eager to climb into my bed that you forgot to take care of the weekly maintenance, didn't you?"

Ted's scalp crawled with horror, and tears of humiliation and regret stung his eyes. "*You* did something to the hydraulic gun?"

"You bet I did, darlin'," she said with the slow smile that had once driven him crazy with desire.

"But why, Fran? Why?"

"Let's just say it's a little matter of getting even." She went to the door and opened it. "Why don't you run along now? I have a lot of packing to do. And Ted, honey, don't bother calling the cops. If you do, I'll just tell them that you put me up to it. And I'll see to it that that name you're so proud of gets dragged through the mud from here to Dallas and back.''

Like a zombie, Ted went to the door and stepped out into the night. He hardly remembered getting into his car or driving to the lake. The silhouettes of moss-draped cypress trees rose up from the placid surface of the water like an army of stringy-haired hags who raised their dresses and tiptoed through the water, their bony knees lifted high. He got out of the car and leaned against the hood, staring out at the night. He couldn't believe what had happened or that his whole life could so easily come crumbling down around him.

When Fran had come back to Calloway Corners from a job in Arkansas shortly after Ben's death and started to work at the plant, he'd liked her immediately. She teased and flattered him, lifting his spirits and ego, both badly in need of boosting after his wife's lengthy illness. It wasn't long before they were having lunch together. A short time later they began to date.

His kids were furious. She was using him, they said. Trying to find some stability. She wanted the farm. She wanted his savings. His retirement. He had refused to listen. He was too deeply under her spell.

And that spell was sex. For the first time in years he felt like a young man. Fran was ready and willing to have sex in the morning, noon or night—all three if he wanted. She knew how, and was willing, to do things in bed he'd only dreamed of. And as she had planned, she became the center of his world. He had neglected his job.

What did they say? That there was no fool like an old fool. It was true. He had let down Ben Calloway's family— hell, he'd let down Ben himself. He'd let down his own family. And he'd let down himself.

Futile tears of shame coursed down Ted's cheeks.

Still, even though he should, he knew he wouldn't call the sheriff or Eden. Not now. Maybe later he would tell what he knew, but right now his own grief was too new, the wounds to his self-esteem too deep.

He would make it up to the Calloway girls somehow. Beginning in the morning, he would give them one hundred percent. Tomorrow, they would find that Fran was gone, and one thing was certain: he wouldn't even have to fake his surprise.

# CHAPTER TEN

SINCE MARIAH AND TESS had spent what was left of the
night with Eden, they all went to the mill together. Nick had
eaten breakfast with them and then left for work, but not
before he had kissed Eden goodbye, a gesture that caused
Tess and Mariah to exchange surprised looks. Eden saw the
byplay and ignored it. Now wasn't the time to be concerned
with who was kissing her.

They got to the mill early, even though they had been up
most of the night. Ensconced in the office that had been
their father's, the Calloway women waited for Fran to come
to work so that they could confront her with her deception.

Ted came in at his usual time. Unlike the impression of
youth and vitality of the night before, this morning Ted
looked tired. Old. Beaten. Eden read the truth in his
haunted, regretful eyes. "Fran isn't coming to work today,
is she?" Eden asked softly.

Ted exhaled a shuddering breath and shook his head.
"No."

Eden knew without a doubt what had happened. Ted had
seen Fran and told her what they had found. A part of Eden
suspected that he would: the other part of her ached with
disappointment...in Ted...in Fran.

"She was already packing when I got there."

"Did she say where she was going?"

Ted shook his head again and met her gaze head on.
"No," he said, his voice hardly above a whisper. He looked
from one sister to the other, his gaze begging them to be-

lieve him. "She told me it was for her mother...that her mother was dying of cancer, and after Barbara, I—" He couldn't go on.

Looking into his pain-ravaged eyes, Eden believed him. The scenario became a little more clear. Fran had somehow used Ted and dumped him. Eden glanced at Mariah and Tess. They both looked as shocked as she felt. The crack in her heart widened as pain poured inside. She couldn't bear to see Ted brought to this, couldn't stand to have him and his family dragged through all the ugliness. "Thank you, Ted," she said.

He nodded and left the office.

"What now? The police?" Tess asked.

Eden shook her head. "No. No police. I say we let it go. A measly fifteen thousand dollars isn't worth the grief we'll all suffer if we try to bring Fran to trial. And I don't think I can bear to implicate Ted. Not after what he's meant to us all these years."

"She's right," Mariah said. "That money is a drop in the bucket to what it would take to get the mill solidly on its feet. I say we forget it."

Tess nodded. "Whatever you think."

AS ALWAYS, WORD GOT AROUND. By noon, news of the embezzlement was on every Shreveport television and radio station. Eden was swamped with calls of sympathy, many of which also added their opinion of Fran Glidden's morals. In the end, she was forced to unplug her phone to have any peace.

She was trying to catch up on her sleep that afternoon when she heard a car in the driveway. Rising, she went to the window and saw Tess's car pulling to a stop.

What now? she wondered, letting the curtain fall into place. Tugging her sweatshirt down over her hips, she went to the front door. Tess looked as tired as she felt. Eden held the door open and she and her sister exchanged wan smiles.

"I tried to call," Tess said, "but the phone just rang and rang. I finally figured out that you had your phone unplugged."

Eden covered a wide yawn. "I was trying to take a nap, and I was thoroughly tired of everyone calling."

"You, too?" Tess asked with raised eyebrows. "I turned on the answering machine."

"Good idea. Coffee?" Eden asked.

"Why not?"

Tess followed Eden into the kitchen and sank down onto one of the walnut chairs.

"Have you talked to Mariah since this morning?" Eden asked, filling the glass carafe with water.

Tess raked her hands through her thick, dark hair, pulling it away from the perfect oval of her face. "I stopped by there on the way over. This has really knocked her for a loop."

"I know," Eden said, turning on the coffee maker. "She shouldn't have to deal with all this right now. I was worried about her last night."

"I think she was just tired," Tess said. "She seemed fine."

"Good." Eden sat down across from Tess and propped her chin in her hand. "Well, we have all the amenities out of the way now, so why did you come?"

Tess looked surprised. She shook her head, laughing softly. "I never could fool you."

"Nope," Eden agreed. "So what's up?"

Tess sighed. "After you left the mill this morning, I looked into some other things."

"And?" Eden prompted.

"And a closer look shows that there are several outstanding accounts, some from as far back as last fall—before Dad died."

"Before Dad died?" Eden echoed.

"Yes. He probably wasn't taking very good care of things, and obviously Fran didn't try to collect them."

"Get to the point, Tess," Eden pressed. "What does it mean?"

"It means that our most immediate problem is cash flow," Tess explained. "If things go well, we have enough money to tide us through the next couple of months—the end of the year, max."

Eden dropped her head in her hands and groaned.

"When and *if* we collect our outstanding debts, we'll be in fair shape. But if anything happens, like the hydraulic gun going out again, we're in deep meadow muffins." She sighed. "In fact, closing the mill or selling will be the only options left."

"Damn!"

"My sentiments exactly. What it amounts to is that Dad must have just given up the last few years. I think he was just biding his time . . . waiting."

*Waiting to join Mama.* Tess didn't say it, but the look in her eyes spoke for her. Eden knew what she meant. She'd thought the same thing. The coffeepot sputtered for the last time and Eden rose to fill the waiting cups. "If we're forced to sell, Mariah will just die."

"I know," Tess said. "Now that it's a real possibility, I can hardly bear to think of it myself." Her eyes glazed with tears. "I can remember Daddy taking us down there and buying us Cokes from the Coke machine. Remember? In the little glass bottles?"

Eden nodded and set the two cups down on the table. "Do you remember the peanut machine?"

Tess laughed; her voice caught on a sob. "Yeah. You put in a penny and a handful of peanuts came out."

The room got very quiet as both women were swamped by a lifetime of memories. Finally, Eden spoke. "I'm not going to let it happen."

"What?"

"I'm not going to let the mill go under."

"What can you do?" Tess asked.

"I don't know," Eden said, rising and striding to the sink. She stared out the window at the woods behind the house. Beyond the stretch of pine and hardwood, completely hidden from view, stood the mill. Even though she couldn't see it, even though she had taken it for granted, it had always been there. "I'll go to the bank. I'll arrange to get some money to tide us over until we can get back on our feet."

"Do you think we can do that?" Tess said, a glimmer of hope shining in her hazel eyes.

"I don't know why not," Eden said, turning to face her sister. "What time is it?"

Tess glanced at her watch. "One-thirty."

"That gives me plenty of time," Eden said, flying out of the room toward her bedroom.

"Time to do what?" Tess called after her.

"Go to the bank."

Tess rose and swept up her coffee cup, following Eden through the house to her room. "You're going today?" she asked, watching as Eden yanked an off-white suit from a padded hanger.

"Why not?"

Why not indeed? Tess wondered, hope rising within her as she watched Eden prepare to do battle. She should have known that Eden would take care of things. Hadn't she always?

*"I'M SORRY, EDEN, but I'm afraid we can't lend you the money. The mill is already mortgaged. So is the house."*

Eden's conversation with the vice-president of the bank her father had done business with for years played over and over in her mind, as if a needle was stuck in the groove of a worn record. She sat on the back patio watching the storm clouds—remnants from a hurricane that had blown into the gulf the day before—and fighting the tears of bitterness rising up inside her.

*"Times are hard. You understand."*

What she understood was that not only the family business but the house—her home—was in jeopardy. What she understood was that not only was she not getting money to keep the mill afloat, but the money Ben had given her years ago, which she had carefully invested for her future, was going to have to go toward paying off money Ben had already borrowed.

Eden had wanted to grab the banker's four-hundred-dollar suit and scream at him that loyalty and friendship and forty-odd years of paying on time should count for something. She wanted to tell him that she hoped he never needed help from a friend who would have to turn him down because of "our policy." And now, an hour after the conversation that had dashed her dreams for saving the mill, she wanted to run out into the yard, lift her face to the angry sky and scream to the roiling heavens that it wasn't fair...it wasn't...

"...fair," she said on a sob. Her carefully guarded composure cracked and two renegade tears scaled the dam of her lashes to tumble heedlessly down her pale cheeks. She laid her head on the patio table and gave over to her tears, something she had never allowed herself to do in front of her sisters.

Eden was so wrapped up in her misery that she was only vaguely aware of the sound of the approaching motorcycle.

But when Nick's hands closed over her upper arms and pulled her to her feet, she went into his embrace and buried her face against his hard chest like a pigeon going home.

"Eden? Baby, what is it?"

Nick took her face between his palms and forced her to look at him. Her makeup was ruined, her mascara running in ebony trails down her face. Her lips trembled, and she caught the bottom one with her teeth in an effort to control the harsh, gulping sobs that tore from her throat.

"I—I can't ... g-get any m-money," she said.

"Money?" he asked with a frown. "Money for what?"

"T-the mill. It's already mortgaged to the hilt and s-so is the h-house!" she wailed. "Nick, what am I g-going to d-do? What will I t-tell M-Mariah and T-Tess? They think I c-can f-fix everything."

Nick felt his heart—the heart he'd encased in bitterness three years before—swell with empathy. He couldn't stand to see her tearing herself apart because she couldn't do something she thought was expected of her.

"Shh," he murmured, drawing her close. "They'll understand. You aren't Superwoman, and it's time everyone realized it. You won't lose the mill or the house, Eden. I promise you that."

Eden didn't even ask herself how he could stop such a calamity. She only knew she believed him. Gradually her crying stopped; slowly her tears dried. She was exhausted. Spent.

"Better?" Nick asked, tipping her head back and looking into her tear-drenched eyes.

She nodded and tried to smile.

Nick wasn't sure he had ever loved her more than he did at that moment, when she was trying so hard to gather the shredded remnants of her composure and dignity. He didn't smile back. He crushed her to him in an embrace so tight it was painful. Then he set her away from him and brushed the wind-blown strands of strawberry-blond hair away from her flushed face with gentle fingers.

"Go wash your face," he said gently, "and we'll talk."

She nodded, gave his hand a hard squeeze and went inside. She returned a few moments later, her face scrubbed free of all traces of makeup, her off-white suit replaced in favor of elastic-waist shorts, a T-shirt and tennis shoes.

Thunder rumbled in the distance. Eden pushed her windswept hair from her face. "Let's walk."

"Sure. Where do you want to go?"

"Anywhere! Just someplace away from here."

Nick cast a worried eye toward the threatening sky. "It looks as if it's going to pour down any minute."

"What's the matter, Logan?" she said with an attempt to lighten the dark mood holding her captive. "Afraid you'll melt?"

Nick was glad to see her trying to regain her equilibrium. "Sugar does, you know," he told her with mock seriousness.

"So does salt," she shot back.

They traded smiles. "Thanks for being here when I needed you," she said softly.

"My pleasure."

"Aren't you home early?" she asked as, hand in hand, they started across the yard toward the bridge and the footpath that led into the woods.

"We finished the job, so Seth told us to take off early."

"Oh. Remind me to tell Seth thank you when I see him."

Eden led the way through the trees and into the dim shadows of the woods. The path had been heavily used when they were children. Farther into the dense growth of trees and vines, it intersected an old logging road that had washed out through the years until it was impassable except on feet. Eden still used the path and the road whenever she needed to get away for a while or was looking for pine boughs and holly for Christmas decorations.

They had walked perhaps a quarter of a mile when they came to a place where small trees looked as if something had mangled them. They were bent and broken and the tender bark had been rubbed away.

Nick lifted his eyebrows questioningly. "Bigfoot?"

Eden stopped. She knew he was trying to make her smile. "It's a deer scrape," she told him.

"A what?"

She smiled teasingly at him. "Not the great white hunter, huh?"

He shrugged noncommittally.

"See that place on the ground?" she asked.

"Where? There?" Nick asked, pointing to a place three of four feet long and half that wide where all the vines and leaves had been pawed away.

"Yes. The trees are where the buck has rubbed the velvet off his horns. It's his way of marking his territory during the rut."

"Yeah?" Nick said.

"Yes. If you have patience, the rut is a good time to bag a trophy buck."

"Why is that?" he asked, leaning against a tree and watching her.

"They get careless," she explained, feeling a little nervous under his close scrutiny. "Their mind is more on . . . mating than the hunter."

"Typical male," Nick offered laconically. "So how does this—" he gestured toward the scrape "—work?"

"Well, he scrapes out a place like that one over there and he . . ." Eden turned away, talking over her shoulder. "He urinates in it. Then he goes off and a doe, tempted by the odor, comes along and urinates in it, too."

"Sort of like men's cologne and pheromones?" Nick interrupted innocently, so innocently that she cast him a quick look over her shoulder to see if he was laughing.

"I suppose," she admitted as a light sprinkling of rain, carried by a gust of wind, pattered through the trees.

"And?"

"He checks his scrapes—usually at night. She's only in heat twenty-four hours. He follows her scent and breeds her."

"No!"

The shocked denial sent Eden spinning around to look at him questioningly.

"I love it when you talk dirty like that," Nick said solemnly, trying his utmost to suppress a smile and failing as a wide white grin threatened to split his handsome features.

Eden's eyes widened as realization dawned. Why, the sorry, no-account beast! He'd been making fun of her all along! She turned as Nick lunged away from the tree. She'd gone no more than three running steps when he caught her around the waist and turned her to face him. Eden made a token struggle, but her senses were already being towed under by the desire she felt every time he touched her.

"You've been putting me on," she accused, tilting her chin up pugnaciously. "You know all about scrapes."

"And breeding," he said, lowering his head and pressing his mouth to the side of her neck. "I've been hunting deer since I was eight years old."

"In other words, I've been had," she said, mock ferocity in her green eyes.

"Not yet, you haven't," he corrected. "But if we hightail it back to the house, we might make it before the storm hits, and then we can curl up in that big bed of yours and make love with the windows open while we listen to the rain."

Eden freed herself from his hold and stepped back, very
deliberately unbuttoning the metal button of his jeans. She
shook her head. "Here."

Nick laughed. "It's raining," he said, as a raindrop
splattered onto his nose. "Let's go to the house."

She hooked her thumbs in the elastic waist of her shorts
and shimmied out of them. They landed at her feet, a pink
puddle of cotton against the carpet of fallen leaves. Nick's
breathing escalated at the sight of the ivory flesh of her
stomach and the shadowy triangle beneath the mint-green
lace of her bikini panties. His heart began to beat faster.

"Come on, Eden, we're going to get . . . drenched." The
last word was barely audible. His voice was stolen by her
nimble fingers, which dragged his zipper downward.

"What's the matter, Nick?" she taunted, looking up at
him through the thicket of her lashes as she eased her hand
inside. "Getting soft?"

"Hardly," he wheezed, as her questing hand breached the
final obstruction and closed gently around him.
"Eden . . . ah, Eden . . ."

Nick buried his face in her damp hair and for long moments let the sweet sensations wash through him. Then,
when he couldn't distinguish the perspiration beading his
face from the rain, he caught her wrist in his strong fingers.
"Enough," he rasped. "Let's go home. It's raining."

An understatement, he thought. The rain had escalated
to a steady downpour. He watched her with eyes half closed
against the rain. She shivered, whether from some emotion
she saw in his eyes or the chill air, he wasn't sure. Her white
shirt clung wetly, transparently, the soft cotton cloth mold-
ing her full breasts like a second skin. Gooseflesh rose on her
arms, and her nipples, clearly visible through the wet fabric, puckered into hard beads of desire. Nick gave a sigh of
acquiescence. They wouldn't be going back to the
house . . . not for a while.

Skillfully, he maneuvered her backward until she felt the rough bark of a tree digging into the flesh of her back. His hand cupped one breast, lifting, kneading, caressing her through the cloth of her shirt. Lowering his head, he took the tip into his mouth, his tongue curling around it with a gentle suckling movement. Flames of desire licked hotly at her.

Eden arched her back and pressed her lower body against his leg, which was wedged between hers, offering him more, offering him all of her. Abandoning her breast, Nick dragged her panties downward. His hand covered her, his fingers searching...seeking. Eden's thighs contracted, and she dragged his head down until their lips met.

The sweet pressure of her open mouth against his effectively stopped all thought and silenced any further objections he might have. As always, he could hardly believe the passion bottled up inside her. Her dueling tongue met his with a thrust and parry that made his blood run as thick and hot as maple syrup in the springtime. His body felt flushed with heat...the same heat that raged inside her, making her hot and melting to his touch, even though the chill rain had drenched them both to the skin.

Nick drew away. "Look at me," he whispered.

Eden's eyelids, heavy with need, swept slowly upward. The jade green of her eyes was softened, blurred by passion. Nick watched the emotions he was arousing chasing each other across her face. He watched as her eyes widened, as sensation gathered, building...building... pushing aside everything but the need to capture the shimmering light of need. Brighter, brighter...until her head fell back and she cried out in pure ecstasy as she surrendered to the feelings exploding like Fourth of July fireworks inside her.

"Easy, easy," Nick murmured softly, his clever fingers wringing every drop of feeling from her.

Eddies of desire were still trembling through her when she felt the touch of his mouth against the side of her neck. His hands slid over her bare bottom, lifting her high against the tree and angling her legs to accommodate him. Driven by the desire to bury himself in the forgetfulness of her love, Nick thrust into her, swallowing her cry of pleasure with his mouth. Her legs closed around him and, bracing his palms against the rough bark of the oak tree, he closed his eyes and concentrated on capturing the feeling that was just out of reach...a feeling that grew closer with every stroke of his body.

It was swelling inside Eden again, too, growing like the strength of the storm. Her mouth scattered wild random kisses over his chest and throat, and her hands clutched him nearer as his body strained against hers.

Lightning cracked loudly, and harsh white light illuminated the gloom of the forest in a display of power and glory as Nick made one hard, final thrust. He chanted her name in wonder and fulfillment as thunder boomed and rumbled, rolling across the countryside, and the earth beneath them trembled like their racing hearts. Nick's head dropped forward onto Eden's breast.

She cradled him close as she lifted her face to the sky. The tears of autumn fell like a benediction onto her face, making her eyelashes cling together in wet spikes that lay against her cheeks. Miraculously she was cleansed of all her doubts and fears. Nick cared. He had to.

Long moments later, he lifted his head and took her lips in a gentle kiss. Then he disengaged himself from her and lowered her to the ground. He smiled then, a smile of tenderness, of happiness, of contentment.

"Let's go home."

Eden's lips quirked upward at the corners. She nodded. Laughing, tripping over each other, they gathered up their clothes, dressed in the driving rain and ran back to the house hand in hand. There, as he'd promised, Nick made love to her again...in a tub full of hot soapy water that chased away the chill of the rain.

The storm lasted all evening and into the night. Near morning, Eden woke to the feel of Nick's mouth against hers. He made love to her again, in the comfort of her bed...with an intensity and passion as frightening as it was pleasurable.

Later, when she lay sleeping beside him, Nick blew smoke rings at the darkened ceiling and wondered what he was going to do. He loved her. That much was fact. She made him happy. She'd restored his faith in mankind, not to mention his faith in women. He blessed the workings of fate that had brought him to Calloway Corners; he cursed the events that had molded his life, a life he wasn't certain a woman like Eden would want to be a part of.

But he definitely wanted to be a part of her life. He wanted to do whatever he could to help her and her sisters out of the jam they were in. If he had to, he would give them the money himself...or maybe he could buy the mill, give it back to them and help them run it. He tossed to his side, thoughts of settling down in one place making him uneasy. On one hand, he wasn't certain he was ready to settle down. On the other, thoughts of a life without Eden seemed bleak.

He stubbed out his cigarette and rolled over, taking her in his arms and holding her tightly. She was exhausted, he thought. It had been a rough thirty-six hours. She murmured his name against his chest. Nick nuzzled the hair at her ear and closed his eyes...ready for sleep at last. He was drifting off when a sudden thought sent his eyes flying open.

He hadn't used any protection. His billfold had been locked in the Harley, where he left it while he was working. A thousand thoughts—all of them panicked—flitted through his mind. He forced himself to calm down, to be realistic. The chances of Eden getting pregnant just because he'd forgotten once were slim to none. He was getting paranoid. It's just that he was always so careful.

WIND HURTLED the sheets of rain at the windows of the hospital. The lights of the parking lot shone through the rain-beaded glass, facets of light splintering off each separate raindrop, creating a psychedelic light show against a black backdrop.

Stuart was propped up in bed asleep—or pretending to be. Theresa sat at his side, supposedly engrossed in a thick paperback book. But instead of seeing the crisp black print of the thriller in her hand, she saw the round, feminine handwriting of Ellie Tanner's diary and the smug smile on Keith's face when he had handed it to her.

"I know all about their affair, Keith, so if you hope to stir up trouble between your father and me, you're wasting your time."

"Read it, Theresa. I think you'll find a little tidbit in there that you didn't know. The catalyst, I'm sure, for Dad's stroke." He laughed, and Theresa's skin crawled. "I'll give him one thing; he knew how to go about getting what he wanted."

Theresa had read. And read. And when she had found what Keith meant, she had felt the same shock Stuart must have felt, but for entirely different reasons.

*Nicole. Oh, Nicole. Did I make you do something I shouldn't have?*

She had closed the diary and gone to bed, wanting to wipe out the memory of the past, wishing she could undo the harm inadvertently done to her daughter and taking little comfort in the knowledge that the decision she had made over eight years before had been, at that time, the right one. The only one.

Even though several days had passed since Keith had given her the diary, Theresa was still thinking of the past. It was amazing how the arrogance and impatience of youth could make you do things you wouldn't do with maturity sitting squarely on your shoulders. If only Stuart hadn't been so certain that he could manipulate Ellie...if only Ellie had been stronger.

*What about yourself, Theresa?*

Oh, she was guilty, too, as well as Gil. And what had seemed so acceptable then had done nothing but cause her heartache for the past thirty years...

Gil, hurt by his wife's duplicity and wanting to pay the mighty Stuart Logan back in kind, had deliberately come to Theresa when he was home on furlough and told her about the affair. Theresa had been particularly vulnerable, already smarting under the knowledge that despite the fact that Stuart had married her, he still—in some strange way—cared for his first wife. Keith's mother.

Handsome and kind, Gil had treated Theresa with all the consideration Stuart never had. Her month-long involvement with her husband's foreman had seemed as natural as breathing. And it satisfied the streak of rebellion inside her, which she had struggled to control all her life in an effort to be the lady her mother always encouraged her to be. She had rationalized that Stuart and Ellie deserved what she and Gil were doing to them. And it was nothing to her, except a way to get back at Stuart for hurting her...again. An eye for an eye, her grandmother had always said.

She hadn't counted on learning to care for Gil Tanner, of coming to count on his strength and his steadfastness. She hadn't counted on *liking* him. And when he broke off their relationship because he realized that despite what had happened between them he still loved Ellie, Theresa hadn't counted on hurting. But she had.

She had never contacted Gil after the day he told her that he was leaving to go back to Germany. Ellie was pregnant, he said, and they had decided to try to work things out.

Theresa never once tried to stop him from doing what he thought was right. Instead, she'd relegated the stolen month to its proper place in her life and decided to give her marriage to Stuart another try.

Unfortunately her efforts to create a happy home hadn't been as rewarding as Gil's and Ellie's. Her marriage had never reached the heights of happiness that theirs apparently had. Even the twins' birth hadn't changed Stuart. He was good to them, was fond of them, but it was still Keith, Keith, Keith.

Once, just as Nick was finishing college, Keith had left Arkansas for the pleasures of Europe. He hadn't come home, and Theresa had hoped he was gone forever. Then, three years ago, Stuart had unexpectedly found out her secret, the secret she thought she had buried forever, and suddenly, irrationally, Nick was jerked from his place of prominence and Keith was back as heir apparent to the Logan empire. Nick had lost his future and his relationship with his father, but Theresa had remained adamant that he and Nicole not lose it all....

With the memories of the hurtful past still filling her mind, Theresa sighed. Given the same circumstances, she would probably make the same choices in her life. She wondered what Stuart would say if she confessed that despite everything they had been through, she loved him. But he would never know...because she wouldn't tell him.

# CHAPTER ELEVEN

"I WANT TO SEE Nick and Nicole," Stuart said almost two weeks later. Though speaking took a great effort, and his speech was still slow and slurred and without much inflection, he was improving daily and doing much better than the doctors had at first anticipated.

Theresa looked up from the magazine she was reading, a frown on her attractive features. "You want to see Nick?" she asked in disbelief.

His gaze locked with hers. "Yes."

Placing the magazine on the bedside table, she rose to stand beside him. "But Stuart, you know that no one knows where Nick is. I haven't seen him since he left three years ago."

"Damn fool," Stuart muttered, his eyes drifting closed as if to block out a picture he'd rather not see.

"Nick?"

Stuart opened his eyes, which burned into hers. "Me."

"You? Why?"

He heaved a deep sigh. "For mistaking money for happiness and letting it rule my life and for letting my damned pride keep me from ... doing what I knew was right."

Theresa's smooth brow furrowed in puzzlement. "I don't know what you mean."

He tried to smile. The side of his face that was still partially paralyzed twisted downward. "How long have we been married, Terry?"

"Thirty-two years," she said without hesitation.

"Thirty-two years," he repeated. "Why?"

"Why?" she echoed, at a loss to know what he was getting at.

"Why did you stay all these years after what I put you through?"

Theresa knew what he meant. Why had she stayed when she knew about his affairs. When she knew that his business practices often bordered on the shady. When she knew he used his power and his money to get what he wanted...when he wanted it, and that included Ellie Tanner.

The way Theresa saw it, their affairs were tit for tat, even though she hadn't indulged with the frequency Stuart had.

"Why did you *let* me stay?" she shot back gently.

"You were my wife."

The words were spoken as if they could—as if they should—explain everything. But they didn't. "So?" she probed.

"So in spite of what I've done, of what you've done, I have always believed that marriage should be forever."

Theresa's eyes stung with unshed tears. What a dichotomy of beliefs he was! How could he claim that marriage vows should remain inviolate when, on the other hand, he appeared to take breaking those vows so lightly?

"Forever? Even if it isn't a happy marriage?" she asked.

Stuart's forehead puckered. For the first time it seemed he tried to put some power behind his words. "But I have been happy, Terry," he told her. "Didn't you know?"

Her eyes widened with disbelief. "How could I know? You never said."

His lips twisted again. "I'm not a...gushy type person."

"No," she said in a shaking voice, "you certainly aren't."

He reached for her hand, slowly, awkwardly. "I've raised my share of hell, had my share—more than my share—of women. But it never meant that I wasn't happy with you...or that I didn't care. It's just...the way I was. Not that it was right."

Theresa's teeth clamped down on her bottom lip to still its quivering. She didn't speak. She couldn't.

"I know that for a long time after you and I married, I still cared for Keith's mother. She was no good, but she had some kind of hold on me. When she got involved with that carnival character, I couldn't believe it. I decided that I needed someone completely different to bring Keith up, and you were perfect. But I still wasn't over caring for her. Unfortunately it took me a long time to see her for what she really was, and that you were nothing like her...thank God."

"Why didn't you ever tell me this?"

His shoulders shrugged beneath his pajama top. "I guess I was afraid of giving too much of myself, of being vulnerable again." His eyes held a wry disillusionment. "I don't like being vulnerable, Terry. Never did. But I was always home for dinner...and I never forgot your birthday...or Nick's and Nicole's."

"No," Theresa choked out, fighting the need to give in to her tears. "No, you didn't."

"I want to talk to Nick and Nicole, Theresa. I want to get things straight before I die."

The possibility of him dying rocked the new and tentative happiness she felt at his confession. "Die?" she echoed. "You aren't going to die. You're better now."

"Yes. Now. They say you can't teach an old dog new tricks, but I learned something from this. We don't have tomorrow. I can't afford to wait for Nick to come to me. And he shouldn't have to. I was the one in the wrong, not him. I lost him because I was trying to hurt you, and I'm sorry. I'm very sorry."

Tears ran unashamedly down Theresa's cheeks. She had never thought she would live long enough to see Stuart humbled by anyone or anything. Leaning over the bed, she pressed her lips to his forehead.

"Will you call Nicole and find out where Nick is? She'll know. I want to straighten this out with them once and for all."

"Yes, she will, I'm sure . . ." Her voice trailed away.

"What is it?" Stuart asked.

"Do you mean to tell them . . . everything?" she asked, her face suddenly blanched of color.

"Everything," he said, no quarter in his eyes.

"But . . . I'll lose him. Maybe Nicole, too."

"We don't have them, now, Terry. We don't have anything to lose. Not really."

Theresa nodded, dreading the confrontation. There was so much to set straight, so much to clear up. And she wasn't certain that either of the kids could forgive them for their silence and the lies. "You're right, but it will have to wait because Nicole isn't here. She went to Dallas for a few days to see some designer or something."

Stuart's eyelids drifted down. "I can wait," he said. "I've waited this long, I can wait a few more days."

"Yes," Theresa said, taking his hand in hers and trying to hold back the fear. "Yes."

"HOLD STILL," Eden said to a squirming Mariah. "You always were such a wiggle wart."

Mariah tried. "Have you finished your outfit?" she asked.

Eden nodded. "Yesterday," she said around a mouthful of straight pins.

"I wish Tess would wear something with a little more élan," Mariah complained, bemoaning Tess's choice of a costume for the Halloween carnival being held at the Platt elementary school gymnasium that evening.

Just as many of the parents of trick-or-treating-age kids were, Ford was concerned about the increasing incidence of Halloween candy being tampered with. He had convinced the school to let him put together a carnival with booths and contests and treats as an alternative to the customary door-to-door quest for fun and goodies. Tess, Mariah and Eden were all going to help run things, and Eden had made everyone's costumes. Obviously Mariah didn't like Tess's choice.

"Maybe you're right," Eden said, securing the last pin. "It's not too late. Nick is going to be gone all day, and I'll have time to see what I can do."

"Thank goodness! Honestly, Tess as a turn-of-the-century schoolmarm is a dead giveaway."

"You're right." Eden stepped back a few paces and tilted her head to the side, silently contemplating the costume she had made for Mariah to wear to the carnival. She struggled to control the laughter tickling the corners of her mouth.

"Well?" Mariah asked.

"It's you," Eden said, tongue in cheek.

"What do you mean, it's me?" Mariah cried indignantly, raising her arms up and looking at the orange-ribbed protuberance that stuck out in a three-foot circle all around her. "It's a pumpkin, for heaven's sake!"

"I know," Eden said solemnly, but her eyes danced with mischief.

"Very cute, Ms Smart Aleck."

"I thought so," Eden replied unperturbed. "It sure beats heck out of a skeleton—"

"I thought the black would be slenderizing," Mariah said, defending her earlier choice of costume.

"But, Mariah—a *pregnant* skeleton?"

Mariah shrugged, and her mouth turned down at the corners. "Well, it was better than what Ford suggested."

Eden's eyebrows lifted in inquiry. "Which was?"

"A belly dancer."

"A belly dancer?" Eden chortled. "He wanted you to be a—" She couldn't finish. Instead, she flopped back onto the bed and dissolved into a fit of laughter. Mariah began to see the humor of the situation. She smiled and she, too, began to giggle, easing down onto the bed beside Eden. Lying on her back, the pumpkin ballooned upward, obscuring her view and inciting another round of mirth.

The laughter served as a much-needed relief from the worry and fear that had plagued them for the past ten days. Fran Glidden might just have well disappeared off the face of the earth. Ted was subdued, pitifully anxious to please and extremely unhappy.

As for Eden, Mariah and Tess, it had been a time of trying to figure out what to do to keep the mill, a vital part of the area's economy, from closing down. To top off Fran's defection, they were having trouble with the hydraulic gun again. Though Nick had replaced the pump, which had been slowly ruined when Fran added sand to the hydraulic fluid several weeks ago, the sand had caused other problems. The valves were leaking, and there was excessive wear to the barrel cylinders. Either problem was potentially crippling to the vital piece of machinery.

All in all, there hadn't been much to laugh about, and Eden and Mariah felt their tensions fading with the giggles.

"Look at me," Mariah said, rolling to her feet and putting her hands on the rotund pumpkin costume.

Eden looked at her sister's flushed, happy face, noting the glow of health in her cheeks—cheeks that were more filled out with her advancing pregnancy. "You look wonderful," she said truthfully.

"I'm a cow."

"You're not a cow. You look better than you have in your life, and you were certainly no slouch before," Eden told her.

"I'll be glad when it's over," Mariah said with a soft sigh.

Eden frowned. This was the first time she'd heard that anxiety in Mariah's voice since Mariah had finally overcome the fear that she would die in childbirth. "You aren't getting nervous, are you?"

"A little," Mariah confessed. "But mostly I'm just tired of being pregnant, tired of being tired all the time and tired of the backaches. *And* I'm tired of not being able to fight for my man on equal terms."

Eden smiled. "That sounds like some old country and western, cry-in-your-beer tune: 'Fightin' For Mah Man On Equal Terms.'" Eden drawled the fake title in her best nasal country voice.

"Well, you didn't see the way Dottie Harrison was looking at Ford when we had the meeting for the carnival last night. It was positively disgusting."

Eden couldn't help smiling at Mariah's jealousy. "Face it, sis. Dottie Harrison is positively disgusting."

Mariah's mouth turned up in a reluctant smile.

"So," Eden probed, "what did Ford say?"

Mariah cast her a sideways glance. "He says he didn't notice." Her voice dripped with disbelief.

"And I'm sure he didn't," Eden said, standing up and going to her sister. She took Mariah's hand in hers. "The man is completely, totally, head-over-heels in love with you, so stop all this unnecessary worrying."

Mariah looked deeply into Eden's eyes. She sighed. "Okay. I just don't know why he has to be so darn sexy."

Eden rolled her eyes. "It seems that all of you waited until you could get your hands on the sexiest men in town."

"Including you." The observation was made softly, and to Eden, sounded almost like an accusation.

She didn't answer or even acknowledge Mariah's statement. "Turn around," she said instead. Mariah pivoted obligingly, and Eden began undoing the pins that temporarily closed the costume.

Mariah glanced at Eden over her shoulder. "Where's Nick today?"

"He went to see a friend who lives in Hope."

"What about tonight?"

"He promised to be back in time to go to the carnival," Eden replied, but there was no disguising the worry in her voice.

"If he isn't, you can tell him he's in serious trouble," Mariah warned teasingly.

"He'll be back." He would be back, wouldn't he? He had said he would be.

"You're sleeping with him, aren't you?"

Mariah's bald-faced question took Eden by surprise, and she accidentally jabbed the pin she was unfastening into her finger. Without answering, she stared at the drop of blood oozing from the pinprick and popped the finger into her mouth.

Mariah stepped out of the pumpkin outfit and placed it on the bed. She was left wearing nothing but green leotards and a frilly bra.

"Eden?"

Eden drew the finger from her mouth. It had stopped bleeding, but it still stung. She turned away and went to the window that overlooked the front lawn, the lawn where Nick had made love to her beneath the live oak and a silver moon three short weeks ago. The place where she had at long last blossomed into a real flesh-and-blood woman.

"I love him," she said simply, staring out at the clear autumn day.

"I know that. I've known that for a long time, but I warned you about him, Edie," Mariah said, a frown pleating her brow. "He's a nice guy... but he isn't husband material."

Eden turned and met her gaze squarely, steadily. "But I'm not asking him to marry me, Mariah. I'm not asking him to stay. To do that would kill the very thing that makes him the man he is...the man who taught me about being a woman."

Mariah stepped into her maternity jeans. "That's awfully generous of you," she said, unable to hide the sarcasm in her voice. "And I'm sure Nick loves the arrangement. What man wouldn't? But what about you, Eden? I don't think you're the kind of person who can go into a casual affair and come out unscathed when it's over and the dust clears."

"But it isn't a casual affair...at least not for me. Besides, I don't know what you mean."

"People are starting to talk."

Eden's face paled. She lifted her chin. "I don't care. I've lived my whole life for other people, and it's time I thought about myself for a change."

"We all have to live in this town," Mariah reminded her sister gently. "It isn't like you to be so unconcerned about people's opinions."

"Well, it's certainly strange to hear you telling me to toe the mark," Eden snapped. "Especially since you've caused more than your share of gossip in this town."

Mariah gasped. This wasn't the Eden she knew. The Eden she'd grown up with would never have thrown past indiscretions back in anyone's face.

"Did it ever occur to you—to any of you—that maybe I'm sick and tired of being good little Eden Calloway? Did it?" Eden cried, venting the frustrations that had gnawed at her the past few months.

"Need your kids tended? Call Eden. Need cookies for the church bake sale? Eden will bake them. How about a shoulder to cry on? Eden's is available. Well, I'm tired of being so damned dependable!''

As suddenly as it had come, Eden's anger fled, and her eyes filled with tears. ''All I want,'' she said in a small voice that begged Mariah to understand, ''is to be loved the way you and Tess and Jo are...even if it's only for a short while. Is that so terrible?''

''No,'' Mariah said, crossing the short space between them and putting her arms around Eden. ''That isn't so bad. And I never meant to criticize. It's just that I worry about you. We all do.'' She laughed. ''That's one of the curses of having a family as close-knit as ours. We tend to take more interest than we should in each other's business.'' She met Eden's gaze, her own remorse clearly defined in the depths of her clear green eyes. ''I'm sorry if you feel that I'm meddling, but I only want you to be happy.''

Eden's heart filled with regret for taking her frustrations out on her sister. ''I know.''

''Forgive me?''

Eden nodded. ''If you'll forgive me.''

Mariah appeared to be thinking it over. ''Only if you'll do something to Tess's outfit.''

Eden began to laugh, her animosity forgotten. ''What do you have in mind?''

Mariah grinned mischievously. ''I was thinking about a belly dancer.''

They laughed together again, the angry words forgotten. The subject of Nick Logan was dropped but definitely not forgotten. During the rest of the time they were together, Mariah watched her sister closely and worried about Eden's future. It wasn't the first time she had seen a woman respond to Nick's considerable and apparent charms. Nor, she feared, would it be the last.

It wasn't until she was standing at the front door ready to leave that she brought up the subject again. Clutching her pumpkin outfit to her breast, she looked up at Eden and tried one last time to make her see reason.

"He's going to hurt you." The statement was bold and filled with conviction.

This time Eden's reaction was different. She smiled, a strange, bittersweet sort of smile that settled in her jade-green eyes as sadness. "I know," she said. "I knew that going in. But feeling pain is better than not feeling at all. At least if you're hurting, you know you're alive."

NICK SAT ACROSS from Nicole at the Kettle Restaurant just off the interstate in Hope, Arkansas. Nicole, looking chic and classy in a wool-blend suit of cranberry red, also looked a little out of place in a chain restaurant. With the pearl and ruby earrings studding her ears and the sleek pageboy that brushed her chin, she looked as if she had just stepped from the pages of *Women's Wear Daily*.

When they first arrived, they had hugged and kissed and looked each other over from head to toe. Then they had laughed at the sheer joy of being together again, each admitting that the other looked great. Chatting about her trip to Dallas and his job, they had eaten lunch—hamburgers and fries—and then the talk had grown more serious.

"How's Dad?"

Nicole's luscious red lips tugged at the straw in her diet cola. Then she blotted her mouth on the napkin and pushed her plate aside.

"He seems to be doing fine. The paralysis is leaving gradually. He can talk, but it's slow and sort of slurred," she told him.

"That's good," Nick said, and realized he meant it.

Nicole looked as if she wanted to tell him something but couldn't find the right words.

"What is it?" Nick asked.

"Keith is gone," Nicole said.

"What!"

"He left a few days ago, supposedly to go to California for a few days. No one has seen or heard from him since."

"Keith has never been one to check in," Nick said.

"I know, but this is really fishy."

"Why? Do you think something has happened to him?"

Nicole shook her head. "I think he's afraid the investigation is getting too hot. They've found some companies that Keith set up that Daddy didn't know about."

"You're kidding!"

Nicole shook her head. "It doesn't look good."

"What about Mom?"

"She's holding up better than I expected. I called her last night to tell her I'd be home this evening, and she told me that he—both of them, actually—want to see us."

"Us?" Nick asked. "You and me? He hasn't asked to see the two of us together since right before they shipped us off to college. What do you think is going on?"

"I don't have any idea," Nicole said. "Mother sounded...strange. There was a sort of...lilt in her voice, but on the other hand, she sounded almost nervous."

Nick took a deep drag from his cigarette and blew the smoke toward the ceiling. "She's always been nervous."

"True." Nicole swirled her straw in the cola. "Well?" she asked.

"Well, what?"

"Are you going to come back and see what he wants?"

Nicole could see the agony on Nick's face...the remnants of past pain lingering in his dark eyes. He shook his head. "I don't think so, Nicci."

Surprise glittered in Nicole's blacker-than-black eyes. "Why? It sounds as if he's trying to make an effort to get closer."

"Well, it's a little late for that. Besides, I don't trust him. This sounds a lot like the same scenario we went through when Keith stayed in Europe and Dad brought me in to run things. Since he's out of commission, he probably needs me to come home and take over some job or another. Then when he's able, he'll step back into harness and jerk it out from under me the way he did the last time." Nick's voice held the remnants of past bitterness. "Thanks, but no thanks. It's taken me three years to put myself together after what he did to me when Keith came home. Three years, Nicole! And I might not have recovered by now if it wasn't for—"

He stopped abruptly and turned his head to look out at the traffic going by. Fool! he chided himself. You should leave Eden out of this.

"What, Nick?" Nicole probed. "If it wasn't for what?"

Nick stared across the crowded restaurant and conjured up the memory of the softness of Eden's body pressed against his, the peace he felt lying beside her at night. Just thinking of her took the edge off his anger. He'd rather have Eden than all of Logan Enterprises. She made him happier than he'd ever been in his life, and he didn't want to keep her or the happiness she gave him a secret—at least not from Nicole.

"Not what, Nicci. Who."

"Who?" Nicole's eyes brightened. "A woman, right? Oh, Nick, I knew you'd find someone else! I just knew it! Who is she?"

Nick smiled at Nicole's enthusiasm. "Slow down, slow down. Her name is Eden Calloway, and she—"

"Is she pretty?" Nicole interrupted.

"She's beautiful," he told her in a voice that bordered on reverence.

Nicole's eyes shimmered with tears. "Oh, Nick! I'm so happy for you." She smiled, a smile that was like sunshine breaking through the clouds on a dreary day. "Tell me about her."

Nick laughed, suddenly glad he was sharing Eden with Nicole. After all, weren't they the two most important women in his life? "What do you want to know?"

Nicole rested her elbows on the table and leaned forward. "How did you meet her?"

"She's the sister of someone I met a few years ago in Aruba," he explained. Then, with a smile, he added, "She's my landlady."

"Landlady? My goodness! How old is she?"

"Thirty-three."

"Ah," she said with a nod. "Older than you."

"So?" he challenged.

"So nothing," Nicole said with a smile. "Go on."

"She's never been married. She's a fantastic cook. And she has red hair. Strawberry-blond, actually," he corrected. "She has a great figure and she is absolutely the most warm, funny and feminine woman I've ever met."

"She sounds wonderful," Nicole said, genuine happiness glittering in her eyes.

"She is."

"So when do we get to meet her?" Nicole asked. "I can hardly wait."

The pleasure on Nick's face died. "I don't know."

"Why? What's the matter?"

"She doesn't know who I am," he confessed.

"What are you talking about?" Nicole asked, a frown drawing her perfectly arched eyebrows together.

Nick ground out his cigarette. "She thinks I'm a motorcycle bum. A friend of her sister's who has just blown into town for a while. She doesn't know that I'm one of the Logans whose family is under investigation."

"But if she's accepted you as a drifter, why wouldn't she accept the problems with the family? That doesn't even make sense."

Nick leaned against the back of the padded booth and crossed his brawny arms over his broad chest. "Does it help you to understand if I tell you that her family is in timber?"

"It gives you a common bond," Nicole said, her slim shoulders moving in a shrug. "I still don't see the problem."

"They're in a bit of financial trouble right now, Nicole," he explained. Looking her squarely in the eye, he asked, "If you owned a floundering timber company and you heard about a family accused of putting small companies out of business and then swallowing them up, what would you think if their son just *happened* to come to town and *happened* to fall in love with you?"

Nicole's eyes dilated in surprise as she grasped his predicament. "What are you going to do?"

He looked at Nicole with tormented eyes. "I don't know. One part of me says that she'll understand, the other tells me to get the hell out of Calloway Corners before it all comes tumbling down around me again."

"I'M THIRSTY, DAD." Marla Morgan made the complaint as they approached the outskirts of Hope. Dan and his daughters had spent the previous night and all of Saturday with his mother, who lived just north of the Arkansas town.

"Why didn't you get something at Grandma's?" Dan asked his younger daughter.

"I didn't think about it."

He sighed in exasperation. It was times like these he missed their mother the most. "All right," he said. "We'll drive through Andy's."

"Why don't we stop there?" Marla said, pointing to the Kettle Restaurant just ahead on the left.

Dan looked toward the restaurant parking lot. He couldn't help noticing the gleaming black motorcycle sitting there. He didn't know one kind from another, but the very sight of it made his blood boil. Even though time was supposed to heal all wounds, he still hadn't got over Eden's rejection of his proposal, and he knew that Nick Logan was the reason she had turned him down. Several people had mentioned seeing them around town together.

As the car neared the restaurant, a couple came through the door with their arms around each other's waists, smiles wreathing their faces. Both had dark hair. There was something familiar about the woman, but Dan knew without a doubt that he'd never seen her before. Slim and elegant, she had the kind of looks that made you do a double take, the kind of woman you wouldn't forget meeting. The man was a head taller than she was, dressed in black jeans and a black leather jacket. Something about him was familiar, too. Familiar enough to make Dan slow the car.

"Are we going to stop here, Dad?" Marla queried, assuming that he'd changed his mind about going to Andy's.

"Why not?" Dan said, pulling into the entrance even though satisfying his daughter's thirst was the furthest thing from his mind. He turned into a parking space out of the couple's line of vision and ordered the girls to stay put. As he moved toward the restaurant's entrance he took a closer look at the motorcycle. It was a Harley, the same kind Nick Logan rode. He took a surreptitious look at the man and almost stopped short.

Nick Logan! No doubt about it. Nick came into the store on a regular basis to pick up things for his lunch. Dan ducked inside before Nick caught sight of him and peered out the door. He couldn't believe it. If he'd left his mother's earlier as he'd planned, or if Marla hadn't wanted something to drink, he would never have witnessed Nick Logan's meeting with the unknown woman.

Even as surprise and disbelief washed through him, Dan saw Nick take the woman's face in his hands and say some-

thing to her. That he cared for her was apparent, even from
this distance. She smiled and they embraced, holding each
other close for long moments. It was much more than a casual embrace, Dan thought uncomfortably, feeling both
pain for Eden and a strange embarrassment for witnessing
what was obviously a private moment. He watched as Nick
kissed the woman on the cheek and threw his leg across the
seat of the Harley. Then he put on his helmet, started the
engine and, giving a final wave, pulled out onto the highway.

"May I help you, sir?"

Dan turned. The voice belonged to a young waitress who
was looking at him curiously. "Uh, yes. Two Cokes to go,
please," he said with a vacant smile. He didn't hear her reply; his attention was already focused on the parking lot.

The dark-haired woman still stood in the same spot, hugging herself against the slight chill in the afternoon breeze
and watching the disappearing motorcycle and rider. He saw
her reach up and brush at her eyes with her fingertips. Then
she turned and got into a silver Saab, tearing out of the
parking lot and zipping toward the interstate with no regard for the state troopers' headquarters a block away.

"Sir, your Cokes are ready."

Dan turned toward the sound of the voice. The waitress
stood at the cash register; two Cokes sat nearby. He paid her
and started toward the car, wondering if Eden would regret
her decision not to marry him if she knew that Nick Logan
was seeing someone else.

THE RIDE BACK to Calloway Corners went by in a blur.
Nick's thoughts whirled like the Harley's tires, and like the
tires, they seemed to have no end.

He didn't know what to think about his parents wanting
to see him and Nicole. He couldn't imagine what it could be

about, and Nicole didn't have a clue. While he could sympathize with Stuart having a change of heart—even though it might be temporary—he didn't think he wanted any part of whatever plan his father might have up his sleeve. He had tried to please his father all his life, and nothing had made Stuart think any more of him—not good grades, loyalty or dedication. He was through trying to please. Stuart Logan was synonymous with heartache, and Nick had suffered enough of that at his father's hands.

He had decided something while he was talking with Nicole: he had to tell Eden who he was and hope that what they felt for each other would carry them through her surprise. Putting it off any longer would only make it seem as if he was trying to hide something. Surely she knew him well enough by now to trust him when he told her he had nothing to do with his family's schemes to get ahead. And maybe, if the plan he had dreamed up with Nicole's help worked, the Calloways would realize that his heart was in the right place no matter what his family did.

EDEN DRESSED FOR THE CARNIVAL, her forehead furrowed with worry, her heart beating heavily in dread and disappointment.

"I'll be back. I promise." Nick had spoken the words earlier that day, before he started out for Hope and his visit with his friend. They played through Eden's mind, a talisman she held close to her heart. Yet as the afternoon shadows lengthened and dusk closed in on the day, she found the words held little comfort and, in their stead, she heard over and over, "He'll hurt you . . . hurt you . . . hurt you."

Eden regretted the argument more than she could say. She and her sisters hardly ever argued, but she supposed it was to be expected. Everyone was worried right now. Everyone was on edge and tempers were short . . . especially hers.

Mariah's reminder of what Eden already knew had taken the sunshine from her day as did her sister's warning. *"People are starting to talk."*

As she'd told Mariah, she didn't expect Nick to stay, but more and more lately—ever since the problems with the mill had come about—she wondered if her safe, secure world was coming to an end. She was torn whether to take each day and the happiness it held as it came, or to start trying to prepare herself for the ever-nearing inevitable heartbreak...not to mention the pity and the censure that was bound to follow.

She had told Mariah she didn't care what people thought, and on one level she didn't. But a lifetime of habits and values was hard to deny and, though she had gambled and found the happiness and excitement she'd longed for, Eden now wondered how she was going to manage when it was gone....

Even though Eden did her best to join in, her mood hadn't improved an hour later when she arrived at the carnival alone. Mariah's pumpkin costume was the butt of several corny jokes. Ford—who was to take a turn in the dunking booth set up outside the gym—was dressed in an old-fashioned swimming suit that managed to make him look as dashing as ever.

The belly-dancer costume Eden had whipped up for Tess on such short notice that afternoon brought a whistle from Ford, "That's more like it," from Mariah and "You're not wearing that in public," from Seth who was, of course, an outlaw—complete with mustache, low-slung gun belt and long black duster.

Eden surprised them all by wearing a tiger suit that fit her like a sleek second skin. She slicked her bright copper-colored hair back from her face and put on feline ears made from an old pair of earmuffs. A plain black mask covered her eyes, and glued-on whiskers completed her outfit. While everyone said that they couldn't believe she was going as a tiger, Ford, who did more observing than talking, thought the costume fit the new Eden to a tee.

Ghosts and goblins roamed the gymnasium, and pirates and princesses vied for prizes in their category. Balloons escaped from careless hands and floated to the ceiling or were popped unexpectedly, eliciting startled shrieks and laughter. Happy voices mingled with music, and the air was redolent with the aroma of buttered popcorn and funnel cakes. A cakewalk had been marked off at one end of the large room, and booths with crafts and games were set up along each wall.

Eden took charge of the cakewalk, trying not to think of the pitying glances Mariah and Tess bestowed upon her as she did her best to throw herself into the festivities. When Ford suggested that she take a break and go see Stella, the fortune teller, Eden demurred. Only when Mariah and Tess said they would go first did she reluctantly agree.

They all laughed over the exotic-looking woman's prediction that an unexpected visitor would be coming to stay with Tess. Mariah was told she was expecting a baby—not much of a prediction since her condition was well known all over town and her platinum-blond hair was hard to mistake for anyone else's in the Haughton area. Eden was told to "beware the tall, dark stranger" and warned that "lies lead to heartache."

Though clichéd, Eden's fortune was too close to the truth to be ignored. They were still laughing over the predictable summations when a strange feeling came over Eden.

Without knowing why, her gazed was drawn to the double doors that led outside to the dunking booth and the parking area. Standing in the doorway was a James Dean look-alike—jeans, leather jacket, sunglasses and slicked-back hair.

Eden's heart smiled. Though it was full dark outside, sunshine flooded her. Doubts fled and worries vanished. Ignoring the questions about where she was going, Eden started across the crowded room . . . toward Nick. . . .

SHE WAS DRESSED like a tiger. And she was one. A gentle tiger who purred at his slightest touch, yet could become like a wild thing when he made love to her. She came to a stop a foot from him, her jade-green eyes glittering behind the mask. Her mouth curved upward in a tremulous smile and, without a word, Nick put his arm around her shoulders and turned toward the open door. Silently, they left the noise and activity inside the gymnasium and headed around the building toward the playground. There, in the mammoth shadow of the wall, she threw her arms around his neck. Between scattered, random kisses she murmured feverishly, "I didn't think you were coming, I didn't think you were coming."

Nick heard the fear in her voice. It was very much like the fear he felt every time he thought of telling her who he was. If only she realized that he couldn't stay away. He held her tightly, as if he were trying to absorb her doubts and fears, as if he were trying to absorb her into his very soul.

He wanted to tell her he loved her, but he couldn't, not until he could tell her about his family. It wouldn't be fair. And there was no way he could do it now, no way he would ruin the rest of Eden's evening. He was, as Gil Tanner used to say, between a rock and a hard place.

## CHAPTER TWELVE

MONDAY MORNING DAWNED crisp and clear, everything an early November morning should be. A light breeze danced among the branches and sent the fallen leaves racing across the yard. It was the kind of brisk day that made the horses in the front pasture kick up their heels and run. But for the first time in years, Eden failed to derive pleasure from her favorite season.

Nick had been gone for a couple of hours and, after throwing in a few loads of laundry and straightening up, Eden had put two apple pies in the oven. She was tired, but she knew that even if she went back to bed she wouldn't be able to sleep.

The problem of what to do about the mill was seldom far from her mind, and even Nick had commented on her perpetual frown and the fact that she wasn't sleeping well. Her nerves were shaky and tears were so close to the surface most of the time that she felt like bawling if anyone looked cross-eyed at her.

She knew her state of mind was nothing but the stress of worrying about the mill and the constant fear that Nick would leave one morning and not come back. Telling herself there was nothing she could do about Nick didn't help. But there was something she could do about the mill—maybe. She sipped her hot chocolate and chewed her bottom lip, dreading the call she had to make but knowing that she'd put it off as long as she could.

It had been almost two weeks since things at the Calloway mill had fallen apart and the banker had refused her the money to set things right. According to Tess, they could go on until the first of the year—maybe. If possible, she needed to make some kind of arrangements to keep the mill going before funds ran out. Though she had racked her mind for some other alternative, she now believed that there was only one possible source of getting the money. E.Z. and Jo.

As much as she hated going begging, Eden didn't know anyone else to ask. Surely, she reasoned, anyone as successful as E.Z. was either had the money or could get it. She sighed. There was nothing to do but put the call through to the apartment Jo and E.Z. stayed at when they were in New Orleans. She punched in the number and waited for the call to go through.

"Hello." The breathless voice answered the phone on the second ring.

"Hi, Jo. It's Eden."

"Eden! Hi!" Jo said. "How is everyone?"

"Fine." Eden gave Jo a progress report, telling her about the carnival, Mariah's latest doctor's report and Tess's progress with Jason and her teaching position.

"What about you? Mariah tells me you've been seeing that good-looking friend of hers—Nick Logan."

"Yes," Eden said with a slight smile. It seemed that the family grapevine was working well, as usual.

Jo laughed. "He's a handsome devil, but you watch yourself. He's out of your league."

"So everyone keeps telling me," Eden said dryly.

"Butt out, huh?" Jo said.

"If you don't mind. Go save the whales or something and leave my love life alone," Eden said with mock irritation.

"Okay, okay," Jo said with a laugh. "We should be home any time now. By Thanksgiving, for sure. E.Z. is almost finished here, and we're anxious to get home and stay in one spot for a while," Jo said in an attempt to change the subject.

"I'm glad," Eden told her. "We miss you."

"How is everything with the mill? Fran didn't have a change of heart and bring the money back, did she?"

"Hardly," Eden said. She was glad the pleasantries were out of the way and the subject of the mill had been broached indirectly. "Speaking of the mill, I need to ask you something."

"Sure. What is it?"

Eden drew a deep breath and plunged in. "Is there any way you and E.Z. can get your hands on some money to tide us through until we can get some outstanding debts collected?" Eden rushed through her rehearsed speech in double time, and then tacked on hurriedly, "You know I wouldn't ask if we weren't desperate."

"I know." Jo's voice had lost it's bounce. "E.Z. and I have talked about this already, Eden. We figured out that things would probably go downhill in a hurry after you told us about Fran, but frankly, it couldn't have happened at a worse time for us."

Eden's heart sank. The weariness that had dogged her heels the past few days elicited a soul-deep sigh.

"We're tapped out," Jo confessed. "E.Z. put up the money for that halfway house for the homeless in California, and he's promised a huge amount to get things going here. He's sunk a tremendous amount of money in his new record label and studio, and we're already committed to building the house...."

"I understand," Eden said, blinking back the ever-threatening tears. She was sick with disappointment but awed by the amount of money E.Z. had already spent on helping people. "I thought it was worth a try."

"I'm sorry," Jo said. "I'll talk to E.Z. again. Maybe he can figure out how to get something short term. Or maybe he knows someone—"

"Thanks, Jo," Eden interrupted. "I appreciate it. I really do. It's just that Christmas is coming up, and . . ." She swallowed the emotion rising in her throat.

"I know," Jo said. "I can't stand to think about it, either. I'll be in touch, okay?"

"Yeah. Thanks, Jo."

"Sure."

"Give Carmen a kiss for me?" Eden said.

"I will," Jo promised. "Bye."

"Goodbye."

That was that. Her last resort, her hidden ace. If E.Z. couldn't figure out something, the mill would have to shut down in December. It wasn't fair, Eden thought, cradling the receiver. It just wasn't fair.

NICK RAN THE BOARD through the table saw and handed it to the waiting carpenter. He was worried about Eden. She was pale, and there were dark circles beneath her eyes from her sleepless nights. The last night she had slept without waking before morning was the night of the storm almost two weeks ago, when they had made love in the woods.

She was worried about the mill, and there wasn't a damn thing he could do to ease her fears.

*Is that why you haven't told her who you are, Logan?*

An uncomfortable feeling swept through him even though he told himself his reasons were valid. He hadn't realized how close she was to breaking until the night of the carnival. When she had clung to him and said over and over, "I didn't think you were coming, I didn't think you were coming," Nick thought he would die. He had known then that he would rather die than cause her any more hurt. So instead of telling her the truth, he had just held her and won-

dered how long he could keep his secret...and how far away
he would have to run to forget her.

EDEN WAS JUST TAKING the pies from the oven when she
heard someone at the door. She pulled off the padded mitts
and turned off the oven. She went to the front door, hoping that it was a salesman she could get rid of in a hurry and
praying that her face didn't still bear the ravages of her tears.

A familiar figure was visible through the lacy curtains
covering the leaded oval pane in the front door. Dan. She
sighed. She wasn't crazy about seeing Dan. As a matter of
fact, ever since she'd broken off with him she had done her
best to avoid him. Whenever possible she drove into
Haughton to shop for milk and bread and other groceries
she ran out of during the week instead of getting them from
the Calloway Corners store. She didn't like hurting people,
and Dan's hang-dog attitude was more than she could bear.
She plastered a welcoming smile on her face and swung open
the door.

"Dan!" she said, stepping aside for him. "Come in."

"Hello, Eden," he said, his blue eyes sweeping her from
head to toe. "You look tired. How are you?"

Eden forced a laugh. "Flattery will get you nowhere."

Dan had the grace to look embarrassed. "I didn't
mean—"

"No offense taken, Dan," Eden said, wondering how she
could have ever seriously entertained the possibility of
marrying him. He was stable, he was nice and he was attractive enough, but he just wasn't...Nick. "I just took
some apple pies from the oven. Would you like a slice with
some coffee?"

"No, thanks," he said, shifting from one foot to the
other. "I need to get back to the store. I just stopped by to
tell you something I think you should know."

He looked uncomfortable, but there was a stubborn glint in his eyes, as if he had taken it upon himself to tell her whatever was bothering him, but he didn't like having to do it. "Please," she said. "Sit down."

He sat in Ben's old recliner and rested his elbows on his spread knees, his clasped hands dangling between them. "I hate to be the one to tell you, Eden," he hedged, "but I feel you need to know."

"What is it, Dan?" she asked.

"I know that you've been seeing that Logan guy."

Eden frowned. What could he possibly have to say about Nick? She nodded. "Yes."

Dan cleared his throat. "The girls and I went to Hope to see my mother Friday night, and when we were coming home for the carnival Saturday evening, we stopped to get something to drink at the Kettle. You know, that place by the interstate that used to be the Pitt Grill?" When Eden nodded, he continued. "Well, I saw this motorcycle sitting there, and I thought it was Nick's."

"It could have been Nick's," Eden explained, wondering what he was leading up to. "He went to see a friend who lives in Hope."

Dan looked surprised momentarily, and then he blurted out, "Was it a woman friend?"

It took a second for the implications of the question to sink in. Eden looked at him, a nebulous fear sprouting in the nether regions of her heart.

Dan's eyes held pain—for her. "Eden, I hate to break it to you like this, but I felt you should know...before you get too serious."

Eden didn't know whether to laugh or cry. *Serious? How serious would you call making out in the woods, Dan? How serious is moving all his things from the apartment to my room?*

Her heart beat crazily. "Are you certain it was Nick? I mean, there are a lot of black—"

"I was close enough to see for sure, Eden. I know who he is because he comes in the store a lot."

"Oh." She drew in a deep breath and met his troubled gaze. "I'm sure it was an innocent meeting," she said in Nick's defense. "He told me he was going, and a lot of people have friends of the opposite sex. Why, Seth and I have been friends for years, and I—"

"He had his arms around her, Eden," Dan told her with an implacable look on his face. "And he kissed her. He looked—" Dan recalled the expression he'd seen on Nick's face as he had held the unknown woman "—as if he couldn't bear to have to leave her."

The words tumbled around inside Eden's head and heart, battering her newly found belief in herself, his words a death knell to everything good and happy that loving Nick had brought to her life. She felt suddenly bereft. As if she had lost her best—her only—friend. Jerky, wooden movements brought her to her feet. "I appreciate your coming, Dan. Really."

Without being rude, her actions clearly indicated that his presence was no longer welcome. The burning need Dan had felt to tell her, to make her see the truth about Nick Logan died beneath the anguish dulling the jade-green of her eyes. Dan rose and preceded her to the door, anxious now to be gone.

At the door, he turned to look at her. "I'm sorry, Eden. I never meant to hurt you."

"I know." Her voice held no reproach, only a deep sorrow. Dan didn't doubt that she meant what she said. He turned and went down the steps, the sound of the door closing behind him echoing hollowly in his heart.

"So you couldn't get Nick to come?" Stuart asked that same Monday morning.

Nicole shook her head, thinking how his speech had improved the last week or so. "I'm sorry, Daddy, but he's just...afraid it will be—"

"I know why," Stuart said gruffly, interrupting her faltering apology. He sighed and stared at the ceiling. "I should have known it would take more than my asking to get him to come back. I can't say that I blame him."

Nicole didn't say anything.

"Sit down, Nicci," Stuart offered, the subject of Nick obviously finished as he gave Nicole his full attention. "Where's your mother?"

"She followed me in her car. She should be along any minute," Nicole explained, smoothing the skirt of her pearl-gray suit and sitting down in the brown and tan striped chair next to the bed. Glancing up, she saw that Stuart was looking at her as if he were seeing her for the first time. There was appreciation in his eyes, and the barest hint of sadness.

"How is he?" he asked at last, resurrecting the subject of Nick without warning.

A bit taken aback that he hadn't dropped the subject of her brother, she said, "Nick's fine. Happy. He's met a woman and seems crazy about her."

"That's good," Stuart said with a satisfied nod. "Belinda was never right for him. She wasn't good enough for Nick and was way too good for Keith."

Nicole tried to hide her surprise at hearing any hint of censure from their father about her oldest brother, though there was no denying that Stuart was hurt by Keith's defection.

"I've always been sorry I put Keith back in charge when I called him home from Europe," Stuart said thoughtfully.

"Called him home? You *asked* him to come back?" Nicole was incredulous. Like everyone else, she had always thought that Keith had decided to come home and that Stuart had put him in charge to make up for whatever rift there was between them. "Why?"

Unfortunately Stuart wasn't thinking as clearly as he should have been. He was so anxious to get at the truth that he forgot that it should be told a certain way—and in the right order. "I brought him back. But it was all a mistake, all for nothing," he said enigmatically. "If only I knew then what I do now, I would never have let them take Lucas, never have hurt your mother the way I did."

Lucas! Hearing the name of the man who had raped her on her father's lips didn't make any sense. What did her mother and Lucas have to do with Keith? Stuart hardly knew Luke was alive. No one ever talked about the Tanners, not since Luke and his family had moved away from Colbert eight years ago... after the attack.

Nicole's head began to throb as it always did when she thought of Luke. She prayed that her mother would come and help her to comprehend Stuart's words because nothing her father was saying made any sense. "I don't understand, Daddy," she confessed.

There was a strange look in Stuart's eyes. "I lost Nick, but I gained Luke. Luke is a Logan, Nicole."

"What?" she whispered, certain she hadn't heard right.

On one level of her mind, she heard the soft moans of two people making love—who?—and on another level she heard Stuart's reply, tinged with incredulity and conviction. "Lucas is a Logan, Nicole. He's my son, not Gil Tanner's."

The room whirled, and a part of her mind spun backward in time. She might have been alone in the hospital room. Her eyes drifted closed, and the doors in her mind opened a crack. Stuart's voice droned on, but she didn't hear it. From some place where it had been buried for eight long years came the memory of being with Luke in a tangle of arms and legs with her face resting against his chest. *"I love you, Nicole. I love you so much."*

Stuart looked at her, wondering why she had grown so quiet suddenly. There was as strange look in her eyes. She was deathly pale, and her breathing was shallow and fast as she rocked. "Nicole? Are you all right?"

She didn't answer.

She could almost feel the warm breeze drifting over their sweat-slickened bodies, could hear the sound of a dove cooing in the distance. Behind her closed eyelids, her mind roiled with visions from her past: Luke undressing her. Kissing her. Making love to her.

She recalled Lucas's soft words of love, the gentleness of his touch. Luke loved her. Why would he have raped her? But even more important than that, wouldn't she have *known* if they were related?

Nicole's stomach churned in rebellion at the news that had been tossed so callously out to her. She crossed her arms tightly across her middle, as if the action could stop her from flying to pieces. Her head moved slowly from side to side in denial and she rocked back and forth, back and forth.

"Nicole?" Stuart's voice, filled with concern, was as distant to her as her memories. It didn't even register.

She recalled hearing a sound. Remembered being surprised. And then Luke was gone... A sob rose in her throat and she fought to hold it back. *I would have known, Luke. I would have known.*

A knock at the door penetrated her misery, causing her eyes to fly wide open and bringing her painfully to the present.

A white-frocked nurse stepped inside. "Time for your medication, Mr. Logan," she said cheerfully.

"Can't you see I have company?" Stuart snapped, his eyes never leaving Nicole's face. "I don't want your damned medicine!"

"Come on, Mr. Logan," the nurse cajoled, "don't give me any flack."

The simple, innocent words had the effect of a stick of dynamite, exploding into Nicole's subconscious and jarring loose the last stubborn memories. They rushed through her mind, flooding her with recollections that were painfully clear.

*"Dammit, Keith! Leave her alone!"*

Luke and Keith rolling around on the ground grunting and groaning as they beat at each other with furious fists, and a memory of herself, screaming and screaming for them to stop...

Luke lying silent beneath the trees, and hands, Keith's hands, touching her where they shouldn't be. *"Don't give me any flack, Nicole...don't give me...don't, Keith, don't..."* It was wrong, wrong, because Keith was her brother!

Keith had raped her, not Luke.

Nicole leaped from the chair, trying to escape from the truth that clawed at her mind. "No," she screamed. "No!"

Theresa heard the screams as the elevator doors slid open. Her heart plummeted to her toes as she recognized the voice as Nicole's. No! she thought. *Please, God, not now.* Not now, when they were so close to getting things straightened out. Breaking into a run, Theresa tried to dodge the nurses who were already rushing down the hall toward Stuart's room.

She burst through the door behind a blond R.N., trying to take in what had happened in one sweeping glance. Stuart lay propped up in bed, his face an ashen gray. Standing in the corner, her eyes dilated darkly with raw, liquid fear,

stood Nicole. A Nicole Theresa thought they had left behind forever in a swank California sanatorium.

The past had caught up to them with a vengeance.

"Oh, God," Theresa whispered as pain sluiced throughout her body in cold, sobering waves.

But God must have been otherwise occupied; it was obvious that he hadn't heard her prayer.


"WHAT'S THE MATTER?" Nick asked, as he helped Eden
load the dishwasher after dinner that night. "You haven't
said ten words to me all evening."

*You lied to me! You didn't go see a friend. You went to see
a woman.*

"I'm just tired," she hedged, refusing to look at him as
she scrubbed a pan with unnecessary force.

Nick braced his hands on the countertop, effectively im-
prisoning her with his arms. His lips touched the side of her
neck and she stiffened in his embrace. Frowning, he
straightened, grasping her by the shoulders and turning her
resisting body around to face him. "What's going on,
Eden?" he asked in a puzzled voice.

She lifted her chin a fraction of an inch and met his questioning gaze head-on. "You tell me," she countered, her
voice skirting the edges of iciness.

He released his hold on her. "Gladly," he said, striving
to control his irritation. "If you'll at least give me a clue to
what the hell this is all about."

"Hope."

"Hope?" he echoed, uncomprehendingly.

"Why did you go?"

Like the sinister shadows in a horror movie, a premoni-
tion of something terrible flitted through him. Something
was wrong here. Bad wrong. "I went to see a friend," he
said, recounting the same story he'd told her the previous
Saturday morning.

"A friend?" she probed.

"Yes." He stuck to his story, even though something told him it was about to hit the fan.

Eden shook her head in disbelief. "A woman friend."

It wasn't a question. It was a statement. She knew. Somehow, she *knew*. Nick felt the happiness he'd experienced the past few weeks slipping ever so slightly from his grasp. It was obvious that the time for truth had arrived . . . or at least part of the truth.

"Yes," he said, surprising her with his candor. "A woman friend. My sister."

The shock Eden felt at his admission was drowned in anger by his obviously trite explanation. "Your *sister*?" she repeated in patent disbelief. "Oh, Nick, I would have thought that with your vast, worldly experience, you could come up with something a little more original than that."

This was an Eden he had never seen before. The rarely furious Eden whom Mariah had warned him about. One thing was very clear. If she didn't trust him and what they had together enough to give him the benefit of the doubt about this, there was no way she would be sympathetic about his family. His hold on happiness slipped another notch.

"I don't lie, Eden," he said quietly. "If I can't tell the truth, I don't say anything. I thought you would know that about me by now."

Eden had the grace to look ashamed at his gentle reprimand.

"The woman is my twin sister, Nicole," he told her coolly. "She was on her way back to Arkansas from Dallas, and we agreed to meet in Hope for the day. And that's the truth, whether you believe it or not."

Eden was silent as she watched him go to the door. He was either telling the truth or he was the greatest liar in the world. She preferred to believe the former.

He opened the door and turned back suddenly. "Who told you?"

"Dan," Eden admitted.

"Dan," Nick said with a nod. "Why doesn't that surprise me?"

The door was almost closed behind him when the sound of Eden's voice made him pause. "Nick!"

He turned.

"If you were going to see your sister, why didn't you just say so?"

"Maybe because I didn't think you'd believe me."

EDEN LAY IN HER solitary bed, the sound of a gentle rain whispering against the windowpanes, her eyes long dried from her tears. Rolling to her side, she reached out to the place beside her, the place where Nick had slept for several weeks now. Like her heart, it was empty.

*"It was my twin sister, Nicole. I didn't think you'd believe me . . . believe me . . . believe me."*

It made sense that if the unknown woman was his sister he would have hated to leave her as Dan suggested. Why had she been so eager to believe what Dan had to say? Was it because, deep down, she had so little faith in herself as a woman—and less in Nick's dependability? Or was it because she had felt from the very beginning that what they shared must come to an end? Hadn't she expected it?

Why? She'd never been negative before. Why now? Because he was worldly and she was a homebody? Because he was younger? Maybe it was because she had been going through so many upheavals in the past ten months that her usual equilibrium had been knocked out of kilter. But no more. Tomorrow she would sit down with Nick and really talk . . . about their pasts, and their future—if they had one. She wouldn't put any pressure on him, but the time had come when they had to either go ahead with their relationship or put an end to it.

Her decision made, Eden closed her eyes, ready to sleep. The patter of the rain was so soothing. What a surprise, she thought drowsily, to find that Nick had a twin sister. Actually, she knew precious little about him except that he made her feel so whole, so happy. Her fingertips caressed the empty place next to her. What she did know was that after sharing a bed with him, she didn't like to sleep alone....

HE FELT SO ALONE.

The rain, which had started slow and gentle, now lashed at the windows in sudden fury. The soft glow of the security light in the yard invaded the dark sanctity of the garage apartment, causing the furniture to appear as shadowy lumps. The sofa bed, with which he'd had no previous complaints, was uncomfortable after sharing Eden's bed and warmth.

*Ah, Eden, I miss you.*

He missed her the way he had known he would when it all came falling down. He sighed and folded his arms behind his head. He supposed he should be thankful that it had lasted as long as it had, long enough to get him through the toughest time of his life.

No. If it was really over with Eden, all the rest of his life would be the toughest time. He swore, unable to face the fact that what they shared might be over, unable to believe that he would never be able to lose himself in the delicious warmth of her body again and never hear her say the words he longed to hear her say...the same words he longed to say to her, but was afraid to: I love you.

TED PACED AROUND his small living room, wondering when Bart would hear something, wondering if he should call

Eden and tell her about the offer he'd received for the mill
a few days before and wondering why the offer bothered
him so much. Was it guilt that was making him so wary, or
the fact that the offer had been made through him and not
one of the Calloways? Was he extra sensitive now that he'd
so recently been taken for a fool?

Even after the fiasco with Fran and his dereliction of
duty, Eden had let him stay. To make up for it—if he could
ever achieve that goal—he owed it to the Calloways to do his
best, which meant going the extra mile and checking out
everything, including any offers to purchase the mill. That's
why he was having Bart at the sheriff's office check out this
unexpected offer.

If this company was a legit operation, then and only then
would he put the offer before Eden and her sisters. After
that, it was up to them whether they decided to sell.

Loyalty meant something to Ben's girls. It meant something to Ted Vincent, too. And he damn sure wasn't going
to let them down again.

# CHAPTER THIRTEEN

WHEN THE TELEPHONE on the bedside table rang early Tuesday morning, it interrupted Eden's tormenting dreams of Nick. Reaching out a lethargic hand, she groped for the offending instrument.

"Hello," she murmured in a sleep-husky voice.

"Eden Calloway, please."

The words were clearly enunciated, though the feminine voice was soft and very Southern. Something in the tone of the unfamiliar voice swept the remnants of sleep from Eden's mind and set warning bells to ringing. She propped herself up on one elbow. "This is she."

A relieved sigh originated at the other end of the phone line. "Thank goodness!" the woman said. "I've asked information for the phone number of every Eden or E. Calloway in every town in the Shreveport-Bossier City area."

Eden was growing more confused by the minute. "May I ask who's calling, please?"

"Oh, my dear, forgive me. It's just that this has been such a terrible night! I'm afraid I'm not thinking straight. This is Theresa Logan, Nick's mother."

If Eden hadn't been lying down, she probably would have fallen. Nick's mother! How had she found out about her? And why on earth would Nick's mother be calling?

"I hate to bother you," Theresa Logan was saying, "but I had no idea how else to get hold of Nick. Thank God Nicole told me about you and Nick after she saw him on Saturday."

Though Eden still had no idea of what was going on, one thing was clear. Nick had been telling the truth. He had seen Nicole on Saturday.

"Does he have a telephone?"

"No, I'm sorry, but—"

"Well, do you have any idea how I can get hold of him?" she asked, breathlessly, interrupting before Eden could answer. "It's a family emergency."

Eden's heart sprinted into a faster rhythm. She sat up and reached into the nightstand drawer for a pad and pen. "If you'll leave me a number where Nick can call you back, I'll go get him. He's nearby, so it shouldn't take but five minutes."

"Would you mind?"

"Not at all," Eden said.

She took down the number and assured Nick's mother that he would be returning her call in a few minutes. She was just about to hang up when Theresa said, "Oh, and Eden. Be sure and tell Nick that it's about Nicole."

THE POUNDING ON THE DOOR woke Nick abruptly and brought him to a sitting position. He scrubbed a hand down his face and glanced around the room to get his bearings. Misery, left over from the night before, swept through him. He was in the garage apartment, not Eden's bed, and someone was pounding on the door.

"Nick!"

Eden! Had she come to apologize? he wondered. He threw back the sheet and leaped up, crossed the room and flung open the door.

Her hair was sleep-tousled, and her eyes held a hurt, vulnerable look. She wore nothing but a soft cotton nightshirt that hit her midthigh. The rosy tips of her breasts were clearly visible through the opaque fabric, and in spite of their argument, his body reacted in typical male fashion.

Eden, too, was achingly aware of Nick. His face was covered with a day's growth of beard, a trend that was in vogue, thanks to George Michaels and Sonny Crockett. Eden found it incredibly sexy. His chest—broad and naturally dark—was bare, the black hair sprawling over his pectorals and down his stomach in a way that robbed her of breath and reason. He wore nothing but a pair of low-cut navy-hued briefs that cling to his narrow hips and the heart-stopping fullness of his manhood. She ached to touch him him, wished they hadn't argued....

"Eden? What is it?" he asked gruffly, wanting her so much he hurt, but unwilling to forgive her so easily.

"Your mother," Eden said, forcing her wayward thoughts away from wants and wishes and facing the reality of the moment.

"My mother?" Nick said, his heavy brows snapping together in a frown. "What about my mother?"

"She called just now."

"My mother doesn't know where I am," he told her, even as the memory of telling Nicole that he was near Bossier City flashed through his mind. He'd also told Nicole Eden's full name on Saturday.

Eden was growing more puzzled by the moment. Why wouldn't Nick's mother know where he was? "She said she was Theresa Logan. Is that your mother?"

"Yes." The admission seemed forced from between gritted teeth.

"Well, I told her you'd call her back."

"I'm not interested in anything she or any of the other Logans have to say," Nick told her, starting to close the door.

"Nick! Wait!" Eden said, pushing against the door. She was appalled by his apparent callousness. "She said to tell you that it's about Nicole."

The opposing pressure gave away without warning. Nick reached out and grabbed Eden's upper arm, dragging her into the room. "Nicole!" he said roughly. "What is it? What's the matter with her?"

Eden shook her head. The quicksilver changes in his attitude were dizzying and confusing. "I don't know. You'll have to call her to find out."

"Damn!" Nick released Eden and crossed the room to where his clothes lay draped over the back of a chair. He drew the clean jeans up his muscular, hair-dusted legs and zipped them, not bothering with the metal button.

"If they're pulling something else, I'll..." His threat trailed off to silence as he slid his bare feet into brown loafers. "Come on," he said, snatching his shirt from the arm of the chair and shrugging into it as he neared the door. "Let's go."

TED LET THE PHONE RING eight times before hanging up. Where on earth could Eden be at this hour of the morning? he wondered, rubbing at his whisker-stubbled cheek and frowning at the cup of chicory-flavored coffee in his other hand.

A thought came to him, one he didn't really want to consider, especially now. Like everyone else in town, he'd heard the rumors. Was Eden—heaven forbid—with that Logan fellow? Had she spent the night with him?

Restlessly, Ted stood up and strode the length of the room. What should he do now? He was thankful that he'd checked on the offer the NiLole Company had made for the Calloway lumber mill. He looked at the phone and wondered again what to do.

Mariah, he thought suddenly. He'd get dressed and go to work, and when he got there, he'd tell Mariah everything he knew. Everything.

"HELLO." THE SOUND of his mother's voice after three years brought a strange and inexplicable sadness to Nick.

"It's Nick, Mom."

"Oh, Nick!" Theresa cried softly. "It's so good to hear your voice."

He heard the thickness of tears and the unmistakable sound of her voice breaking. It occurred to him that maybe he'd been wrong in judging her along with his father and Keith.

"Are you all right?" she asked. "Are you well?"

"I'm fine," he assured her. "What about you?"

"I'm coping."

Coping. A strange word, but one he realized fit her perfectly. Coping was something Theresa had been doing all her life. And doing well. "How's Dad?" he asked, uncertain if he was asking because it was expected of him, or because he really cared.

"He's better. He…wants to see you, Nick. We both do."

"Nicole told me. Is that what this is all about, Mom? Nicole couldn't talk me into coming back so you thought you'd give it a try?"

"No, Nick," she told him. "As much as I'd like to see you and have things straight between us, I would never try to coerce you into coming back. And neither would your father."

The words seeped into his mind slowly, telling him more than he would have ever believed. It sounded as if they did want to make things right, but that if he chose not to return, they respected his decision. It even sounded if they cared about him. But did he dare to believe the implications of his mother's statement? Did he dare trust anything the other Logans said?

"I called about Nicole."

"What's the matter?" he asked, unable to believe that his own concerns had blocked out the real reason for her call. "She hasn't been in an accident, has she?"

"No," Theresa said, "nothing like that."

"Then what— Oh, no," he said, as a sudden thought struck him. "She hasn't had another breakdown, has she?"

"Yes."

"What happened?" Nick demanded roughly, his heart pounding in slow, painful rhythm.

"It's too much to go into over the phone, Nick. It's...very complicated, and in a roundabout way, what has happened concerns you, too."

"Me?" His mind raced with possibilities, regarding and rejecting them one after another. What could possibly concern him and Nicole and send her off the deep end again?

"Yes. Will you come home, Nick?"

Go home? Go home and face his father and all the bad blood between them? Could he do it?

"She's asking for you," Theresa told him, throwing in her trump.

The four small words made up his mind, as she had known they would. He would do anything for Nicole. Anything. At least he wouldn't have to deal with Keith. He drew in a deep breath and let it out slowly, almost as if he were fortifying himself for the ordeal ahead.

"Tell her I'm coming," he said. "I'll be there as soon as I can."

WHEN NICK ENTERED THE KITCHEN, he was immediately assailed with random images and sensations. Images and sensations that seemed more vivid than he could ever recall.

The scent of freshly dripped coffee and frying bacon.

The sound of the early morning banter between the radio deejays.

The sight of Eden standing at the stove, still wearing the nightshirt.

She must have sensed his presence, because she turned, the two-pronged fork in her hand. The look on her face was a careful balance of concern and uneasiness. "Breakfast is almost ready."

"I have to leave."

Eden felt the new world she had purposefully carved out for herself since Nick arrived begin to splinter apart. "Is something wrong?"

There was no denying the look on her face, in her eyes. Just as Nick himself had realized, Eden knew that the phone call from his mother was the beginning of the end.

"It's my sister. Nicole. She's . . . ill." How could he tell Eden about Nicole's breakdown, about the ugliness of her past that wasn't really her fault? And what could he tell her, when he didn't know the details himself? How could Eden, whose past had been good and filled with love, understand?

"Oh. I see."

She didn't see. She couldn't. Nick wanted to go to her and hold her, to tell her that it was all right, that he was leaving, but that he would come back, if she wanted him to. But he didn't move to touch her, simply because he wanted to so badly. He was afraid that if he did, he would never be able to bring himself to leave her or the happiness and peace he had found in her arms. He was afraid that if he heard one word of encouragement from her to stay, he wouldn't be able to bring himself to go and face whatever it was that was waiting for him in Arkansas.

"Where do you have to go?" Eden asked.

"Arkansas," he told her. "Colbert. It's only a wide spot in the road, sort of to the north, between Hot Springs and Little Rock."

She nodded. "Oh."

Nick plunged his fingers into his back pockets to keep from going to her and taking her into his arms. "Will you do something for me?"

"Of course."

"Call Seth and tell him what's happened, so he'll know why I didn't show up for work. Tell him I'll call him tonight and let him know what's going on."

*Will you tell him how long you'll be gone? If you're coming back at all?*

"Okay," she agreed.

Nick withdrew his hands and started toward the door.

Eden watched him go, a sense of futility and emptiness filling her. The door was partially closed behind him when she called his name.

He paused. The line of his back was straight, rigid. He turned stiffly, as if he was braced for something he might not want to hear. "Yeah?"

Her eyes clung to his. Eden neared him, wanting desperately to say something that would break down the wall that had sprung up between them the day before. She thought of her promise to herself that she would try to make up for her accusation. But he was worried about his sister, and now wasn't the time to try to hash out their problems. In the end, she didn't say anything except, "I'm sorry."

*Sorry that your sister is sick. Sorry that you have to go. Sorry that I didn't trust you.*

Nick nodded slowly. "I know."

She watched him leave then, without another word. In less than fifteen minutes, he had loaded his belongings into the Harley's compartments. Eden heard him crank the engine and watched him growing smaller and smaller as he negotiated the long driveway. Tears pooled in her eyes, and a sob fought its way free of her throat. He hadn't said it, but something told her that this would be the very last time she would watch the Harley disappear down the lane. This time she knew he wasn't coming back.

BY BREAKING EVERY SPEED LIMIT in two states, Nick pulled into the Little Rock hospital where his father and Nicole were patients by eleven o'clock that morning. He had made the trip in a daze, his thoughts vacillating between what was happening with his family and his misery over leaving Eden with so many things unsettled between them.

He knocked on Stuart's door and, without waiting for an answer, let himself in. His father was propped up in bed watching television. His mother was sitting in a nearby chair, working on a crossword puzzle, looking poised and chic in a rose-colored wool dress. They looked older, he thought in the split second before Theresa leaped to her feet.

"Nick!" she cried, a smile lighting her still-beautiful face. She took a step toward him and then stopped as if suddenly remembering that he might not welcome an embrace from her.

"Hello, Mom," he said, approaching the bed. He held out his hand to Stuart. "Sir."

Stuart took Nick's hand firmly, warmly, his shrewd eyes giving him a thorough once-over. "I'm glad you came home, boy," he said. "Things are in a damn mess around here."

Nick noticed that Stuart's words were slow, a bit slurred, but the look in his blue eyes was as sharp as ever. Stuart Logan was still a man it would be better not to cross.

"So I hear," Nick told him. "What happened to Nicole?"

Stuart looked at Theresa. She took his hand in hers in a silent symbol of support, an action that surprised Nick, who had seen few gestures of affection between the two.

"It's complicated, Nick," his mother said, repeating what she had told him on the phone that morning. "And it might take a while. Maybe you should sit down."

"No, thanks," Nick said, growing more confused by the second.

"Very well, then," Stuart said. He cleared his throat nervously. "First off, I want you to know that my wanting you to come back has nothing to with the fact that Keith has skipped out and I need a replacement. I have regretted a million times over what I did to you three years ago. It wasn't right. I knew it then, but I—" he sighed deeply "—I wanted to get back at your mother. I wanted to hurt her."

"What?" Nick's face wore an expression of total shock. Nothing Stuart could have said would have surprised him more. "Why would you want to hurt Mom? And how could you hurt her through me?"

"I guess it's my turn," Theresa said with a wry smile. "But I honestly don't know where to start."

"Well, I don't know what in hell is going on here, so how about starting at the beginning?" he suggested.

"All right," Stuart agreed. "All right. First of all, right or wrong, I have always doted on Keith. Because he was my firstborn, I suppose, and partly because he was a link to Frances." He shook his head. "It took me years to realize what a scheming, conniving bitch she was, and by that time my life had grown so complicated it was easier to keep on going the way I was than to try to straighten out the mess I'd made of things. But when I had this stroke, I knew that the lies and deceptions had gone on long enough. Too long, in fact. I knew that it was wrong for me to keep punishing you and Nicole and your mother for something that was as much my fault as it was hers."

"Which was?" Nick queried.

"My affair with Gil Tanner." The brief confession was dropped into the conversation with all the impact of a corpse being dropped through the ceiling.

Nick's gaze snapped to his mother. "Your *what*?"

"My affair with Gil Tanner," she repeated.

Nick sat down in the chair he had refused a few moments before and let that piece of news soak in for a few seconds. "But why?" he asked his mother. Then, before she could answer, he turned to Stuart. "That's what you meant when you said you were getting at Mom through me. That's why you kicked me out, and brought Keith back in, isn't it?"

Stuart nodded. "My finding out was an accident. When we got word that Gil was in that bad car accident in Tennessee three years ago, your mother took it pretty hard. She got to drinking one night, and as I was putting her to bed, she was rambling on about herself and Gil, saying things she would never have spoken of if she'd been sober. I confronted her with it the following day. When she admitted it, I wanted to hurt her. So I asked Keith to come home."

Nick sat thoughtfully a moment, still trying to piece things together. He looked at his mother. "How could you have had an affair with Gil three years ago? They had moved away five years before that."

Theresa shook her head. "The affair with Gil was a long time ago," she said. "Before you and Nicole were born."

"Before . . . ?" Nick couldn't go on. It was all too bizarre, too unbelievable.

Theresa left Stuart's side and rounded the foot of the bed, stopping a few feet from Nick. She stooped down so that she would be at eye level with him. There was fear in her eyes, and shame. Her perfectly outlined lips trembled. "Nick, you and Nicole are not Stuart's children," she said. "Your father is Gil Tanner."

Nick's eyes widened in shock as he stared disbelievingly into his mother's eyes. The room spun for a moment, and then settled. No wonder Nicole had gone to pieces.

"Is that what happened to Nicole? She found out that—" Nick's voice stopped short, another horrifying explanation exploding in his mind. He looked from Stuart to Theresa. "Oh, no," he said, his voice hardly above a whisper. "Nicole figured out that if Gil is our father, Luke was her—our—brother."

"No," Stuart said emphatically, with a wry twist of his lips. "That's the strange part. I don't know what happened to set Nicole off. I didn't tell her about Gil. I told her what I found out the day I had my stroke. Lucas Tanner is *my* son."

Nick pushed himself up from the chair, nearly knocking his mother down in his effort to get to the window, away from the mind-boggling news he was hearing. He planted his hands on his hips and stared down at the slow-moving traffic, struggling to grasp what his parents had just told him. After several moments, during which he tried to control the ragged tenor of his breathing, he turned at last and met Stuart's concerned gaze.

"You're putting me on, right? I mean this is the craziest story I've ever heard. It's so damned convoluted and clichéd that Sidney Sheldon couldn't even sell it."

"I know it's a lot to grasp, but it's the truth. Finding out about Luke is what triggered your father's—Stuart's—stroke," Theresa said. "Someone sent him Ellie's diary after she died. We don't know who. Maybe Gil decided that it was time everything was out in the open, time we all stopped living a lie."

Gil Tanner, the man who had been almost like a father to him, was indeed his father. He was Gil Tanner's son. And Luke was actually Stuart's and Ellie's. It was crazy. He could almost see why his mother would turn to someone like Gil, but who would have ever thought that Ellie Tanner...

"How did you get hooked up with Ellie?" Nick asked.

Stuart had the grace to look embarrassed. "It's a part of my life I'm not proud of, Nick. If you want a real reason to hate me, why don't you read Ellie's diary? Your mother has it."

Nick looked at the man he had called father all his life. The man he had thought he hated for the past three years. Now that he had more reason than ever to despise Stuart, the hate was gone.

"Did Gil know about Luke all these years?" Nick asked.

"Yes."

"You'd never have known it," he said. "He always treated Luke just fine. Like he really was his son."

"Gil Tanner is a good man," Theresa said. "Even Stuart knows that. When Gil and Ellie decided to give their marriage a chance, they put the past behind them and started fresh."

"Did Gil know about me and Nicole?" Nick asked curiously.

Theresa shook her head. "No. He still doesn't know. If you and Nicole want to tell him, I won't stop you. It's your right. And maybe his."

"Whew!" Nick said, throwing his head back and staring at the ceiling. "I don't know what to think... what to say."

"If you say you'll forgive us, it would be a start," Theresa told him. "We can't change the past, Nick. Stuart and I can't undo what's been done, or take away the heartache. But if you and Nicole and even Luke can forgive us and give us another chance, we can do what Ellie and Gil did. We can go on from here."

"Have you talked to Luke?" Nick asked.

Stuart's eyes filled with pain. "I had Theresa write a letter for me. I haven't heard a word."

Nick didn't say anything. He couldn't. It was all just too much to grasp in the span of a few minutes...or a few days.

"Well?" Stuart prompted.

"I don't know," Nick said honestly. "I just don't know."

Stuart nodded. "I understand. Will you at least stick around a while... until Nicole gets out of the woods?"

"You know I'd never leave Nicole," Nick said. "Of course I'll stay until then."

"I'd like for you to do something else for me, too, Nick."

"What's that?" Nick asked, surprised again. Stuart hardly ever asked for anything. He demanded.

"This investigation has really got me worried," he said. "You know that Logan Enterprises has been accused of sabotaging small companies and then buying them for a song. They've uncovered some companies that have had money diverted to them from Logan Enterprises. I have no knowledge of any of that. But I don't oversee things the way I used to."

Nick couldn't help the look of skepticism that crossed his face.

"Don't get me wrong, boy. I've made some enemies in my lifetime. When I hear a company is in trouble, I'm not above offering them a price so low it'll knock them to their knees. I've bought many an operation for a little or nothing just because the owners were desperate. I've gone in after a takeover and put my own people in, knocking the other workers out of jobs. I'm no damned saint, but I know how to make money. And I swear to you that I have never set out to put someone out of business. I'm telling you that if this really has happened, it happened without my knowledge or my sanction."

Nick looked into the intense blue of Stuart's eyes for long, measuring moments. He turned away abruptly, wondering if this crazy day was affecting him, making him crazy.

Though he had no reason to, though every bit of intelligence in him protested, Nick believed Stuart.

"If it's true," he began slowly, "and you aren't responsible, there's only one other person it could be."

Stuart lost what color there was in his face. Pain flared in his blue eyes. "I know," he said in a voice devoid of all feeling. "Keith."

AT NOON, MARIAH got into her white car and drove the short distance from the mill to the house. She had called Tess at school earlier to ask if she would meet her at Eden's during her lunch hour, explaining the situation as Ted had told it to her. Tess had been furious. Mariah hoped she could keep her cool until she arrived to act as a buffer. When she drove across the railroad tracks, Tess was just getting out of the car. She waited for Mariah before going in.

"Thanks for coming Tess," Mariah said, giving her older sister a hug. "I'm not certain I can do this without a backup."

"It's not going to be easy," Tess stated.

Mariah's platinum hair glistened in the sunlight as she shook her head. "No. It isn't going to be easy."

Side by side, they made their way to the front door. It was unlocked as usual. No sound came from Eden's domain, the kitchen. The radio was silent, and so was the television. Mariah and Tess exchanged questioning glances.

"Eden!" Mariah called, heading toward Eden's bedroom door. "Are you here?" She swung the door open and poked her head inside. Tess heard her gasp of surprise from where she was standing. Her pulse quickened in a rush of fear, and she followed Mariah inside.

Eden, still wearing her nightclothes, was in bed. It was obvious that she'd been crying...for a long time. "Edie, what's the matter?" Mariah asked, her concern over Eden's state overriding her reason for coming to see her.

"N-Nick's gone," Eden wailed, the moisture in her eyes spilling over.

Tess's surprised gaze met Mariah's. "Gone?" Tess said. "What do you mean he's gone?"

"He got a c-call from his mother this m-morning," Eden said, wiping her red nose on a tissue and adding it to the growing pile on the nightstand. "He had to go back to Arkansas." She saw Mariah and Tess exchange a what-do-we-do-now look. "He didn't say it, but I'm afraid t-that he w-won't come back."

Like mother hens protecting their chicks, Tess and Mariah moved to the side of the bed and sat down, each taking one of Eden's hands in theirs.

Eden was upset, but not so upset that she couldn't tell something was in the wind. "What is it?" she asked, looking from one sister to the other. "What's wrong?"

"Eden, we—" Mariah began.

The telephone pealed, interrupting Mariah's faltering beginning and causing all three women to jump in surprise. Freeing her hands, Eden reached across Tess for the receiver.

"Hello."

"Eden!" Jo cried without preamble. "What in the world is going on up there? Where are Mariah and Tess? I've been trying to get hold of them ever since I heard."

Eden frowned. What on earth was going on? "Jo . . . Jo, calm down. Mariah and Tess are here. What are you talking about? What's wrong?"

For a moment there was silence at the other end of the line. Then Jo said softly. "Do you mean you haven't heard? And it's happened right on your back doorstep?"

"I don't have the slightest notion of what you're talking about," Eden said, dabbing at her still leaking eyes.

"I'm talking about the Logans making an offer on the mill, that's what I'm talking about."

"The Logans?" Eden echoed, her startled gaze flying to Mariah's. Suddenly her sisters' visit began to make sense. "Do you mean *the* Logans?"

She turned her head and looked into Tess's hazel eyes, which were glittering with a sheen of tears. Eden didn't like the pity she saw there.

"*The* Logans," Jo said. "And more specifically, *Nick* Logan."

# CHAPTER FOURTEEN

"WHAT ARE YOU TALKING ABOUT?" Eden asked.

"Eden, it's all over the news," Jo told her with a sigh. "Look, I'll let Mariah and Tess explain things to you since they're there. But we'll be home just as soon as E.Z. comes back from his meeting."

Eden's mind whirled with questions and fear and a painful disappointment. She had no idea what was going on, so what could she say? "All right."

She hung up and looked at her sisters, confusion evident on her features. "Will someone please tell me what's going on and why you think Nick is involved with the Arkansas Logans?"

"I'd be glad to," Mariah said, pulling a tea bag from her pocket and holding it up. "If you'll put the kettle on. I have a raging headache."

A few minutes later, Mariah and Tess sat at the table, waiting for the teakettle to boil while Eden got down the mugs. She had pulled on a lightweight sweater and a pair of faded jeans, but her hair was still uncombed. With her red eyes and the trembling vulnerability of her mouth, she looked like a lost waif.

When the cups were filled, she sat down across the walnut table from her sisters and demanded, "What in the sweet hell is going on?"

Tess looked at Mariah. Neither of them had ever heard Eden swear before. Taking a quick gulp of tea to fortify her, Mariah spoke up. "Ted was waiting for me when I got to work this morning. He said he tried to call you, but you didn't answer.''

Eden frowned. ''I've been here all morning—except for the few minutes I went to the apartment to get Nick when his mother called.''

''His mother called?'' Tess asked.

''Yeah,'' Eden said, pushing her tousled hair from her face. ''Something was wrong with his sister. He had to go back to Colbert.''

Tess and Mariah exchanged another of those private glances.

''Look, you two, why don't you get to the point? Obviously everyone thinks Nick is guilty of something dark and devious, so stop beating around the bush and tell me.''

''All right, all right,'' Mariah said. ''Remember when we got that offer a couple of weeks ago from the NiLole Company?''

Eden nodded. ''We thought it was fair—maybe a little low—but we didn't really want to sell, so we decided to shelve making a decision until after the first of the year.''

''Right.''

''Well, poor Ted has been so paranoid since the deal with Fran and so thankful we didn't can him on the spot that he has set himself up as our official watchdog.''

''Meaning?''

''Meaning that he called Bart Reynolds at the sheriff's office and had NiLole checked out—unofficially, of course.''

''And?'' Eden prodded.

Abject apology filled Mariah's eyes.

''The NiLole Company belongs to Nicole and Nicholas Logan, and they are the children of Stuart Logan, sole owner of Logan Enterprises.''

Whatever color remained in Eden's face from her sleepless night and tear-filled morning faded, leaving her face as pale as a magnolia petal. "I don't believe it," she said, pushing herself away from the table and striding to the sink. She stared out the window at the woods beyond the lawn, the trail she and Nick had taken blurring as she struggled to hold back the tears filling her eyes.

"Bart has no reason to lie, Edie," Mariah said.

"He could have kept his mouth shut, though," Tess tacked on, her voice filled with disgust.

"What are you talking about?" Eden asked, turning around and swiping at her tears with trembling fingertips.

"Someone blabbed it to the news."

"What!" Eden screeched, even though Jo's comment lurked in the back of her mind.

"It's all over the television and radio that NiLole made the offer, and who NiLole actually is. Ted must have told Bart about Fran, because speculation among the press is that Fran was sent here to help us along the way to financial ruin so that the Logans could snap us up the way they did Anderson," Mariah told her.

"But that's crazy!"

"Is it?" Tess asked, rising and going to put her hands on Eden's shoulders. "Eden, we hardly know Nick Logan. And his family is pretty unsavory."

"I don't want to hear it!" Eden said savagely, breaking free of her sister's hold. She looked at Mariah, her eyes filled with pleading. "Tell her, Mariah. Tell her that Nick isn't like that. You've known him for a long time. You must know that he wouldn't do that to us. Not to you, or me."

Mariah's face held a sad look, one closely akin to resignation. "I never thought he would, but—"

"Face it, Eden," Tess interrupted, thoroughly put out with her sister and wanting to make her see reason. "Fran came to work for us after Daddy died. Nick has been here several times since then, too, probably checking things out and meeting with Fran—who was conveniently taking money hand over fist. Old man Logan probably set it all up.''

"You missed your calling, Tess," Eden said, her voice laced with sarcasm. "You should be writing commercial fiction."

But Tess wouldn't stop. Things were starting to jell in her mind. "The day the hydraulic gun went down and Ted couldn't fix it, Nick was sitting on the patio when I came, and I remember that he was mighty interested in your phone conversation with Mariah. Who fixed the machinery that time, Eden? Nick Logan, that's who."

"You're crazy," Eden said softly.

"Ted also admitted that the hydraulic gun went on the blink because someone put sand in the fluid, which causes excessive wear on the pump and the valves. Fran admitted to doing it. That isn't the kind of thing a woman would think to do on her own. Who do you think planned it?"

Eden didn't answer. She only stared at Tess, her anger growing.

"Do you want to know what I think?" Tess said, continuing with her version of the Calloway mill downfall. "I don't think there was a thing wrong with Nick's sister. Someone called—probably Fran—and told him that things were about to fall apart, so he split. Face it, Eden," she finished. "Some men are users. I know. I was married to one. And just because Nick Logan was good in bed doesn't mean he's innocent."

Eden didn't think; she reacted. The sound of her open palm hitting Tess's cheek was deafening in the quiet of the kitchen.

"Eden!" Mariah's horrified voice mingled with Tess's sharp gasp.

Eden's hands moved involuntarily to her mouth in an effort to stifle her own cry of shock at what she'd done. Her

eyes, awash with brimming moisture, clung to Tess's, bright
and shining with tears of pain.

Without another word, Tess turned and ran from the
kitchen while Eden and Mariah watched in silence. The
front door slammed and they heard the sound of her car
engine starting and then growing faint as she drove away.

"Are you going to go, too?" Eden asked at last when the
silence had grown heavy with unspoken words.

"No," Mariah said with a shake of her head. "But I think
you owe her an apology."

"I owe *her* an apology?" Eden cried. "What about me?
What about the terrible things she said about Nick?"

"I know. But you can't deny that what she said is true.
Everything points to him, Eden, as much as I hate to say it."
Mariah rose and began to pace the room. "How do you
think I feel? Everyone is going to blame me for bringing him
here. You know—wild Mariah Calloway's biker friend. I
can't guess what Ford is going to think."

Eden saw Mariah's point. She was just beginning to gain
the respect of the older people in the community, just beginning to live down her unusual life-style. The town would
probably never let either of them forget getting involved
with someone like Nick.

"It'll be all right," she said, going to Mariah and putting
her hands on her shoulders. "Ford will support you through
this. When you love someone, you stand behind them
through everything."

Unexpectedly Eden remembered her accusations against
Nick after she'd heard Dan's story about seeing him with the
woman in Hope. Accusations that had been false, groundless. She had learned the hard way that sometimes things
weren't what they seemed. Surely her sisters knew that as
well.

"I don't know what's going, on, Mariah," she said
thoughtfully. "Maybe Nick is one of those Logans. I don't

know why he didn't tell us, or why he made an offer for the mill, but I do know that he didn't do it to hurt us.''

"NICOLE," NICK SAID SOFTLY, brushing back his sister's uncombed hair with a gentle hand.

He had left Stuart's room only moments before, still reeling from the multiple shocks that had been dealt him. He wasn't sure he could take any more just now, yet he was driven to see what was wrong with his sister. His mother had warned him that Nicole had been given an antidepressant and a tranquilizer, but Nick was determined to find out what was the matter... if she was awake and calm enough to be coherent.

"Baby," he said softly. "Can you hear me? It's Nick."

Nicole's eyelids fluttered open, and she struggled to focus on his face. "Nick." Her voice was hardly more than a whisper that tugged at his heartstrings. She clutched at his hand, holding onto it as if she would never let go. Her eyes filled with tears, and a sob fought its way into the quiet of the room.

"Shh," he soothed. "It's okay, Nicci. I'm here."

"You won't...go away?"

"No," he promised. "I won't go away."

"I'm glad," she said as her eyes drifted shut again.

Nick stood beside the bed for long moments, squeezing her hand and willing her to know how much he loved her. Her tears dried. Her grip on his hand relaxed. Her breathing slowed to an even rhythm.

He thought she had drifted back to sleep when she whispered, "I remember what happened, Nick."

She opened her eyes and looked up at him. There was pain there, and self-loathing. Nick's heart faltered and then picked up an accelerated beat. Instinctively he knew what it was she remembered. "You remember what happened that night with Luke?"

She nodded. Uncertainty marred her features, and her
tongue skimmed over her dry lips. "I never could remember before," she said. "All I really knew was what everyone told me."

"And that was?" Nick prompted.

"That I was in love with Luke and Daddy didn't approve, so I had been sneaking out to meet him. Keith found
me and Luke together, and Luke was—" she paused
"—that Luke had...raped me. Keith beat him up and
Daddy told Luke's family to get out of town or he'd press
charges and have Luke sent to prison. Then while I was at
the hospital they found out that I was...pregnant. Mama
thought I ought not to have the baby because I wasn't
very...stable."

Nick shook his head in the affirmative. That was the story
he'd been told. "What really happened, Nicole?"

Nicole clasped her hands tightly together and her eyes
pleaded, as though she were begging him to understand...and forgive. "I was with Luke, Nick. But it wasn't
rape. At least it wasn't with Luke."

Nick's frown deepened. "What do you mean, it wasn't
rape with *Luke*?"

"Luke and I had made love. Keith came along and found
us, and he—" She looked at him, her anguished eyes filling
with tears, unable to finish. She pressed her fist to her
mouth and bit down on her knuckle to stifle the sudden
harsh sob that racked her slender body.

"My God," Nick said in sudden comprehension. "Keith?
It was Keith who raped you and beat Luke up to make it
look the other way around?"

"Yes," she said with a soft expulsion of air. "I think—I
guess—I blocked it out of my mind because of who he was.
Nick, Keith is my *half brother*." She shuddered. "I've
wondered so many times why I couldn't stand to be in a
room alone with him."

"The bastard," Nick said, his voice filled with venom.

Nicole's eyes begged him to understand. "It was different with Luke. I loved him, Nick. I did. But until last night, I didn't know it was wrong for us to be together, and neither did he."

"Wrong? Why was it wrong?"

"Last night, Daddy told me that Luke wasn't Gil Tanner's son," Nicole said in a rush. "He said that he was really a Logan, and then I thought that they were *both* my brothers."

Nick was speechless. He hadn't realized that Nicole hadn't been told the other half of the incredible double affair their parents had indulged in. He began to laugh, sad, sorrowful laughter that was totally out of place considering what she had just told him. How many lives their parents' indiscretions had touched!

"Nick?" she said fearfully.

He took Nicole's hand and carried it to his lips. "Oh, Nicci," he said in a voice of unutterable weariness. "I can't change what Keith did to you, but I can set you free of one problem."

"What?"

"Keith is not your half brother."

Nicole's eyes widened in shock.

Nick nodded. "It's true. Stuart Logan is not our father. Mom told me not more than a half hour ago."

"Then who is?" Nicole asked, her eyes reflecting her confusion.

"Gil."

"Gil Tanner?" she cried softly.

"Yes."

Nicole stared at him, trying to absorb the facts she'd just heard. "Daddy said that Luke was *his* son, and if you and I are Gil's . . ." She shook her head as if she couldn't believe it, and tried once again to get the situation straight in her mind. "Keith and Luke are Logans. We're Tanners. So...so even if I was raped by Keith, he wasn't my brother?"

"Right."

Slowly, the shadows in her eyes began to dissipate. "And it was okay for me to make love with Luke, because we aren't related either?" she asked, as if she wanted to make certain that she understood.

"Yes."

"How? I mean—" she attempted a smile "—how?"

Nick shook his head and smiled back, thankful that she could see the strange humor in it all. "I'm not sure I know. I'm as confused as you are. But it's all mixed up with Dad—Stuart, I mean—and Mom trying to get back at each other."

Nicole stared at a spot across the room. "Mom and Gil Tanner," she said wonderingly. "Who would have ever thought it?"

"Even more unbelievable, can you see Stuart and Ellie together?"

"Sweet, kind Ellie and Stuart?" Nicole giggled. Actually giggled. Nick's heart soared. His laughter mingled with her. She was going to be all right. *Thank you, God.* She was going to be all right.

When their laughter had changed to smiles, Nicole grew quiet again. "I think about him, sometimes," she confessed, plucking at the sheet with nervous fingers. "Luke, I mean."

"Do you?"

She glanced up at him from beneath her eyelashes. "The baby, too."

"Don't," Nick told her, stilling her hand with his. "At the time, Mom did what she thought was right. She knew we were Gil's, and she thought Luke was, too."

"I know," she said.

Nick didn't want to argue with her. It didn't matter now. "Don't dwell on it, Nicci. It's okay to mourn the loss of the baby and Luke, but don't let it ruin your life. It's like Mom says. We can't undo what's been done, but we can start fresh and go on from this point.''

"She's right," Nicole said. "Keith Logan has already robbed me of so much. The ability to love someone. My memories of Luke. So many happy times. It's going to be hard, Nick, but I swear to you that he's not going to cheat me of anything else.''

STUART AND THERESA were pretending to watch television when Nick returned. They were on pins and needles, waiting to hear the outcome of his talk with Nicole.

"I'm not sure you can take it, Dad," Nick told him, afraid that the stress of hearing the truth about Keith would cause him to suffer another stroke. "It isn't pretty.''

"I'm a tougher old bird than you think," Stuart said with a wry twist of his lips.

Nick drew in a deep breath and released it slowly. "All right," he said. "I'll give it to you straight." He glanced at Theresa. "When Dad told Nicole about Luke being his son, she started thinking, remembering, and everything came back to her." He looked from his mother's worried face to Stuart's. "It was Keith who raped Nicole, not Luke," he said bluntly.

Theresa gasped.

"Damn his soul to an everlasting hell," Stuart muttered, pounding the bed in impotent rage. His eyes closed and, if Nick didn't know better, he might have thought the glitter he saw on Stuart's short, thick lashes was an errant tear. Stuart opened his eyes and looked at him beseechingly.

Nick knew Stuart was thinking of how much he loved Keith and silently asking him how that love could have gone so wrong. Nick didn't have any answers.

"She didn't tell me any of the details, and I didn't ask. Maybe she needs to talk to a counselor about it, but I think she's all right. Or, she will be, in time."

"What a mess," Stuart said heavily. "What a rotten, damned mess."

"Stuart," Theresa said, approaching the bed anxiously. "What are we going to do?"

Stuart reached out a gentle hand and lifted her chin until their eyes met. "I taught Keith everything he knows, Terry," he told her. "But I've forgotten more than he'll learn in a lifetime." He looked at Nick, and the light of decision gleamed in his blue eyes. "With Nick's help, I'm going to bury the bastard."

For a moment, Nick was so shocked he couldn't answer. The room was still, waiting, even though the pretty blonde doing the noon news chattered on and the sound of an airplane droned in the distance. The only sound Nick registered was the heavy beating of his heart. He couldn't believe how the tables had turned. Was it real? Could he trust Stuart this time?

"There is a new development in the continuing investigation of the business affairs of Logan Enterprises."

The unexpected comment burst into the quiet of the room like a ton of TNT. Nick and Theresa turned toward the television, which was mounted on a swivel rack on the far wall, and Stuart stared straight ahead, his blue eyes as cold as ice chips.

"An undisclosed source says that an offer was made by the NiLole company to the owners of the Calloway lumber mill in Calloway Corners, Louisiana."

Nick swore.

"The family-owned mill," the newscaster continued, "which has been in existence for approximately forty years, is suffering financial setbacks following the death of the owner last December and the rumored embezzlement of thousands of dollars by bookkeeper Fran Glidden.''

A picture of Fran flashed on the screen. Nick wasn't sure who was more surprised—Stuart or Theresa.

"Authorities, learning that NiLole is a corporation belonging to Nicholas and Nicole Logan, both children of Stuart Logan, speculate that the Calloway operation had been targeted by Logan Enterprises, and was due to suffer the same fate as the Anderson company, which was bought out last July.''

"What in the hell is going on?" Stuart demanded, his eyes wild with doubts, his brow furrowed with fresh disbelief. "Why would you and Nicole try to buy out the Calloway mill—now, when all hell is breaking loose?''

"Stuart," Theresa said, turning a dazed gaze to him. "I think it's more important to figure out what Keith's mother was doing acting as a bookkeeper for those poor people.''

"What are you talking about?" Nick asked.

Stuart's eyes flashed blue fire. "Fran Glidden is none other than Frances Glidden Logan. Keith's mother, and my ex-wife.''

# CHAPTER FIFTEEN

ALL HELL BROKE LOOSE after the noon news report.

With the knowledge that Fran was involved, Stuart decided that she and Keith had probably skipped out to parts unknown. Nick could tell that the news had shaken the older man deeply, but he was proud of the way Stuart handled himself in the face of his disappointment and hurt.

The hospital was besieged with reporters and investigators wanting to speak to the president of Logan Enterprises. Stuart denied the reporters an interview but promised the investigators his full cooperation. Nick, too, promised his help, which included giving both Stuart and the investigators a full disclosure about the NiLole Company.

Tired to the bone, he had gone to his parents' house that night and called Seth to tell him that he wouldn't be back to work, and why. He wasn't prepared for Seth's fury over the supposed plan to take Eden and her sisters to the cleaners. Nick tried to explain that he only wanted to buy the mill to help; Seth refused to listen, listing all the incidents that Tess had cited to Eden earlier that afternoon. He had finished by telling Nick to never set foot in Calloway Corners again, and not to try to contact Eden.

"Is that what Eden wants?" Nick asked.

"That's what we all want."

Nick had hung up and gone to his bedroom, the same bedroom he'd slept in most of his life, and crawled into the double bed. He had stared at the ceiling and smoked until dawn, reliving every moment he'd spent with Eden and wondering how he was going to make it through the rest of his life without her. It was for the best, he told himself. There was no way a woman like Eden would want to be tied to a family like his.

The next few days were hectic, the killing pace the only thing that kept him from going crazy over worrying about Eden and how she was handling the news of his identity and his supposed plot to buy the mill out from under her and her sisters. The days were filled with questions and more questions, hard work and patent disbelief at what they were uncovering. The duplicity Keith and Fran had used was unbelievable, their bookkeeping so convoluted that even the experts were amazed. Money had been diverted to several small operations, all of which could be traced to Keith or Fran. It seemed that even while Keith was carefully siphoning money from his father's company he was working in subtle ways to destroy him, and Stuart was at a loss to understand why his oldest son had turned on him. There were no leads to Keith's and Fran's whereabouts. It was a bleak time for the Logans.

Trying to help Stuart all he could, Nick divided his time between the Logan offices, the hospital and the house in Colbert. Besides his improving relationship with his mother, the only positive thing that was happening was Nicole's steady progress as she slowly accepted what had happened to her eight years before.

The third night he was back, Nick took Stuart's suggestion and looked through Ellie's diary, hoping to learn more about the man he'd called father for so long. Ellie's handwriting made fast reading, and the entire affair was summed up in scattered, random sentences. Nick read about Stuart's initial approach to her and her refusal, and then the blackmail that led to Ellie's capitulation.

*I have to do it,* she had written. *I don't know of any way to fight him. How do you fight that kind of money and power?*

And an entry dated March twelfth said:

*It is done. I feel so dirty, as if I've prostituted myself, and I suppose, in a way, I have. I tell myself that my reasons were sound. The knowledge that Gil will come back to a family, a home and to a wife who loves him with all her heart is my only consolation.*

The next few pages held brief notations of Stuart's visits—the entire affair being of short duration—and Ellie's guilt and despair. Then, when she realized that Stuart wasn't coming back, there was a feeling of joyous happiness to the entries. Finally, Nick came to the section the diary had been opened to the afternoon of Stuart's stroke.

April 25: *I'm pregnant. Oh, God, what am I going to do?*

May 3: *Gil is coming home on furlough at the end of the month. Thank goodness. This way, if the Lord and luck are with me, he will never know what I have done.*

May 30: *I told him the truth. I couldn't help it. I have been deathly sick, and I'm afraid that I am not a good actress. Gil was furious, as well he should be. He threw a chair through the television and swore that he would get even. I worry about what he might do. I worry that he will confront Stuart, and Gil is no match for Stuart Logan's power.*

Nick closed the diary so that he wouldn't have to look at the tear-stained pages any more. His heart ached in sympathy for Ellie Tanner, a woman caught up in a powerful man's desires. He laid the battered book down. Reading any further to find out what Gil had done was unnecessary. Nick already knew. Gil had fought fire with fire. He had seduced Stuart Logan's wife.

The much-needed talks with his mother had cleared up a lot of things for him and Nicole. Theresa had explained how her relationship with Gil Tanner had begun and how it ended. She explained how her love for the man who had now been her husband for thirty-two years had evolved from hero worship to near hate, which had caused her to retaliate in kind. From there her feelings had mutated to tolerance and finally acceptance for his actions, which she learned were no better and no worse than those of many men. Nick had been satisfied with her answers. He was a grown man and, right or wrong, he knew that desperate people did desperate things.

He put Ellie's diary in the desk drawer and went to the window. Dark clouds raced across the face of the harvest moon hanging low in the November sky. He plunged his hands into the pockets of his twill slacks. It had been three days since he had left Calloway Corners. Three days since he had seen Eden. He wondered if she believed the tales being broadcast over the airwaves. Wondered if she missed him...loved him. And he wondered if she would be the kind of woman who would stand behind the man she loved for thirty-two years and longer.

"I LOVE HIM." The dogged look on Eden's face hadn't changed one whit in five days, nor had her belief in Nick's innocence.

"You're crazy!" Jo exploded, throwing her hands up into the air. "All the evidence points to Nick Logan."

"Jo!" Eden cried. "You of all people should know that things aren't always what they seem. Don't you remember those suggestive lyrics to E.Z.'s songs? You were ready to have him tarred and feathered for corrupting all those innocent teenagers until you found out the words didn't mean what you thought they did. Can't you at least check out the evidence against Nick a little better before making a judgment?"

Jo shook her flaming red head in despair and turned to Mariah. "See if you can talk some sense into her," she pleaded. "Tell her you know nothing about the man."

"I have," Mariah said.

"And what about Seth?" Eden asked.

"What about Seth?" Jo asked.

"Everyone thought he was a nothing, a nobody, just because his parents weren't legally married and his father was a drunk. Look at him! In spite of the fact that he won't speak to me, he's one of the nicest guys I know, and the best builder in the area. Tess should have at least been willing to give Nick the benefit of the doubt."

"Let's don't talk about Tess," Jo said, sinking into a chair. "It's too depressing."

For the first time in their lives there was a serious rift in the Calloway sisters' relationship. Mariah still couldn't believe Nick was guilty, but on the other hand, she couldn't completely discount the evidence they had. Predictably, E.Z. sided with Jo; Jo sided with the evidence. Ford was making no judgments. Tess and Eden hadn't spoken to each other since their fight on Tuesday, and though Seth thought the world of Eden, he refused to listen to her arguments for Nick until she apologized to his wife.

"You need to apologize to her," Mariah said again, for the dozenth time.

"Mariah," Eden warned. "Don't start."

"All right, all right."

"Listen to me," Eden pleaded. "I don't doubt that he's *the* Nick Logan. But doesn't it seem strange that this Keith Logan has taken off to who knows where with Fran—his mother, according to the news—who, if you'll recall, embezzled a lot of money from us? Isn't that strange, when Nick stayed put to help the police get to the bottom of things?

"Maybe his family is involved in all kinds of dirty deeds, but he doesn't have to be. Mariah, didn't you say that Nick never talked about his family, and that you felt he was running away from something?"

"Yes," Mariah said, "I did."

"Be honest. You liked him. *Everyone* liked him. You said yourself that you'd trust him with your life—didn't you?" When Mariah nodded, Eden continued. "Don't you think that the something he was trying to escape could have been his family?"

"I suppose it's a possibility," Mariah conceded.

"Jo?"

"Maybe. But—"

"No buts," Eden said, waving her hand in a gesture of dismissal. "Listen. I've been thinking about some things that Nick said the morning he left."

"Like what?" Jo asked.

"Well, when I told him his mother wanted to talk to him he almost slammed the door in my face and said he wasn't interested in anything any of the Logans had to say if they were pulling something else."

Jo sighed. Shrugged. "I don't know. I just don't know. I think the best thing for you to do is forget him. Make up with Dan. Marry him and go on with your life."

"I can't."

"For goodness' sake, why?" Jo asked. "Nick came; Nick went. Nothing's really changed."

"*I've* changed," Eden said earnestly. "I could never be happy with Dan Morgan. Not after Nick."

"Well, darlin', I hate to break it to you, but you're going to have to be happy without him, because it's for darn sure he won't be back—not after what Seth told him."

Eden grew very still. She looked from Jo to Mariah and back to Jo. "What do you mean—after what Seth told him?"

"I told you to keep your mouth shut, Jo," Mariah said.

"Well, he only did it for her own good," Jo said.

"What did Seth do?" Eden asked.

Jo raked a hand through her vibrant red hair and leaned her elbow on the table. "He told him not to come back here."

"What!" Eden screeched. "How dare he!"

"Now calm down, Edie," Mariah begged as Eden flew from the room. "Eden, where are you going?" she asked as she and Jo jumped up to follow.

"I wondered why I hadn't heard from him," Eden flung over her shoulder angrily. "And now I know." She whirled around in the middle of the living room. Mariah and Jo almost ran into her. "You can tell my brother-in-law that I'll apologize to his wife when he apologizes to Nick. Now both of you go on home like good little girls and leave me alone."

"What are you doing to do?" Mariah asked.

"First thing in the morning, I'm going to go to Colbert, Arkansas, to see Nick."

"Eden!" Jo gasped in shock. "You can't!"

"Hide and watch me, sister dear. And after he tells me what's going on, I'm going to ask him to marry me."

"What!"

Jo, seldom at a loss for words and always in command, looked as if she were about to faint. Mariah shook her platinum-blond head, a resigned look in her emerald-green eyes.

"Someone told me once that if the man I loved didn't ask me to marry him, then I should ask him," Eden said, a reminiscent look in her eyes.

"My word!" Jo stormed. "Who was the idiot?"

Eden's smile was sweetly false. She leaned over and pressed a kiss to Mariah's cheek. "Thanks for the advice, sis."

EDEN GOT A LATE START. By the time she got packed and
had the station wagon—which needed a tuneup—checked
out, it was noon. She was just outside Lewisville, Arkansas, when she heard that Keith Logan and his mother had
been picked up in Ohio. The news only made Eden more
confident that she was right and that Nick was innocent of
everything her family was accusing him of.

She arrived in Colbert just before three and stopped at a
combination gas station and grocery store to ask directions
to the Logan house. The closer she got, the more she felt her
resolve failing. To kill time and to calm the queasy feeling
in her stomach, she got a hamburger at a small café across
the street from the bank. She wasted almost forty minutes.

Gathering up her flagging courage, she drove the ten miles
to the house, an imposing Georgian-style home set a quarter of a mile from the highway. A long blacktopped drive
was bordered on both sides with multi-trunked crape myrtles and huge azalea bushes, which were no doubt breath-
taking in the spring and late summer.

Eden parked on the grassy shoulder of the highway and
stared at the house. It was hard for her to grasp the fact that
this was where Nick lived. Where he'd grown up. It was so
big. So grand. So *rich*! Nick wasn't a typical motorcycle
bum, and they should have all realized it. There had been
hints that he had money, lots of money. It took money to be
able to drive in the Grand Prix. And money to scuba dive in
Aruba. His clothes, while few, were of excellent quality,
expensive brands. And according to E.Z. even the Harley he
rode cost upward of ten thousand dollars.

Panic hit Eden then, like a punch in the stomach, which
was already churning madly. Why had she assumed that
Nick thought she was special? Why had she supposed he
loved her, when it was painfully obvious that a Logan,
especially one who looked like Nick, could have anyone he
wanted? And why had she thought he might want her when

Mariah had warned her all along that Nick had no intention of settling down? Had she thought that she—plain-Jane, country-bred, exciting-as-yesterday's-casserole Eden Calloway—could make him want to settle down? She shook her head. How had she ever imagined that she was anything to him but a pleasurable pastime while he was frittering away an autumn in Louisiana?

Eden cranked the engine and drove the car onto the road, pulling into the driveway so that she could turn around and head home. Coming had been a fool's errand, an impulse, like so many others she'd given in to since Nick had come into her life. Thank goodness she had come to her senses before she'd made a complete and total fool of herself. She might not have Nick, but at least she had salvaged her pride from the whole affair.

NICK DOZED WHILE NICOLE maneuvered the silver-gray Saab through the winding pine-bordered highway that led to the house. He was tired. Exhausted. Stuart had been released from the hospital earlier in the day, and close on the heels of that had come a call from the state police that a trio of troopers near Columbus, Ohio, had arrested Keith and Fran. In one of those stranger-than-fiction, nobody-would-believe-it coincidences, Keith had been stopped during a routine driver's license check. Recognizing who he was from the A.P.B. out on him and Fran, the trooper and his partners had quickly taken them in. They would be flown to Little Rock the following day.

It was almost over, Nick thought. And when it was, he could go on with his life...whatever that might be. The evidence against Keith was staggering, and Stuart had already asked Nick to stay and take his rightful place with Logan Enterprises once more.

Nick was reluctant. It wasn't because he was afraid that history would repeat itself. It was that his place *wasn't* rightfully with Logan Enterprises. That was Luke Tanner's rightful place. Nick didn't know what his was anymore.

Nicole, who had left the hospital after only two days, was like a different person. Just knowing what had happened and facing the truth had made her stronger. She had questions, and a lot of them. Would she ever see Luke again? Would he want to come back to Arkansas and claim any part of the heritage that was truly his? Would he want to have anything to do with Stuart after Stuart had literally driven him and his family away? And did he still think of her?

And what about Gil? What did he think of the whole ordeal? Was he as shocked to find that he had fathered twins as Nick and Nicole had been to learn that he was their father? Would he want to see them? To become a part of their lives? Nick honestly couldn't say what would happen, but he knew that he'd had enough excitement and surprises to satisfy him for the rest of his life.

"Someone's in the drive," Nicole said, breaking into his thoughts and gearing down to make the turn.

"Probably someone having car trouble," Nick said, lifting his head wearily from the back of the seat. "Stop and see if they need . . ." His voice trailed away as he recognized the familiar station wagon sitting in the driveway.

*Don't be ridiculous! There are hundreds of station wagons like Eden's.* Still, his eyes made a quick perusal of the license plates. Louisiana.

"What's wrong?" Nicole asked, glancing at him briefly.

"Stop right here," he commanded, opening the door while the car was still in motion. He stepped out onto the blacktop with his tassled loafers, and Nicole's soft, questioning, "Nick?" was drowned out by the slamming of the car door.

Looking in the rearview mirror, Eden saw the car pull in behind her. Great. She watched as a man got out of the car.

Nick! Her heart sank; her pulse raced. If only she had made
her decision to leave a few minutes earlier, they might have
passed on the highway and he would never have known
about her brief bout of insanity.

He tapped on the window. She had no choice but to roll
it down.

For a moment, he just looked at her. The eternity of the
six days they had been apart faded into nothingness as his
eyes soaked up the sight of her, feature by perfect feature.

Her hair, newly washed, formed a soft, coppery cloud
around her face, which was tilted toward him. Carefully
shaded eyelids were half closed against the glare of the late
afternoon sun, giving her a sultry appearance. Her cheeks
were dusted with earthy color, and her lips were outlined and
glazed a bronze shade that matched the rust tone of the
cowl-necked jersey dress she was wearing. She wore chunky
gold earrings with stones of black jet. She looked wonderful, he thought. Tired, but wonderful.

A sigh of longing lifted Eden's breasts. Nick looked fantastic in the loose-fitting fisherman's sweater of maroon, tan
and dark brown that was pulled down over his brown cor-
duroy slacks. He was devastating in his jeans, but the outfit
he was wearing, though casual, was obviously expensive and
made him look more polished, less approachable.

As she stared at him, Nick placed his hands on the door
above her head and leaned down. "What are you doing
here?" he asked.

The corners of Eden's lips turned up in a self-derisive
smile. "I was just asking myself the same thing."

"Have you been up to the house?" he asked.

"No," she said with a shake of her head. She tried to
laugh, a weak attempt that sounded as if she were about to
burst into tears...again. "I had no idea..." She didn't
finish, but waved her hand in an all-encompassing gesture
toward the stately home and the lush, well-tended grounds.

Nick began to understand what she meant. He nodded. "Yeah. Quite a setup, isn't it?"

"It's gorgeous," she said with a sigh.

The Saab's horn honked loudly, startling both Nick and Eden. He opened the car door. "Scoot over," he commanded.

"What?" she asked.

"Scoot over. Nicci obviously wants to get home."

"Nicci?" she echoed.

"Nicole," he said. "My twin."

"I remember," she said. *How could I forget?* "Look, Nick. This was all a mistake. I don't know why I drove all the way up here. I just thought—" she shrugged "—if you'll close the door, I'll get on back."

"I don't think so. It'll be dark in another hour, and I don't want you on the road after dark. So scoot over."

Sighing, again Eden scooted. Why not? She'd drive to the house so his sister could go in, drop him off and head back to Louisiana. Nick put the station wagon in gear and started up the drive, the silver Saab following close behind.

He stopped in front of the main door and shut off the engine. Then he opened the door and got out, holding out his hand to Eden.

"Oh, I'm not going in," she said, fighting the urge to put her hand in his, just so she could touch him.

"Well, you're not driving back tonight, and you're not staying in the car, so we have a problem."

Knowing that she was fighting a losing battle and feeling the weariness that had been hounding her lately creeping up on her once more, Eden let Nick help her out of the car.

"I like the dress," he said slowly, noting how the soft jersey hugged the fullness of her breasts and her narrow waist. It flared out at her hips to swirl softly around her calves, which were sheathed in soft high-heeled leather boots.

"Thanks."

"Eden Calloway, I presume?"

Both Eden and Nick turned at the question, asked in a husky, lilting voice that belonged to one of the most beautiful women Eden had ever seen. The woman smiled—a surprisingly friendly smile—and held out her hand. "I'm Nicole Logan."

Eden took the proffered hand in hers. "Hello. Yes, I'm Eden."

"I've heard a lot about you," Nicole said.

Eden cast a surprised look at Nick. "Thank you," she said, and added, "I hope you're feeling better."

Something unpleasant momentarily dimmed Nicole's smile and the light in her eyes. "Yes," she said. "I'm definitely better."

"Let's go on in," Nick urged. "You two can get to know each other inside."

"Oh, I can't," Eden demurred. "Really."

"You're spending the night, Eden," Nick told her, and there was no arguing with the firmness she heard in his voice.

*Spending the night.* The simple words held a connotation that set Eden's heart pounding as she recalled the nights they had spent together in her bed. The look in Nick's eyes said that he was remembering, too. She sent up a silent prayer for a miracle to deliver her. Other than cause a scene, there was nothing she could do but let Nick take charge.

Ten minutes later, Eden was ensconced in an upstairs bedroom for the night, while Nick went to check on Stuart's condition. The room, decorated with Queen Anne furniture, was a woman's delight in cream, old rose and moss green. Under any other circumstances, she would have enjoyed the old-world ambience. But it wasn't any other circumstances. Eden sank down onto the coverlet and closed her eyes, wondering again how she had got herself into such a mess.

There was a knock at the door and, before she could answer it, the knob turned and Nick walked in. She pushed herself into a sitting position, feeling suddenly vulnerable. Neither smiled. Eden felt as if he was deliberately putting distance between them, purposefully holding her at arm's length.

"Do you like the room?" he asked, his voice intruding on the gathering silence.

"Who wouldn't?" she responded.

Nick thrust his hands into his pockets and looked around him as if he had never seen the room or its furnishings before. "Yeah," he said at last, "I guess you're right."

His gaze drifted back to Eden. They looked into each other's eyes as if they hoped to find the answers to the dozens of questions racking their minds. Then, because she couldn't think of one other thing to say, Eden said simply, "Why?"

"Why did I come to Calloway Corners?" he shot back. "Why did I lie about who I am? Why did I make love to you? Or why did I try to buy your company?"

Hearing him list all the things she knew her family was accusing him of made it sound like a well-thought-out plan. Eden swallowed thickly and licked her lips. "All of them."

One corner of Nick's mouth kicked upward in a sarcastic smile. "What you really want to know is did I lie about who I was and come to Calloway Corners and make love to you just to find out about your company, isn't it?"

Eden moved her head slowly from side to side in negation of his question. "No. I've never believed you came for that purpose, though," she told him emphatically, "I'm not sure why you . . . made love to me."

*I made love to you because you're incredibly beautiful, incredibly giving, and because I love you.*

"Thank you for that," he said, sitting down in a dainty chair with delicate, cabriole legs, which looked as if they would snap beneath his weight.

Eden didn't miss the fact that he hadn't answered the part of her question about why he had made love to her. She could only assume that he didn't want to talk about it.

Nick laced his fingers together and rested his hands against his hard stomach. "I made the offer through the little corporation Nicole and I set up a few years ago so you *wouldn't* find out that I was in on the deal if you did decide to sell."

The admission should have caused her to worry, but all it did was pique Eden's interest. "Why?"

"Isn't that obvious?" he asked. "First, if I had offered you the money outright, you wouldn't have taken it, because that isn't like Eden Calloway. And second, I would have had to explain how I got it, which would have tied me to the Logans who were under investigation."

Well, that was true enough, she thought, but it still didn't clear up everything. "But why did you want to buy the mill?"

An embarrassed look crossed his handsome face. "I wanted to keep it open because it's important to the community, and it's important to you and Mariah. And because I wanted to do something for you and your family, to... I don't know, thank you, I guess, for accepting me so wholeheartedly."

Eden sifted through her feelings, trying to make them mesh with what he had just told her. Why would he need to thank her family? What had they done?

"How are things with the family now that this has blown wide open?" he asked.

She shook her head. "We're divided over the whole thing."

"Divided?" he asked sharply. "What do you mean?"

"I mean that Tess started making accusations about you, and I didn't like them. We . . . argued, and now neither she nor Seth is speaking to me. But that's okay, because I'm not thrilled with them, either, especially after what Seth told you about not coming back."

Despair washed through him. He recalled wondering what it would take to tear Eden's close-knit family apart. Now he knew.

Nick Logan.

He had done what nothing or no one else had been able to do. Bitter regret swelled alongside the despair rising inside him. "I figured he was speaking for everyone. You included."

"No one speaks for me," Eden told him.

The knowledge was cold comfort, considering that it appeared Eden was on the outs with her whole family. "What about the others?" he asked.

"E.Z. is siding with Jo, who is siding with Tess . . . although Jo might be swayed now that the news is out. Ford says he isn't in the judging business. Mariah still cares for you and wants very badly to believe in your innocence."

"I am innocent."

"I know."

Nick rose and cloistered his hands in his pockets again. He went to the window, a place where he seemed to spend more and more of his time, as if something out there beyond the walls might offer him solace . . . or a place to run.

"I never meant to destroy your family or that special something all of you had," he said, speaking almost to himself. "I only wanted to have it, too, just for a while."

The words said so much more than he realized. Maybe it had been right to come after all, Eden thought, hurting for him. Maybe it had been right to take Mariah's advice to heart. Knowing that in spite of his actions, in spite of the

distance he seemed determined to put between them, Nick
needed closeness, she rose and went to him, sliding her arms
around his waist from behind and resting her cheek against
the warmth of his broad back. He froze at her touch.

She breathed in deeply, inhaling the heady scent of his
cologne. "I love you, Nick," she said lowly, feeling in the
deepest part of her that love was what he needed. "And I
want us to spend the rest of our lives together."

Nick's eyes stung with unshed tears. He tipped his head
back and let them pool in his eyes instead of allowing them
to slip down his cheeks. *Sure, Eden. We spend the rest of our
lives together, but because of me you never have any kind of
relationship with your sisters again. No thanks. You'd grow
to hate me in a year. I can't buy into that, and I won't let
you, either.*

Besides the conflict he had already caused in her family,
there was the problem of his family's shady past. He wished
he could tell her about Keith and Fran and their plot to send
Logan Enterprises down the river. He wanted to tell her
what he'd learned about Gil Tanner being his real father,
and that Luke was Stuart's son, but those were private
things. It was all too ugly, and the wounds left by the initial
telling of them were still too painful for him to share.

A woman with Eden's background would find the story
of his family disgusting and his family itself warped, terrible. Molded into the person she was by a loving, nurturing
parental relationship, she wouldn't understand the selfish
motivations that had driven both his parents to do what they
had done for revenge.

And, as much as he wanted to, he couldn't bring her into
a family like his. He'd known it from the beginning.
Clenching his jaw, he very gently loosened her arms from
around his waist.

"No," he said, his voice as raw as his emotions. Then, turning on his heel, he brushed past her and headed for the door, unable to control his tears any longer and refusing to let her be a witness to them.

Eden watched him leave, heard the dull thud of the door closing behind him. The sound shattered her fragile hopes and sent them crashing at her feet. She didn't know how long she stood in a state of mild shock at the finality of his rejection. Then, from a distance, a familiar sound penetrated her stupor, the sound of the Harley revving up. An act of God was the only thing that could have kept her from going to the window. The taillights of the motorcycle glowed red in the rapidly falling dusk as Eden watched them flashing through the shadows of the crape myrtles crisscrossing the drive. He turned onto the highway, and the Harley disappeared from her sight, from her life.

Without stopping to reconsider or to tell anyone her decision, she grabbed her overnight bag and purse and left the room and the house. Thankfully the car was still sitting where Nick had parked it....

It was ten-thirty when Eden walked into her familiar bedroom and dropped her bags wearily onto the polished wooden floor. She hadn't cried at all. Her tears had dried up days before. All together, she had been on the road for over nine hours, but the blessed numbness holding her in its grip kept her from realizing how exhausted she really was.

Moving automatically, she stepped out of her shoes and peeled off her slip and panty hose. Then she unzipped the dress and drew it over her head, pausing for an instant before drawing it off. She crushed the soft fabric in her hands and buried her face in it, breathing in the scent of Nick that clung to the rust-colored jersey. The tears she hadn't been able to shed rushed unexpectedly to her eyes and trickled down her cheeks. Nick was gone, and she knew without a doubt that he wouldn't be back. There was nothing left of what they had shared.

Nothing but her memories and the faint, elusive scent of his cologne.

## CHAPTER SIXTEEN

ON THE MONDAY before Thanksgiving, the phone rang at eight, waking Eden from an exhausted sleep. She groped for the receiver and tried to force her eyelashes upward. Focusing on the offending instrument, she dragged it to her ear.

"Hello."

"Eden, this is Ted."

Eden struggled to wipe the cobwebs of sleep from her mind and pushed herself to a sitting position. "Oh, hi, Ted. How are you?"

"I could be better," the foreman said.

"What is it?" Eden asked, aware of a sudden queasy feeling.

"I hate to break it to you, Eden, but the damned hydraulic gun has gone again. And this time I think it's down for good."

There was no doubt about it. The piece of equipment had had it. The barrel cylinders were worn and the valves were leaking. Production, which had dwindled as the condition of the machine worsened, had finally ground to a complete halt. Nothing but a new machine would get the Calloway mill back in business this time. And there was no money for a new machine.

Disgusted, discouraged, all the Calloway sisters and their husbands met at Mariah's late that night because Tess, still angry at Eden, had refused to step a foot into her house.

"What can we do?" Eden said.

"I can get my hands on some money to replace it after the first of the year," E.Z. said, "but right now, I'm tapped out."

"Thanks, E.Z.," Mariah said. "We appreciate that."

"But what do we do in the mean time?" The question came from Tess.

"What can you do?" Seth echoed, his eyes flicking to Eden's. "Because of good ol' Fran's handful of sand, you have no choice. You'll have to shut down."

"But Christmas is coming up!" Eden said. "We can't lay off all those men at Christmas!"

Ford walked around the table and put his arm around her shoulders. "I'm afraid Seth is right, Eden. Even if you could afford to replace the hydraulic gun, that would take what little operating money you have."

"True," Mariah said with a sigh.

Eden looked from the troubled face of one sister to the other. "If we close down, we'll never open up again. You all know that."

"Then, as much as I hate to say it, we have no option but to try to find a buyer," Jo said, speaking up for the first time. "This area needs those jobs."

"She's right." Ford sounded as depressed as Eden felt. "Without those jobs, E.Z. is going to have to build a shelter for the homeless right here in Calloway Corners. I think you girls should give serious consideration to selling."

Tears filled Mariah's eyes. "I wanted to have the mill for the baby."

"I'm sorry, honey, but I think it's your only choice. And I wouldn't wait until the first of the year. I'd take the first fair, legitimate offer that came along, for your own peace of mind and for the good of the community."

One by one, the sisters agreed, yet Eden felt as if they had betrayed not only their father but the men who worked for them as well. Without a word, Eden got up and took her jacket from the hall tree. Without a word, everyone else followed, their goodbyes soft and sorrowful, as if a member of the family had just passed away. No one was in the mood for light conversation.

Eden drove home fighting the misery that had plagued her life since Nick left. She vowed that even though the mill was closing, the men and their families wouldn't suffer during the holiday season. If it took every penny she had, she would see to it that they got a generous bonus—or severance pay—to get through the end of the year. She would go to the bank tomorrow and make arrangements to have her money switched to the mill account. She sighed. One thing was for certain. There wasn't much else that could go wrong.

WHEN EDEN AWOKE the next morning, her first thought, as it had been every morning of the three weeks since he'd left, was of Nick. Her second thought was how tired she was. For a nickel she would have rolled over and gone back to sleep, but she had business to tend to. She dreaded the day. First they had to break the news of the layoff to the workers, and then she had to go to the bank and transfer the money from one account to the other.

After that, things got simple. All she had to do was figure out how to bridge the gap between her and Tess and how to live the rest of her life without Nick. A sick feeling, which she attributed to the strain she had been under for the past week, gnawed at her stomach.

Maybe breakfast would help. She swung her feet to the floor and stood up, the sudden movement causing her head to spin. Eden sank down on the bed until the dizzy feeling faded away. Whew! she thought, reaching for her robe. She had heard of people passing out because they got up too fast, but she had never had the problem before. She hadn't been eating well, so maybe food *was* the answer.

Two slices of toast and two cups of coffee later, she realized that eating was the last thing she should have done. If anything, the nausea was worse. Pushing her feelings aside, she showered and dressed and headed for the mill.

With the men gathered around in front of her and her sisters beside her, Eden made her speech about the mill closing temporarily—until after the first of the year, or until they could find a buyer. She could hardly bear to look at the workers. Every face held disbelief. Shock. Panic. Trying to be as upbeat as possible, she encouraged them to file for unemployment and assured them that they would have a generous, early Christmas bonus. She knew it wasn't enough, but it was all they could do.

After her speech the men scattered, shaking their heads and talking softly about what they were going to do.

"I don't know how you're going to pull off all you promised them," Mariah said, as they walked back to the office.

Eden was sick, body and soul. "I'm going to the bank to get my money out."

"Your money?" Jo said. "But how will you pay off the mortgage on the house if you don't have any money?"

"I'll leave enough to get by for a few months, and then I may have to get a real job, but those men are going to have enough money for their families if I have to let the bank have the house. Daddy would have wanted it that way."

Everyone agreed but Tess, who was silent. She only looked at her sister with a thoughtful expression.

"How about going to Johnny's for pizza at noon?" Mariah asked in an effort to cheer them all up. "My treat."

"No, thanks," Eden told her. "I have to go to the bank. And then I'm going home to bed. I'm not feeling well."

"Too much strain," Jo said sympathetically, giving Eden a brief hug. "I know you're...unhappy because of Nick, and we all realize that a lot has fallen on you, but you know we appreciate everything you're doing.''

A knife-sharp pain sliced through Eden's heart at Jo's mention of Nick. She hadn't told anyone what had happened between them, but the fact that she had come home and he hadn't come back to Calloway Corners spoke for itself.

"I know you do." She offered them a wan smile. "Have a slice of Sweep the Kitchen for me," she called over her shoulder as they separated and started toward their cars. Halfway to her car she turned. "Mariah!"

Mariah pivoted toward her. "Yeah?"

"Will you do something for me?"

"Sure. What?"

"Have Ford pray for either a miracle or a buyer."

Mariah nodded, her face a study of solemnity. "I will."

THE NEXT MORNING Eden didn't feel much better. She had felt better as the previous day progressed and by afternoon had been feeling fine. She thought she was over whatever was wrong. But it was another day, and she was queasy again.

Eden went to the kitchen and poured herself a cup of coffee. It had been a rough three weeks—enough to cause anyone to be stressed out—but there wasn't much else that could happen. Nick had gone, the hydraulic gun had finally died on them and the person partially responsible for the mill closing down had been caught.

Thanksgiving was two days away; it was time to look ahead, time to make things right with Tess. Thursday would be a good day, Eden thought. Once they were all together, she would get Tess aside and apologize to her. Then maybe life could go on as usual.

Life as usual. Two short months ago she had craved excitement. Wanted something to happen in her life. Now she longed for the comfort of "normal" and the way things used to be—before Nick.

Eden took a cautious sip of her coffee and grimaced. The holiday season was upon them, and she knew from the past that it would be a busy time. Maybe she would be so busy she wouldn't think about Nick every waking moment. As a matter of fact, Ford was planning something for his youth group on the third of December and wanted her to help. What day was that, anyway?

She poured the coffee down the drain and went to look at the calendar hanging inside the pantry door. The first thing she saw was the big circle around the fifth, the day she should have started her period. Because she was plagued with severe cramps, she was in the habit of figuring out when to expect them so that she could plan her activities around her cycle whenever possible. With her heart beating in her throat, Eden realized that she hadn't had her period on the fifth. She did some quick calculating and figured out that she hadn't had one since before Nick took her to the Revel. She was now over two weeks late.

No big deal, she told herself, fighting back a feeling of panic. She'd been late before.

*But not two weeks late. And that was before there was a man in your life, Eden.*

She counted back to the day in the woods when she and Nick had made love at least three times without any protection. A perfect time to get pregnant. She shook her head. She couldn't be—could she?

Her face flushed with sudden heat, and she raised her cool palms to her flaming cheeks. Oh, no! If it were true, what would people think? What would her family say? And how would she provide for a baby now that she'd given almost all her money to the mill?

*First things first, Eden. Find out if it is true before you fall apart.* There was only one way to find out, she thought. She would try one of those home pregnancy tests, and if it showed positive she would just have to go in to the doctor and see for sure.

An hour later, Eden was calling a clinic she had never been to before. She couldn't bring herself to call the doctor she had used most of her adult life. She was too embarrassed and could hardly talk for wanting to cry. The home pregnancy test showed positive—not borderline. Positive.

She might have known something like this would happen. Eden Calloway wasn't a woman of the world, which was why she had been so careful in the past. She, who had never committed the slightest indiscretion, had been caught. And before long the whole town would know. It wasn't the kind of thing you could hide. Of course, there was always the possibility that the doctor's test would prove the first one false, but deep in her heart Eden knew she was wishing for the moon.

She had thought that everything that could happen *had* happened. She was wrong. Now she was faced with the prospect of having a baby out of wedlock in a town where people gossiped as if there was no tomorrow.

The new Eden Calloway with her permed hair and midnight motorcycle rides hadn't done very well at all.

THE TEST WAS POSITIVE, as Eden had known it would be. She was stunned. She wanted to tell someone, but Mariah hadn't been feeling well lately, and Eden couldn't burden her with the news that she was carrying Nick's baby. Jo would hardly be sympathetic, and gaining some sympathy was a top priority now. Tess, the only one who might have given Eden some support, still wasn't talking to her, even though the news the night before had placed the blame for the black mark against the Logans squarely in Keith's and Fran's laps. What would happen to the pair still had to be decided, but the evidence was overwhelmingly against them.

On the other hand, Stuart Logan seemed innocent of any actual wrongdoing, even though many of his business dealings trod a very fine line between right and wrong. Eden was glad, for Nick's sake.

It looked as if she would have to keep the knowledge that she was carrying his baby to herself, at least for a while. Still, she knew that she would need her sisters' support throughout her pregnancy.

Longing for Thursday to arrive so that she could straighten out things with Tess face-to-face, Eden threw herself into a frenzy of baking and planning for their traditional Thanksgiving dinner.

"HAPPY THANKSGIVING, NICK," Nicole said, reaching up on tiptoe to press a kiss to his smoothly shaven cheek.

"Happy Thanksgiving to you, too."

Nicole hugged his arm to her side as they walked toward the living room where a fire burned cheerfully. "You know," she said, "for the first time I can remember, Thanksgiving feels like a family holiday."

"I know what you mean," Nick said. "I feel closer to Stuart than I ever have. It's strange, but nice."

"I feel the same way. Where do you think Keith is spending the day?" Nicole asked.

"Who knows? Probably with Fran."

"Stuart is pretty upset, isn't he?" she asked.

Nick exhaled a slow breath. "Yeah. He's really hurt."

"It's hard for me to understand how Fran could sway Keith the way she did after all Stuart has done for him."

"I know, but the way I understand it is that when Stuart got custody of Keith after the divorce, Keith felt that he had been cheated out of knowing his mother."

"But Mom told me that Stuart had told him on more than one occasion that Fran wasn't fit to raise a child."

"Yeah," Nick acknowledged, "but Keith's way of thinking is that Stuart was hardly in any position to throw stones."

Nicole shook her head in disbelief. "So all this started because poor little rich boy Keith felt sorry for himself and his mama because she felt cheated by the pittance she got from the divorce settlement?"

Nick nodded. "Evidently she planned and plotted for years, waiting for the right time to put her schemes into action. Incidents like the Anderson buyout where suspicion would be thrown at Stuart were carefully thought out, according to Keith."

"What about the Calloway mill?" Nicole asked, and wished she hadn't when she saw a cloud of despair cross Nick's handsome features.

"When Ben Calloway died, Fran figured the mill was ripe for the plucking. But when I showed up unexpectedly, she didn't know what was going on."

"So when you started helping Eden and her sisters, Fran decided she'd better hightail it out of Louisiana and forget the whole deal."

"So it seems. But she accomplished what she set out to do. She's all but put them out of business."

Nick grew quiet, wondering how things were at the mill and if Eden and her sisters had made up.

"What are you thinking about?" Nicole asked, sensing that his mind was somewhere far away.

He shrugged and went to the window that looked out over the drive. "I was thinking about Eden. Wondering what she's doing today."

"If you love her, Nick, go to her," Nicole urged earnestly, crossing the room toward him.

Nick turned, a tormented look in the depths of his dark eyes. "How can I go to her and tell her about all this mess? You don't understand what kind of person she is. She's good and kind and untouched by all the ugly things that you and I have had to deal with."

Nicole smiled and put her arms around his waist, pressing her face against his sweater and offering him what comfort and love she could. "There's nothing ugly or bad in you, Nick Logan. She must know that. And what our parents have done has nothing to do with us."

Nick grasped her shoulders and pushed her away so that he could look into her troubled eyes. "You're wrong, Nicole. It has everything to do with us. I would owe her an explanation of why I didn't tell her who I was. Do you want me to tell her about what Keith did to you? Do you think Mom wants her affair with Gil broadcast? Do you want people to know you aren't Stuart Logan's real daughter?"

"I want you to be happy. So do Mom and Stuart. And I think this hangup you have about airing our dirty laundry has grown all out of proportion to the real problem."

"You're right. The real problem is that our families are from different worlds with different rules, different values. We might as well have the Pacific separating us."

"Do you know what I think?"

"What?"

"I think you're not giving Eden Calloway enough credit. You've never let distance stop you from what you wanted before. And if she's half the woman you think she is, she's smart enough to separate the gold from the dross."

"WHERE ARE TESS AND SETH?" Eden asked as everyone rushed into the house with a breath of chill air just before lunch.

Jo, her fiery red hair coiled into a sophisticated French twist and dressed in olive green with a pumpkin-colored scarf, glanced at Mariah. Mariah sighed and looked Eden straight in the eye. "They aren't coming."

"What?" Eden asked.

"They aren't coming," she repeated.

"But she always comes for Thanksgiving and Christmas."

"I know, but she still hasn't forgiven you for...what happened when Nick left," Jo said.

"But she was wrong about Nick. Surely she can see that," Eden said.

"She does, but you know how Tess is. She won't apologize first. You're the peacemaker," Mariah reminded.

"Yeah. I guess I am." Eden untied her apron and tossed it at Jo. "Don't let the dressing burn," she ordered. "Ford, you slice the turkey. I'll fix the drinks later. Mariah, have everything on the table in twenty minutes. E.Z., there are toys in the living room for Carmen. I'll be back in a few minutes," Eden said, firing off orders like a drill instructor.

"Where are you going?" Mariah asked.

"Thanksgiving is a time for families. And this family is going to celebrate it together if I have to drag Tess over here."

EDEN TURNED ON the dishwasher and glanced at the kitchen clock. Almost eleven. It was really amazing how time flew! Christmas was just four days away, and Thanksgiving was a month in the past. As Thanksgivings went, it had been special for Eden since it had put an end to the rift between herself and Tess. When Ford had asked the blessing as they'd all held hands, Eden didn't think there had been a single eye that hadn't felt the prick of thankful tears that they were all together again.

Another stroke of luck was that E.Z. had found a partner for the mill, someone who was willing to put out the money to modernize and update the equipment for half ownership and an upper hand in how things were run. He hoped to have the mill in full production by mid-January.

Since they had little or no choice, the sisters had agreed, knowing they would retain half the company. It was better than not owning the mill at all.

Eden sighed and turned out the kitchen light. Now Christmas was upon them, and even though she was worried about her future, it was still a time of wonder and joy. Though it had taken her a while to get used to the idea of having a baby and becoming a mother at thirty-four, it was only lately that she had started looking at the baby as a part of Nick that she would have forever instead of a mistake that would cause her to be the talk of the town. The realization had gone a long way toward helping her accept the situation.

Going to the living room, Eden turned down the heat. She liked sleeping in a cold house and getting up first thing and building a big fire to ward off the chill. Surprisingly, the Louisiana weather was accommodating the season and offering north Louisiana residents some cold holiday weather, which made the caroling sessions more fun, since they were invariably followed by cookies and hot chocolate.

Eden went to the front door to turn off the porch light, which spilled gold incandescence out into the night. She had made her annual trek to the woods, skirting the place she and Nick had made love, and brought back armloads of pine boughs, which she mixed with sprigs of pyracantha berries and then twined around the porch railing. Huge red satin bows accentuated the Christmas greenery. Eden turned off the light, plunging the porch into darkness, and turned into the room.

Inside, the house was redolent with Christmas scents; bayberry and evergreen mingled with the lingering spicy smells of last-minute baking. She was glad to be finished. She and Molly and Jamie had made Christmas cutout cookies and decorated them with colored icing and sugars, silver dragees and mini chocolate chips. Her fruitcake was baked, and so were half a dozen different kinds of cookies. No less than five kinds of candy ripened in closed canisters. All of it waited to be boxed up and given to the many residents she shared her goodies with each year.

Her gaze was drawn to the stairs where Carmen had left one of Mariah's old dolls. Swags of greenery punctuated with bows draped the banister. Her contented gaze moved to the mantle where holly and pine provided a base for a dozen candles. Seth had shot down a gorgeous piece of mistletoe with a surfeit of waxy white berries, which she had conned him into hanging over the living-room light. A huge tree, bought from the East 80 Volunteer Fire Department because Eden liked the short-needled blue spruce, was decorated with traditional ornaments and stood sentinel over a generous pile of brightly wrapped gifts in one corner of the living room.

The old Calloway house wore the season well, she thought, eyeing the decorations with a sense of pleasure and well-being. As well the dwelling should, since it had over forty years of experience.

She turned off the light and went into her bedroom, undressing in the dark. It had been a good evening, even though Mariah and Ford had gone home early because Mariah had been plagued by a nagging backache lately. Ford's youth group had gone out caroling and then stopped by for refreshments.

Eden pulled her gown over her head. The outing would probably go down as the most well attended caroling session in Haughton's history. Most of the teenagers in town had decided to participate once Seth's Jason had let it slip that E. Z. Ellis would be along. Everyone had gone but Eden who, feeling like the odd man out, had elected to stay at home and get things ready. She was glad she had, she thought, crawling into the cold bed and drawing the covers up to her chin. She yawned. It had been a really good party....

IT SEEMED THAT EDEN had no more than closed her eyes when the phone rang. She jumped, instantly awake, and looked at the bedside clock. Twelve-thirty. The phone rang again and she reached for the receiver.

"Hello."

"Eden?"

"Ford?" she said, recognizing the masculine voice.

"Yeah. I'm at the hospital. Mariah's in labor."

"In labor? Is she all right? I mean, it's early."

"They say she's fine. I guess all that walking while we caroled did her in. Would you mind calling everyone and telling them to come on down?" He laughed, but Eden heard the nervousness in his voice. "I could use a little moral support."

"Of course I'll call them. We'll be there as soon as possible. And tell Mariah I love her."

"I will."

A HALF HOUR LATER, Eden pulled her station wagon into the parking lot of Bossier Medical Center, and she and her sisters piled out. They stopped by the desk on the maternity wing and asked if they could see Mariah Dunning.

"I'm sorry, but they're delivering Mrs. Dunning right now," the night nurse said.

"Now?" Jo cried. "But she just barely got here."

"I thought first babies took longer," Tess observed.

The nurse, an older woman with salt-and-pepper hair, smiled. "That's the way it goes sometimes. I got the impression that she'd had some discomfort for several hours. If you'll make yourselves at home in the waiting room, I'll let you know when you can go and see her."

Unable to believe what had happened, Eden, Tess and Jo filed to the waiting room, silent prayers in their hearts. Surely, she would be all right. It was no more than ten minutes when a middle-aged doctor came toward them. "Are you the Calloway sisters?" he asked.

"Yes," Eden said with a nod of her head.

He smiled. "Mariah just gave birth to a beautiful little girl. And I do mean little. Four pounds, twelve ounces."

"Is she all right?" Eden asked fearfully.

The doctor smiled. "They're both just fine. If you go to the nursery, you can probably see them cleaning the baby up. And you can go in and see Mariah in a few minutes."

After he left, Eden looked from Jo to Tess. They looked as dazed as she felt. After all the worry, Mariah had come through like a champ. A baby. A baby girl. Another Calloway woman. Eden smiled tentatively as the news wrapped itself warmly around her heart. Tess and Jo joined her. The smiles got bigger and brighter until they were all laughing and hugging each other in a celebration of a new life in a season of miracles.

CHRISTMAS EVE. Everyone but Eden had gone to the hospital to see Mariah, who was to be released in time for Christmas dinner the next day. Depressed and pleading last-minute preparations, Eden had stayed at home. She didn't think she could stand any more happiness at the moment.

Grace Elizabeth Dunning, named after her grandmother, was doing just fine but would have to remain in the hospital for at least another week or until she got to the five-pound mark, whichever came first.

Mariah, who had refused to have so much as a pain shot because she was afraid of going to sleep and never waking up, had had the baby so easily the nurses were still talking about it. Ford, Mr. Cool, Mr. Always-in-Control, was still downright punchy, and when Mariah had breezily an-

nounced that she would have him a boy the next time, he
had turned as pale as a ghost and told her he wasn't sure
there would be a next time.

Eden was happy for Mariah and Ford. Truly happy. But
at the same time their happiness filled her with sadness.
Tomorrow her sisters would all be there with their husbands and, as usual, she would be alone.

She snapped the seal on the plastic container holding the
fruit salad and put it in the refrigerator. Checking on Carmen, who was asleep on the sofa, Eden decided to make an
early night of it. She left the porch light on for Jo and E.Z.
and went to bed.

Lying in the darkness, she put her hand on her flat stomach and let the tears that had been threatening all day slide
down her temples and into her hair. There would be no celebrating when she told them about her baby...there would
be no husband to pass out cigars and buy a huge bear with
a ribbon to hang on the hospital door. She would have no
one to share the nighttime feedings, no one to help her walk
the floor when this baby had the colic. She was in it alone,
and sometimes that knowledge was more than she thought
she could endure.

She didn't sleep well. She heard Jo and E.Z. come in,
laughing quietly and talking as they checked on Carmen.
Later, a dog somewhere far away barked, and for the first
time in a long time she was actually aware of the train that
passed through about midnight.

He eyes flew open a few minutes before the alarm went
off. Was that the sound of a car in the drive? No. Not at this
time of the morning. She reached out to shut off the alarm,
which was set for five so that she could put the turkey on.
It was a tradition in the Calloway home that Thanksgiving
and Christmas dinner be served at precisely twelve noon,
and there was a lot to be done before then—especially since
Tess and Seth and Jason would be coming at ten, and Ford

was to bring Mariah straight to the house from the hospital.

Rising, Eden slipped her quilted robe over her flannel gown. Then she shoved her feet into her fleecy house slippers and padded toward the kitchen, stopping to turn a lamp on and the thermostat up as she passed through the living room. She glanced at Carmen and smiled. The child slept peacefully, her arms wrapped tightly around a battered bear.

The coffee had been preset to start dripping and was making its last sputtering sigh as she entered the kitchen. Eden went directly to the refrigerator and took the roasting pan out. Already cleaned and resting in a browning bag, the turkey was ready to pop into the oven, which she did, setting the temperature so that the huge bird would cook slowly.

Eden poured herself some coffee and curled her hands around the warmth of the cup. She had all but stopped drinking caffeine since she had learned she was pregnant, but still liked one cup in the morning to get her going. She took a cautious sip of the fragrant brew and carried it to the living room, where she proceeded to stoke up the fire.

When it was blazing cheerfully, Eden settled herself in one corner of the sofa and watched the dancing flames. Radiant heat eddied out into the room, warming her inside and out. She wondered if Nick was spending Christmas with his family, or if he was in some sunny place wreaking havoc with his smile. She wondered if he ever thought of her and Calloway Corners and what he would think if he knew that she carried his child. And she wondered why he couldn't have loved her as much as she loved him.

The sound of the front doorknob turning brought her to her feet. The door opened slowly. Which one of her sisters would be coming in at this hour of the morning? And why? Then she remembered the car she thought she'd heard. Could it be a burglar coming to steal their Christmas?

As she watched, a large mesh bag came into view, filled with an assortment of gaily wrapped Christmas packages. What on earth? The person carrying the bag took another step backward and Eden saw that the presents were slung over the back of a man wearing a black leather motorcycle jacket. Her heart began a low, heavy beating, even as her mind rejected her hope. It couldn't be . . .

He turned then and her heart kicked into a higher gear. Nick. Her fears about what the people in town might say about her pregnancy vanished along with all the worries about how she would manage alone. Nick was back, and for the moment, it was enough. Joy, pure and sweet, blossomed inside her as they stood staring at each other over the width of the living room. Her happiness at seeing him again when she thought she never would manifested itself in a wide tremulous smile.

"St. Nicholas, I presume."

Nick smiled back tentatively, almost timidly. As if he had just remembered, he closed the door and set the bag on the floor. "Nicholas, anyway," he said with a slight shrug. "I'm not so sure about the saint part."

Without wondering if she was doing the right thing, without asking herself if he wanted her, Eden set down the cup she was holding and flew across the room and into his arms, which closed around her slender waist. Her arms circled his neck tightly.

"I love you." His voice sounded fierce, almost angry, as if he challenged anyone to deny him the saying of it. He rained kisses over her face and hair. "Oh, Eden, I love you."

Emotion swelled in her heart, filling every part of her with the soft glow of love. She pulled back to look at him. "Oh, Nick," she said with a sigh, "I love you, too. Why did you turn me down? Why—"

He stopped her question with a kiss. Eden groaned and arched into him, opening her mouth to his questing tongue. After long moments he dragged his mouth from hers. "Not now," he said, breathing hard. "Not until we talk."

Eden was busy trailing hot kisses along his throat. "I don't want to talk."

Nick grasped her shoulders. "Eden, listen to me. Listen carefully."

She heard the seriousness in his voice and sobered abruptly. "What?"

"I have some things to tell you about me, about my family." His eyes held a strange combination of determination and pain. "They aren't pretty."

"It doesn't matter," she assured him.

"It does. Believe me. Before I ask you to marry me, I want you to know everything."

Eden looked up at him in disbelief. "You're going to ask me to marry you?"

"Yes."

Exultation warred with Eden's innate sense of fair play. She had to tell him about the baby before she accepted his proposal. "Nick, I have something to tell you, too."

He shook his head. "No. Me first. Please."

"All right," she said with a nod.

"First of all, I want you to know that *I'm* the new partner of the Calloway mill."

"What?" Eden cried.

He nodded. "When things started looking as if Keith was the culprit, I called Mariah. She told me that things were worse, that you'd had to shut down. I knew you'd contacted E.Z., and he'd said he would try to help. So I called. He thought it was a great idea. Trust me, everything is on the up and up. A whole battalion of lawyers has looked the papers over."

"But why?"

He smiled then, the first real smile she'd seen. "Because I love you, goose. And I love Calloway Corners and—" he paused "—I guess I love the whole Calloway clan."

Tears filled Eden's eyes.

"I'm sorry I caused a split between you and your family. I never meant to."

"It's okay," she told him, placing her palm along his cheek. "Everything is okay. Now tell me what you think you have to say."

"Can I have a cup of coffee first?" he asked. "I started driving at midnight, and I'm bushed."

Eden smiled. "For a bribe, I might consider giving you a cup."

Nick leaned down and kissed her and, with a sigh, she led him to the sofa. "Stay put. I'll be right back."

She was back in a moment and, between kisses and cups of coffee, Nick told her everything. He told her about Keith and Belinda, what Keith had done to Nicole, and about Stuart and Ellie and Theresa and Gil.

When he was finished almost an hour later, she only smiled at him and said, "Is that all? I don't blame you for skipping out."

Nick only looked at her. "It doesn't bother you?"

"Only because I can see that you're hurt by it all."

Nick pulled her closer and held onto her as if he would never let go. "You don't know how thankful I am that Mariah almost drowned that day in Aruba."

Eden giggled and tipped her head back to look at him. "I'm sure she'll appreciate that."

Nick realized what he'd said, and they both laughed. "Shh," Eden warned, "we'll wake Carmen."

Nick glanced over at the sleeping child who was making sucking motions even thought her mouth was empty. "She's so beautiful, and she's really growing. If you decide to take me up on my proposal, could I talk you into having two-point-five kids?"

Eden looked surprised. "You want kids? With me?"

"The sooner the better," he said fervently. "I've wasted too much time already. I promise to trade in the Harley for a station wagon."

Eden suppressed a smile. Maybe things were changing for the better. This promised to be easier than she expected. "I always had a hankering for a mini-van."

"Great. The minute you tell me you're pregnant, I'll buy you one."

"I think the dealers are all closed today."

"What?" he asked, his brow furrowed in perplexity.

"I said I think the—"

"I heard what you said," he interrupted, "I'm just not sure what you—" He stopped, realization dawning. "Oh, Eden, you aren't saying that—"

She nodded.

"You're pregnant?" When she nodded again, Nick leaped to his feet, grabbed her and let out a loud, joyous, "Yee-ha!"

"Nick," Eden said breathlessly glancing at the restless child on the sofa. "Don't wake Carmen."

"Sorry," he said. He looked into her eyes, his own glittering with the sheen of tears. "I love you, Eden. I love you so much."

"What's going on down here?" a feminine voice asked.

Nick and Eden turned to see E.Z. and Jo, still sleepy and rumpled-looking, standing in the doorway.

"Good morning," Eden said.

"Nick! What are you doing here?"

"I came to ask Eden to marry me."

"What?" Jo said.

"And you may as well know that it's a good thing because I'm pregnant," Eden said, glad to have the burden lifted once and for all.

"Eden!" Jo cried. "What's going on?" She glanced at E.Z. as if to say, "Do something." What E.Z. did was swing her up in his arms and start toward the stairs. "What are you doing?" she screeched.

"They're cheating," E.Z. said as he started up the stairs. "Trying to catch up with us. We have a daughter, Jo, but I really would like to have a son." His voice grew fainter as he climbed the steps. "Several in fact. What I'd really like to do is give the Jacksons a run for the money. . . ."

Nick and Eden smiled into each other's eyes as he held her tightly. He knew that he would never, ever let her go. He'd run as far as his heart would let him.

# EPILOGUE

CHRISTMAS THAT YEAR was the best ever, because as the Calloway clan grew, so did the love, the love that had survived even the hardest of times.

Mariah came home from the hospital full of what Ben would have called vim and vinegar, and set about to eat the rest of the family under the table. The next spring the wisteria arbor was so heavily laden with blooms that someone suggested they call Guinness. Instead they snapped pictures of Mariah and Ford standing in the archway with baby Grace Elizabeth, whose name had been shortened to Liza. The church secretary—who was dating Dan Morgan—told him that the Avon lady had heard Mariah was three months pregnant again. Ah, well. She always was a wild one.

Jo's and E.Z.'s adoption of Carmen went through, and E.Z. received recognition in several national magazines for his work with the homeless. They finished their home on Lake Bistineau that spring and, despite the problems connected with the early stages of her pregnancy, Jo got busy stirring up awareness of what greed and carelessness was doing to the environment.

Tess Calloway Taylor was appointed assistant principal of the high school, and everyone agreed she deserved it. They say there must be something in the water, because rumor had it that Tess was expecting, too. Seth was named Builder of the Year in January, and Jason finished the eighth grade with honors. Wasn't it amazing what a difference a good woman could make in a man?

Drifter Nick Logan became a pillar of the community, a devoted father and husband. Of course, Jessamine Hardy had known all along that he was a fine man. Gil Tanner thought so, too, when he came by to get reacquainted with his son in late spring, after he and Luke had stopped by in Arkansas to see Nicole.

Even though she'd married Nick, Eden continued to care for Molly and Jamie three days a week. The people in town didn't seem to mind when she gave birth to a nine-pound boy the following July. She never knew if it was because they figured everyone was entitled to one mistake or because Nick helped get the mill back on its feet. People were still talking about the way she had almost single-handedly taken charge of the company picnic that summer—and her nine months pregnant!

She and Nick can be found most evenings sitting on the front porch of the old Calloway home, one or the other of them rocking baby Ben in Grace Calloway's squeaking rocker, talking about the rest of the two-point-five kids they plan to have, listening to the rumble of the train and watching the cars go by.

The highway still leads from Calloway Corners to Haughton in the west and Doyline in the east. And the interstate still calls the restless to come and see where it might lead. But Eden has found all the excitement she ever wanted or needed in her husband's embrace. And Nick knows that he's found what he was looking for all the time. A belief in who he was. A lodging place for his love. A home for his heart.

And he'd found it all in Eden's arms.

# *Harlequin*
# *Superromance*

# COMING NEXT MONTH

Coming in June…

# PENNY JORDAN

## a reason for being

We invite you to join us in celebrating Harlequin's 40th Anniversary with this very special book we selected to publish worldwide.

While you read this story, millions of women in 100 countries will be reading it, too.

*A Reason for Being* by Penny Jordan is being published in June in the Presents series in 19 languages around the world. Join women around the world in helping us to celebrate 40 years of romance.

Penny Jordan's *A Reason for Being* is Presents June title #1180. Look for it wherever paperbacks are sold.

# Harlequin Regency Romance™

---

## Romance the way it was *always* meant to be!

The time is 1811, when a Regent Prince rules the empire. The place is London, the glittering capital where rakish dukes and dazzling debutantes scheme and flirt in a dangerously exciting game. Where marriage is the passport to wealth and power, yet every girl hopes secretly for love....

Welcome to Harlequin Regency Romance where reading is an adventure and romance is *not* just a thing of the past! Two delightful books a month, beginning May '89.

Available wherever Harlequin Books are sold.